CARDS
YOU'RE
DEALT

To Sheila,

J. J. MARR

Play well

The Book Guild Ltd

First published in Great Britain in 2024 by
The Book Guild Ltd
Unit E2 Airfield Business Park,
Harrison Road, Market Harborough,
Leicestershire. LE16 7UL
Tel: 0116 2792299
www.bookguild.co.uk
Email: info@bookguild.co.uk
X: @bookguild

This work is entirely fictitious and bears no resemblance to any persons living or dead.

Typeset in 11pt Minion Pro

Printed and bound by CPI Group (UK) Ltd, Croydon, CR0 4YY

ISBN 978 1835740 514

British Library Cataloguing in Publication Data.
A catalogue record for this book is available from the British Library.

For my loving parents and husband for the investment of their love and all that means.

And for me, for betting on myself.

PROLOGUE

Tessa

Neutrality was the most dangerous position anyone could find themselves in. Having a side gave you allies, a team, a direction. Tessa had learned these lessons the hard way. She always thought you wouldn't be a target of either if you didn't choose. She was wrong.

When you positioned yourself in the middle, you got attacked from both sides.

Tessa looked down at the cards in her hand and knew that she was going to lose. She called, trading in a single card in the hope her opponent didn't see right through her. She'd noted the large stack of poker chips on the felted table. They were symbolic, of course. Nothing so individual as money was on the line. Tessa had come to make systematic changes, to right the wrongs of the Game she was born to win. She did this for everybody else, and she realised she was about to die.

She risked a glance at the door, flicking her eyes over the shoulder of her opponent.

"You know, it isn't too late." He looked as arrogant as ever as he repositioned the cards in his hand. She had loved the way he looked at her once.

"Trying to make a deal before you lose, Anthony?" She managed to keep her nervousness out of her voice, and she shifted in her seat instead.

He chuckled lightly, a small smirk forming as he laid his hand face down in a small, neatly stacked pile. Folding his hands, he laid them on top of it. Was he bored? She couldn't tell. However, she needed to stall as long as she could, so she was happy for the pause. Where the hell *was* he?

Tessa looked up at Anthony from under her lashes, sat up straighter and matched his stance. She, too, closed her hand and put it face down on the table; they were just as good there, anyway. A humble pair of twos, ten-high.

"Will I lose, Tess? I think no matter what, I win here."

"What makes you say that?" Tessa put a bit of power behind her scoff, attempting to portray a form of amusement or, at the very least, a lack of panic.

"You win, you live. Long term? I'll get you to join the rebellion – for real this time. I would likely make you fall *desperately* in love with me, and you would become my partner in the Game."

She rolled her eyes. Leave it to Anthony to bring the dramatics to her life-and-death situation. For the second option, she demanded his eye contact. She wanted to see him squirm when he said it.

"Option two?" His eyes darkened. The icy blue she could get lost in shifted to a storm on the sea. He reached for her hands, and to her surprise, she accepted. Both of her hands were now folded into his warmth, his strength, his power over her. Neither broke their gaze; in this game of wills, neither was going to give up easily. "You lose? You die. The risk of your existence is eliminated."

She couldn't help but swallow hard. He removed his hands from hers and she immediately felt the absence of him. She was confused by this sensation. Why did she want to trust him?

Tessa took her hands and folded them in her lap, gripping them together to regain the sensation of touch.

That was it. Tessa couldn't stall any longer. She looked again at the door and knew help wasn't going to come. Her stomach sank.

Anthony flipped his cards and fanned them out. She knew he was arrogant, but he had bluffed well: ten-pair. However, that didn't matter; he had still won, he just didn't know it yet.

As soon as her cards were down, she was dead. That much she knew. This was to be her last game, though she knew what many people didn't, the truth she had been hanging on to in her quest for change:

You're not only as good as the cards you're dealt. You just have to change the game.

CHAPTER 1

Tessa

There was a nervous anticipation in the air. There usually was this time of the year in the run-up to the Draw. This year's age group was smaller than most. The Region had announced that the population decline was related to rebellion uprisings around Cassino. Due to this, they acted on the will of the Fates and now required all citizens from the age groups twenty-five to thirty to participate.

Most years, young adults would have participated in the Draw together in their thirtieth year. These young adults would have grown up together, been through education, competed and networked inwardly their entire lives.

Tessa believed that she would have years left of her freedom.

"Looks like we'll Draw together this year, Squirt," Dante, Tessa's older brother, remarked after they stepped down from their household broadcasting screen.

To ensure everyone in the Region had heard the announcements and the will of the Fates, the reel would repeat until all members of the family simultaneously stood on the acknowledgement pad for the duration of the announcement. Until this happened, the broadcast would keep playing.

Across their village they heard the broadcast repeat out of family homes, waiting for the adults of the household to return from work or the children to arrive home from their education.

Tessa was in her freedom years, the period of time between her education and her Draw, or so she thought.

"Why would they do this? So soon." Tessa couldn't wrap her head around it. In a single broadcast, she had effectively lost years of her life. The years she was meant to use travelling, experimenting, finding her passions, being with Alex. "We do not question the judgements made," she breathed to herself, repeating what had been ingrained into her.

Though Tessa questioned judgements and rules constantly, she rarely let those thoughts be spoken out loud. She believed in the Fates and in the leaders who worked on their behalf. She trusted the system.

The Gamble family was well known and established among the Elite. The luck of the Draw was with them, always. This meant they needed to maintain a certain level of trust and loyalty to the Region.

Anything else would be considered an act of rebellion.

"These are the cards we are dealt," Dante, Tessa and their mother said in unison.

"I guess we are both big kids now!" Dante always tried to make light of any situation, especially if it helped Tessa feel better.

After offering him a polite smile, Tessa looked over at her mother who was playing with her necklace. On it, was their father's wedding band. One of the many losses to the rebel cause.

"It'll be okay, Mum. This is the hand I was dealt, and I will play well," Tessa said lightly, offering her mum a slight grin of reassurance. She only got a slight nod in agreement.

Tessa sighed. "So, how does one prepare for this then?" She turned to her brother who, in his thirtieth year, was already set to be doing the Draw. He had spent the majority of his freedom years volunteering at the Activities Complex and for local sporting events. He was always one to entertain, and the Fates knew the Region needed the distraction.

"In such a short time? I don't know, Squirt... At this point it is just gearing down, staying sober—"

"Dante!" their mum chastised. She turned to Tessa. "Never mind him, Tessa, love. I'm sure the Dealers have already thought of how to get you all ready. They wouldn't do this if it wasn't fated. You are a Gamble. The luck of the Draw will be with you, and you will play well. Your brother will be doing this with you as well, remember! Maybe you can help one another. You won't know many people due to the age range, but you have your brother, and you have Alex." She offered a smile at Alex's name.

Alex was an honorary member of the family as he was always around. Tessa did her best to convince her mum that they were just friends, but, as mums do, she knew better than that.

"In the morning, I will get you over to the bank and transfer your trust... goodness, assuming they are allowing them to transfer early? Never mind." Her mum seemed more stressed than she was. "Let's start your preparations tomorrow. Why not go out and enjoy one last day of your freedom years, hmm?" She was leading Tessa out of the door by the end of her rambling, but Tessa didn't argue.

As soon as the door was open, Tessa felt like running.

In her twenty-seventh year, Tessa wasn't expecting this responsibility so soon. The house she had just left, she would be required to move out of. She would then need to get a job dictated by her Draw. She began to worry.

Tessa Gamble was born and raised an Elite. It was the only life she knew, but in order to keep her Elite ranking, and the lifestyle she was accustomed to, she would need to Draw a jack, queen, king or ace of any suit. Under a third of the deck was in her favour, and it wasn't enough for comfort. The majority of

Draws fell within the Working-Class; for that she would need to get anything from a six to a ten. Below that rank were the Low-Borns, and she didn't even want to think about that. She couldn't.

While walking, her mind raced. Perhaps this Draw would be different. Surely, they couldn't expect people with such little freedom experience, let alone preparation, to be tied down so soon? They had not yet learned how to exist within themselves, let alone exist to contribute to the wider Game.

"I am a Gamble," she said out loud to herself. She turned the corner and her stomach dropped. "Alex!" Simultaneously the first and last person she wanted to see.

Alex had been walking over to the Gamble household. He was a regular piece of the furniture. Frequenting dinners and outings, he and Tessa had developed a special friendship and had planned to spend their final freedom years travelling together. There were so few people in their age group, but she had always been particularly fond of his company.

"Tessa! I was just coming around to see you. Shocking, isn't it?" He brought her in for a hug which calmed her nerves while also tightening her chest.

Terrifying more like, she thought, but wouldn't say it. She couldn't risk being mistaken for being opposed to the Dealers' decisions. Alexander Avarice was the only son of one of the Dealers. There were times he went against the code of conduct out of spite for his last name, but he was usually loyal to his father and the Region. He was an Elite and acted accordingly. It was better to keep her opinions to herself.

"How are you feeling?" he asked, releasing from the hug but keeping his hands gently placed on her arms. She noticed he was practically excited. Tessa wondered if he knew the news before the broadcast.

"Surprised, I guess. I thought I would have more time to prepare."

He let his hands slide down to hers and took the hands in his. Her breath caught at the gentleness of it. "We will play well, Tessa Gamble."

Tessa schooled her emotions from a young age, as all were taught in Elite education. However, she had very little control of the shock on her face. "We?"

Her face went flush. Playing with someone else was the peak of adulthood. Sharing stakes in homes and accounts, making all decisions together and all the complicated entanglement that came with it seemed daunting. They hadn't even started playing yet.

Alex smiled, his cheeks pushing up under his eyes. "We don't have to do anything. I just figured since we were hoping to spend our freedom years together, we wouldn't need to give that up just because of an early Draw." He made it sound so simple. "Just think about it. It has been a big day and a lot to take in." His thumb circled the back of her hand, causing her breath to hitch.

"Did you know?" Tessa knew that he was often privy to information he likely shouldn't know. He was his father's favourite and always had a seat at the table.

He shook his head. "I heard that there potentially wouldn't be enough entering the Game this year to maintain the Region long term."

She felt the thought was incomplete. She had no idea if he was being completely honest with her and she never truly did, but now? He had more stake in the Game now. His Draw was just as close as hers was, and though she was a Gamble, the Avarice name was even greater. He'd likely keep his cards close to his chest.

Options are advantages in the Game of Life.

She knew she was an option on the table. An avenue. A play. Since Tessa hadn't immediately agreed to his proposal to play the Game together, she knew he wouldn't tell her everything he had. However, she didn't want to just be an option on the table. There had to be more.

Tessa had nothing going into this Draw. She felt nowhere near ready. Her family was well connected but she wanted to stand and make her own name in the Game. Three years were taken from her, and she ground her teeth at the thought of it. Three years of exploring, networking, finding passions and having fun turned into just a couple of weeks.

She swallowed back her feelings. "Let's not dwell on the change in direction. These are the cards we are dealt. My mum says I should use today as the culmination of my freedom years. One last day before I begin preparations for the Draw. Want to spend my last day of freedom with me?"

A wide, goofy grin spread across his face. His brown eyes softened to a honey brown and took her in. All of her.

"I'm with you, Tessa, as always. There's likely some sort of party to go to later. I cannot imagine our age group not drinking themselves near to death after the news."

He was right, but she was not in the mood to be angry or stressed with a bunch of other people.

"Let's go to the lake," she said decidedly. It was a regular spot for them and she needed the familiarity. The space to think and the fresh air were added benefits.

"That sounds perfect. I'd like to borrow my father's bike if that's okay?"

Tessa was relieved that he recognised how nervous the motorcycle made her. If this was, however, the final day of freedom, why not use the very thing they were going to use to travel together? In a few weeks, there was likely not to be borrowing of anything anymore. Alex also loved the bike and was likely going to miss it the most out of anything as a result of the closer Draw. She understood missing something that wasn't yours to begin with.

The twists and turns of this Game made it hard to count on anything. Maybe she could count on Alex.

"Penny for your thoughts?" Alex asked, seeing the cogs of her mind turn. He could read her better than anyone which made him her least favourite person to play anything against. Perhaps that was another reason to play the Game with him.

Tessa nodded and he grinned, pulling a coin from his pocket. His hands went behind his back for a moment before he stretched them out in front of him, closed fists down. She pointed at his left, he upturned it and opened his palm, exposing a penny and smiled. He never lost this game.

She grinned, too. She wanted to tell him what she was thinking but he liked winning, so she let him. The prize for this game? Honesty.

She reached out and grabbed for his coinless hand. "Let's borrow your dad's bike, and go camping at the lake, just the two of us. The way we imagined our freedom years squished into a single night. I don't want to go to a party. I want to spend this day, and this night, with you. One on one." She felt bashful saying it, but the truth felt good.

Tessa knew this sounded like an acceptance of his offer. But to her, it was a trial, the only trial they were going to get. This was the last day for her to be stupid, reckless and uncalculated. The time for odds and evens was not that day. It shouldn't have been for the next few years, but those were the cards she was dealt, and in front of her, an option. In a few weeks, everything could, and likely would, change. Not knowing what would be drawn was difficult, but that was the design of it. Gambling on the rest of one's life was meant to be hard. But today? She could bet on herself.

Today, she was free.

CHAPTER 2

Tessa

"Miss Gamble." Alex's father seemed to be expecting them and regarded Tessa with the regular amount of formality she came to expect from the Dealer.

"Dealer Avarice, how are you today?" Tessa was intimidated by him and always had been. If he knew, he never let on. Perhaps he came to expect it. Dealers were the most important role in the Cassino Region. They were the keepers, protectors and dealers of the Fates. They, largely, controlled the Game. The Dealers also facilitated the Draw so it was likely the man standing in front of her would be the one to seal her fate with a singular card.

If his role hadn't made her nervous, his stature did. Alex was tall himself, but his father was easily a head above him. The Dealer had dark eyes that seemed to always be evaluating whatever, or whomever, they fell upon. Tessa always felt judged and appraised but appreciated their hospitality nonetheless, particularly when she lost her father.

"As well as to be expected. We have received some concerns regarding the Draw this year. This was to be expected, of course…" He allowed the end of his sentence to trail off. Tessa saw it for the bait it was as if he was expecting similar arguments from her.

Was this all a test? The younger age groups did lean more towards being independent and free-spirited to be sure. Particularly in the lower ranks, noting some of the disparity between the social groups of the Region. The education curriculum changed to suit the needs of the Elite soon after. It was all a game, after all. Of course, there would be winners and losers. Perhaps this was a way of weeding out those who were not promptly corrected and were more sympathetic to the rebel cause.

She found this thought interesting but did not let on. "I will admit I was surprised." That much she had already said to Alex, should he report back later to his father. "But this life, this Game, is always so full of surprises. We have been raised to see the cards we are dealt and play them well and I intend to do just that."

Alex's hand squeezed hers for reassurance. He approved of her answer, though she did forget until that moment that they had walked up holding hands. His father seemed to notice then as well, looking down and slightly cocking his head to the side. She noted the tension in his jaw, but that could have been from his trying day as a Dealer.

"Tess and I have decided to have one last day of freedom on her mother's advice. We intend to resume preparations for the Draw in the morning." He sounded so sure. She had never seen this version of him in front of his father.

Though his confidence swiftly drained from him when Dealer Avarice turned to Tessa. "Your mother, Miss Gamble, recommended less preparation? With such a short time frame to prepare, I find that intriguing."

She heard the dig and was quite protective of her mother. She felt the swirl of Alex's thumb on her palm. He was there for her, but she couldn't expect backup from him. She needed to answer and answer well.

"My *mother*, Dealer…" Tessa started but a firm squeeze of her hand warned her to regulate her tone, "…merely understands me. I had intended to spend three more of my years towards freedom and had woken with that set of mind. Putting all of my unspent energies into a day instead of being potentially absent-minded during all important preparations is a better gamble. The luck of the cards has always been with us, but would you not agree that focus and drive are not helpful to a player in any game?" She was proud of that answer until Dealer Avarice spoke.

"Would you say that you are unfocused and unable to be flexible, Miss Gamble?" Shit. This was not going well.

She recognised that she needed a change of strategy, and fast. Odds were, his father already knew or had gathered information between Tessa and his son. The only option she had was holding her hand and it was time to play.

"I would say I am focused on securing my future and no outcome arrives better when rushed. If we are to play the Game together…" She paused to look at Alex and swung their arms. His face flushed but he didn't let the joy in his eyes spread to his lips, not in front of his father. She immediately felt guilty. He wanted this and she was using it, but wasn't that what playing a game was? "… then I would say that we have a lot to discuss before our separate and independent doings in the next couple of weeks."

Alex beamed and she could feel his vibrations of excitement through her core.

"Yes, I would be inclined to agree, Miss Gamble. Many, *many* conversations will need to be had." His father eyed Alex. This came as a surprise to Tessa. He would not have defied his father, but perhaps this was a situation of asking for forgiveness rather than permission. She, though, felt like she didn't want to be something to be forgiven.

Was she one to complain? She had used Alex in her Game, as she was going to allow him to use her in his. A pairing plays the Game of Life together to ensure there are no weaknesses between them.

"We wondered if we could borrow your motorbike one last time for our last day of freedom?" Alex using collective pronouns grated on her slightly. She had made the decision herself, but for whatever reason it didn't feel right coming from Alex.

"Well, you cannot possibly borrow something that is yours." Dealer Avarice gently tossed the keys to an openly-stunned Alex. It was a big day for him.

"This… what?" Alex stuttered out, releasing Tessa's hand and approaching the bike.

His father provided a forced half-grin, the closest thing to a smile Tessa had seen from the Dealer. "It is not uncommon for parents to give Drawing gifts to their children. I know you will appreciate and care for the bike as I have. This is your first asset and not your only gift from me and your mother. We wanted to provide you with some more independence for the coming weeks." He turned his attention to Tessa. "Should you decide to play together, I suppose this gift would be for you as well. However, I do not encourage any permanence to be made until after the Draw. One never knows what the Fates will decide."

She wasn't sure if that was approval or a threat.

"Of course, Father, thank you for your guidance."

Though Alex spoke to his father, the Dealer remained looking at Tessa. The motorbike made her feel even more confused about the decision to be together. A joint asset, one of many they were likely to have together if they were going to go through with this.

Why wouldn't she play with Alex? He was her favourite person in their age group, she knew him well, they grew up together and could rely on him to play the Game well. What more would one want in a partner?

The Dealer had made some parting remarks to Alex while Tessa was deep in thought about her acceptance. She only came back to the present when she saw the Dealer retreat up the front steps of the Avarice home.

Alex reached his hand out for Tessa and she closed the distance with a tentative few steps. He led her to his bike, *their* bike. She straddled the seat and accepted the offered helmet from him and clipped it under her chin. The soft click gave her the assurance she needed that she was going to be okay.

"Could we go to mine first? I want to grab a few things and we could use my tent." Tessa wrapped her arms around Alex from behind him.

He responded by grabbing her hand from his belly, reaching it up to his face and kissing the back of it. He placed it back down on her other hand and adjusted a pedal with his foot.

Their closeness felt strange, but not uncomfortable. They had been in this exact positioning before, but it was different now. There was an expectation, a future they had agreed on. A future Tessa had no idea if she was ready for. She would use this time to become accustomed to closeness. She would use this last day and not worry about the commitment of tomorrow, but the freedom of today.

She shifted her weight, put her chest into his back and brought her arms tighter around him. He looked down and placed his hand on hers, moving them both from his belly to his chest and paused for a moment.

This was the closest thing to intimacy that they had ever had, an intimacy Tessa had always craved. But now that she had it, did she want it?

With a firm kick and releasing her hands, Alex started the bike and they shot away from the Avarice home.

CHAPTER 3

Tessa

Alex held the door open for Tessa when they arrived at the Gamble residence. He didn't knock anymore; he would just enter with it being a second home to him.

"Hey Squirt, Mum's upstairs in your room lamenting. She mumbled something about being an empty nester before dragging herself up the stairs." Dante had just left the kitchen; Tessa noticed the tea towel draped over his shoulder and that usually meant he was stress-cleaning.

"Gamble."

"Avarice."

Dante and Alex had this false rivalry that had been ongoing since they were children. The only reason they knew one another was because of Tessa. It was uncommon for people in different age groups to interact, but Alex frequented the Gamble household. It was a far more welcoming environment for kids to be kids. The Gamble family, though a highly regarded family in its own right, didn't enforce the same indoctrinated behaviour or expectations as most families in their station. This was, though, perhaps why Tessa had felt so underprepared for her independence.

Alex was drilled in strategy, probabilities and predictions since birth. He could count cards by the wise age of three, whereas Tessa had barely touched a deck by the time she entered her education.

Dante strolled over and gave Alex a side hug which quickly escalated into a headlock. Well-earned brotherly affection.

"Big adult on the block, eh? We'd better watch out! Another Avarice has entered the Game. Luckily my sister has you to help her – your friendship will make an important ally to her."

"Partnership even more so, wouldn't you say?" Alex gruffed while attempting to release himself from Dante's grip. He didn't have to fight very hard after this though, because Dante loosened his grip and looked up to his sister.

"Tess." The tone and use of her real name made her wince.

"Tessa, could I see you upstairs, please?" Saved by her mum, Tessa sprinted up the stairs towards the beckoning call. She left Dante staring after her with a loose grip around Alex's shoulders. Alex was a big boy, he could handle himself.

When she entered her bedroom, she immediately knew that this was not the reprieve she had just been thankful for. Her mother stared at her, clutching the stuffed frog which normally lived on her bed.

"Mum, are you—"

"What is this I just overheard about a partnership between you and Alex Avarice?" Tessa had rarely got such an indecipherable tone from her mother.

"We are going to the lake today and plan to talk about it further. We wanted to have our freedom years together anyway so, I don't know…" She was trying to convince herself at the same time as convincing her mother. She got the distinct feeling that she wasn't doing a good job on either of them.

"Tessa, you aren't even playing the Game yet. What happens if you or Alex Draw poorly? Or potentially both of you!"

"Mum, I don't think—"

"What you think is irrelevant," her mum snapped at her. Tessa was not in the driving seat of this conversation and her mother's interruption cemented that. "Tessa, you both know one another well. However, that is only from your education and your such limited freedom years. After the Draw, everything changes. People change. Priorities change."

Tessa softened her tone. "I know, Mum. Dealer Avarice encouraged us not to make any final decisions until after the Draw as well. But, come *on*, Mum. You know Alex. He is a good guy and would make a good partner." She was pleading for her mother to understand when she didn't even feel sold on the idea herself.

"If you're going to spend the day up at the lake, please take those." Her mum pointed at a small box of condoms that Tessa had in her headboard cubby.

"Oh, Mum," Tessa groaned.

"Listen, Tessa. I lived my freedom years once before. I have also decided to enter a partnership before." She sighed. "I just want you to have options. Options are power. If you get pregnant before you Draw, especially to a man you aren't in a formal partnership with—"

"Mum." Tessa didn't want to listen to that line of thinking anymore.

"Just take them. You may not need them. I don't know or need to know what… activities… you have planned. Take the option."

Tessa reached back and grabbed the unopened box of condoms from her cubby. Her mother had spoken to her about pregnancy before, which was how she got the condoms. This was spurred on by a girl within her age group falling pregnant. She was from a good family but even if she Drew well she was considered to be a step behind everyone else. Financially this impacted the risks she could take as well as her options for her career.

Her mother was right. Options were power.

"Drive safely, please. I saw the bike out front. It always makes me nervous, seeing you on the back of that."

"To be honest, Mum, me too." Tessa offered a weary smile, and her mother returned it and placed her frog back on the bed where it belonged.

"Now, go and enjoy your last day of freedom." Her mother ushered her out of the door and tailed her going down the stairs.

When they went down to the lower level, they found that Alex and Dante were engaged in an arm-wrestling match on the coffee table. Tessa figured the conversation couldn't have gone too poorly, then.

Alex became distracted by their entrance and Dante used that to his advantage. He slammed Alex's hand onto the marble coffee table with more force than necessary. Tessa narrowed her eyes at her brother.

"Can't let my sister distract you like that, Avarice, there are games to be played!" Dante used the table to hoist himself up and Alex just looked up at Tessa, rubbing his wrist.

"Let's grab our stuff and enjoy our freedom before your brother breaks my arm." Alex attempted a light-hearted smile, but Tessa knew better.

He was a sore loser because he had very little practice at it. Avarices didn't lose.

CHAPTER 4

Tessa

They arrived at the lake and set up camp in their usual spot. When they were younger and had come with Tessa's family, they found a small clearing surrounded by red cedars not too far from the water. It was still close enough that you heard the loons call in the morning, but you had the privacy from any boaters or people fishing for sport.

It wasn't common to find anyone this far out. There was no pier, only a shallow beach protected by rocks from the wakes of the boats. When the tide went out, the two would enjoy searching the rock pools. They never found much, but it was jumping from rock to rock, trying not to slip on the green slime that coated them that made Tessa feel adventurous. It made her think and feel as though she was walking on water.

She and Alex had shared this tent before, but it seemed smaller today. She rolled out her sleeping mat, barely a finger-width distance away from his. Alex didn't seem to notice or care. This was going through the motions, after all. So why did it feel so different to Tessa? It was the same khaki green tent with blue trim with the water-resistant fly that looked like it once belonged to something else, but it did the trick in the woods.

Most Elite families wouldn't be interested in spending time out here unless they were hunting or surveying for land to own. But Tessa felt peace here, and she was sure Alex did too.

She reached over to her window and unzipped it, leaving nothing but a thin mesh between her and the outside world. The breeze rustled through the trees and carried their scent to her. She closed her eyes and took a deep breath.

Being out here was Tessa's idea of perfection. It was safe. She wasn't a Gamble; he wasn't an Avarice. They were barely even Tessa and Alex. They just *were.* They existed as the fish in the lake did, as the deer in the woods, as the worms in the soil below.

As free as she was, there was never escaping all risk. There was never escaping fate. Tessa watched a bird peck at the grass and wondered why birds would ever spend time on the ground at all. They could go anywhere with the wings they, themselves, owned. They had options.

She turned to see Alex watching her. "Would you like to go for a walk?" he asked gently. "You could go yourself. I could finish setting things up here and give you some time to think. It has been a big day." He grabbed her hand and stroked her knuckles with his thumb.

He was so kind and gentle about it all. He was patient with her and always had been. In a single day, she had lost her freedom and tied herself down further to a partnership.

"No, I'd like you to come with me. As we said to your father, we have a few things to talk about." She looked down at their hands noting that it felt right, but also wrong. She couldn't explain it.

"We don't have to talk about any of that if you don't want to. I was thrilled of course when you accepted my offer in front of my father, but we can talk when we know more after the Draw.

We will know what we are looking at then, and know what our options are."

"And if they aren't good? What happens then?"

He shrugged his shoulders. "Then we play well."

As if that would be enough. What if one of them Drew a two or a three? There were so few options in terms of jobs, places to live, investment opportunities...

As if he saw her spiralling, Alex dropped his face to be in line with hers. "Hey. It is all going to be okay, okay? What if you Draw well? That's just as likely. Think of being an ace! You'd be the only one in the Region with unlimited options. You could work where you want, live where you want, *marry* whomever you want. You'd even outrank my father." He chuckled lightly.

As much as she knew he was attempting to make her feel better, the idea of even more options that she wasn't in control of made her feel sick to her stomach. She nodded and gently removed her hand and decided to keep busy by unpacking.

Tessa removed the bug spray from the bottom of her pack, causing the bag to fall on its side. The box of condoms she was forced to bring fell out as Alex tried to stand it back up.

She was mortified when his eyes locked on the box and quickly snapped back to her.

"My mum made me bring condoms!" she blurted out, reaching for the box and immediately stuffing it back into her bag.

The shocked amusement was clear on Alex's face; he likely had not seen this conversation going in such a direction.

He laughed as he spoke, rubbing the back of his neck. "Oh, uh, Tess, we don't... I mean, we can, of course..." Somehow his being unable to string together a sentence made Tessa wish the ground had eaten her whole.

"No, I know. I don't know why I said anything. She just doesn't want me to lose my options."

"Do you think you would lose options by sleeping with me?"

The already small tent somehow managed to seem even more claustrophobic.

"Alex, I think it is more the natural consequence sex might end up with."

"A baby? Would that be the worst thing?"

Tessa's head snapped up in shock. She was both surprised and concerned about this line of thinking. "We haven't even started playing separately yet, let alone together, and without any formal union, Alex! It also limits me far more than it would limit you."

He held her hand and he looked at their connection when he spoke. "Tess, we both want this. We have said as much and I want you to know that we would figure it all out, no matter what, okay?"

Tessa was silent. She didn't know how to think or feel other than her options quickly dwindling in front of her. She was holding the hand of the most strategic, calculated person she had ever met. Yet, somehow, he was sitting there and acting as if adding a child to the mix was a minor eventuality.

"Tess, we don't have to sleep together today. That isn't why we came out here. It never has been the reason we come out to the lake. If we do decide to, which I would be more than happy to oblige, by the way, with or without protection, it doesn't change anything for me. I want *you.*"

Those last three words were so sure, so steady. With his admission, she knew he wanted her. In more ways than just playing the Game, but did she want him?

"Let's go for that walk." Tessa breathed out. She needed out of that tent.

CHAPTER 5

Dealer Avarice

Dante seemed speechless when he opened the door to find Dealer Avarice standing there.

"Mr Gamble, I do hope your preparations have been going well. I have heard great things of you from those at the Complex."

Dante seemed to be reacquainted with his senses by the Dealer's line of questioning. "Yes, sir. I like to think everything is in order, but you and I always know that you cannot possibly prepare for every single possibility."

"That is where I disagree," the Dealer said plainly, getting bored of the conversation through the doorway. "Is your mother in?"

"Yes, Dealer Avarice, I am. Please come in."

Mrs Gamble had come to greet their guest, but in doing so made Dante stand between them. He took the distracted opportunity to get out of the house and did so with speed. He collected his jacket which hung on his designated hook by the door and squeezed past the Dealer, nodding in acknowledgement before going out of sight.

"Mrs Gamble, I apologise for intruding on you like this. How have you been keeping?"

He was well versed in feigning care and interest, but it seemed that his efforts had little impact on Mrs Gamble.

"As well as one might expect, and to be without both of my children so soon."

"You disagree with our decision then." He said it as a statement, not a question.

"Would it help to?" she asked simply.

There was a slight stand-off between them before Mrs Gamble went to take a seat in a studded brown leather armchair. Once she was seated, she gestured at the identical seat across from her. "Though I take it you are not here to discuss the Draw?"

"Quite right. It seems as though your daughter has decided—"

"My apologies, Dealer, but I do believe it was Alex who asked Tessa."

The Dealer grimaced at this. He was unaccustomed to being interrupted due to his seniority, and he had other plans for his son than for him to get involved with a Gamble. He doubted his Alexander would do such a thing. "Are you quite certain?"

"Quite so, Dealer. We have taught our children to do what they enjoy and to appreciate their freedoms when and where possible. Perhaps, to a fault. I will say that there are no solid plans at present. I have been assured by my daughter that nothing will be official until after the Draw. This, she said, was on your advice. It seems you knew before I did and still you come to my home and speak as if my daughter had ensnared your son."

He elected to ignore the bulk of what she had to say. He would be fixing this. "Where is it you think they went?"

"They went to the lake as they usually do. I don't *think* anything."

"While you are in the thrills of not thinking, do you also lack thought towards the advisability of their little plan?" He had a history with the Gamble family. He doubted she supported this any more than he did.

"On that, I do think, *Raymond.*" She hissed his forename through her teeth, a deliberate act of disrespect not only to him but to his rank as well as his position in the Region. "I think these are the actions of two children, with urges, who think they know the world. The few years they had to figure it out and be ready for it have been removed from their resources. They act accordingly."

Dealer Avarice stood from his seat appalled at her discord. Mrs Gamble stood slowly and met his gaze.

"You *will* hold your opinions, Mrs Gamble. You wouldn't want to see the same fate as your darling husband, would you? Or perhaps your daughter to see the same fate?"

She went rigid and clenched her fists at her sides. "You would hold the actions of her father against her?"

He stepped towards her, closing the gap. She didn't step back, so his chest lined up with her face as he looked down. Beatrice was paying no attention to the importance and power of the man in front of her and it angered him.

"Not only can I hold them against her, but I would even say that her future could already be in jeopardy due to it."

Her breath caught in surprise. "You tell me to hold my opinions and you stand there as though you have control over the Fates. The luck is in the cards and the luck of the Draw has always been with the Gambles."

"You forget who I am and just what I am capable of, Beatrice." He sounded amused. A game within the Game.

"I remember every night that I go to bed alone and awake in the morning just indeed what you are capable of," she spat.

She did not follow him as he reached the door, but he needed to have the final word. He turned the handle and stepped one foot through it before turning back.

"Then you will know, Mrs Gamble, that I am the Fates."

CHAPTER 6

Tessa

Tessa was finding that her hand was fitting more comfortably in Alex's as they walked and spoke regarding their Draw readiness. As it turned out, she had nearly nothing compared to Alex. This was to be expected; he had likely been preparing to enter the Game his whole life.

"I'm sure your mum will want to do this with you, but maybe we can get you an account set up at the same bank I have? Then we can start looking at programming."

"Programming?"

"Courses, charities… odds are you won't go straight into working. What are your savings like? Are you able to access them?"

She couldn't have been more embarrassed during this conversation if she tried. She was Elite, growing up without worries and cares. She wanted for nothing, but she was starting to think that was a disadvantage. Her money had always been controlled by her parents; for all she knew she had nothing, or could be a millionaire.

"I know I have a trust, but we aren't sure if I will be able to access that now that I won't be in my thirtieth year when I Draw." At least she had something to offer the conversation, but she had only taken note when her mum said it earlier.

Alex nodded his head. "It will be tough for a lot of people if they can't. I assume you will be benefitting from Drawing gifts?"

"My mum never said anything about giving me or Dante anything and we've never asked. Did your father ever mention the bike?"

He took a moment to think. "I don't think he did." He turned to her and made a right ass of himself by saying, "You really are starting from scratch tomorrow, aren't you?"

She wanted to scream. Tessa had such a loving and fun childhood. Her parents allowed her freedom so long as she did well in her education, which she always did. Tessa sighed in defeat. "It would seem like it."

"Hey." Alex turned to her while blocking her path down the trail. He raised his arms and held her shoulders lightly. "We've got this, okay?"

That 'we' word wasn't settling nicely, but she swallowed her pride. She needed Alex more than she thought. "We will play well."

She wanted to get off the topic of her and her lack of, well, anything.

"Does a larger age group, or Drawing group, I guess, mean the odds of Drawing well are less?"

Alex shook his head and took his place back beside her but didn't take her hand again. He put his hands in his pockets instead. "No, not at all. Remember, the system is designed to be fair and give equal opportunity for everyone." He sounded so sure, as though he were reciting it straight from a playbook. "Once someone Draws, the cards are reshuffled into the deck and you will cut anywhere within it. Though, we do know that nothing is ever truly random. That would go against the laws of probability."

"I don't even know how it all works or even what happens afterwards…" Tessa mumbled, kicking a stone in her path.

"We learned all of this in our education." He seemed concerned at her lack of knowledge.

"No, I know the functions of it. I guess I was just looking forward to watching Dante do it first. It seems cowardly, but to be in the room, watch it happen, see the reactions without the pressure of it yourself… Also, how the ranking will impact me, *truly* impact me. I won't know that until I Draw, though."

"I get what you mean." Alex seemed to relax a bit at her admission and nodded his head. "I've been lucky that I have my sisters. I obviously went and watched, and we spoke of their Draw afterwards and celebrated their entrance into the Game and their adulthood. Though, maybe it is even more special that you, Dante, and I will be doing it all together. Also, since it is done alphabetically, both your brother and I will go before you."

He was right, of course. Being a Gamble, her surname sat her comfortably in the order of things. She wouldn't be first, but she also wouldn't have too much time to get antsy.

"I also wouldn't worry about the rank. Statistically, Elite-born adults Draw Elite-ranked cards. Fates as well as the luck of the Draw are on our side." He smiled lightly. "Never in the history of the Region has an Elite-Born pulled a Low-Born ranking. Those are the things that I keep remembering to tell myself."

"How are you feeling? Do you feel ready?" She was so focused on her own Draw, that she even forgot how this might impact him.

After a pause, he offered, "I don't know." He swiped his hand through his hair. "I guess Avarices are well trained. I also got to see the luck of the cards was on my sisters' side. I watched them become Elite in their own right. Using their ranks to invest, use their banking options and connections, and generally thrive.

They have partners and children now, and Laura is set to be a Junior Dealer soon working under my father."

"Is that what you want?" This was a big question, and she knew it. He was his father's golden child, but that didn't mean he liked his father very much. This was the point of the freedom years. Take opportunities, try new things, meet new people, *live.* They needed to fill in the blanks of their education which primarily focused on facts, figures, politics and of course, economics.

"What is it *you* want, Tess?" The tone suggested that he was done answering questions.

"If I could stay out here, forever, I would." She let out a deep exhale and turned to the lake. The sun was getting lower, but the sky was still blue, but turning grey. The dull sun sparkled across the water which was lapping at the rocks on the shore.

Suddenly, Alex was taking his shirt off over his head.

"Alex! What?"

"Let's be free, Tessa! We have the rest of our lives to worry about all this... shit." He waved his arms, gesturing generally. "We decided to have this one day to do what we want."

"Your big act of freedom is swimming in the lake?" Tessa laughed, unsure how to react to Alex stripping down to his boxers.

"My act of freedom is being with you." He cupped her face in his hands. "Can I kiss you, Tess?"

If it wasn't for the hands on her face, she could have sworn she went numb. She had noticed then her own hands had somehow ended up on his bare waist. She still wasn't sure what she wanted, but she supposed that it was the time to figure that out.

"Yes."

He leaned in closer, and their noses touched. She felt their breathing mingle and realised she had never been this close to anyone before.

"I meant what I said. I want to be partners with you, Tessa Gamble. No matter what happens today or in a couple of weeks from now. Nothing will change my mind. We will play, and we will play well."

"We will play well," she repeated against his lips before he pressed them firmly into hers.

Her breath caught and she found herself surprised at the tingling feeling that resonated through her. She found it easy to work her lips in cadence with his and she pulled herself closer to his bare chest.

Alex wove his fingers through the back of her hair and tilted her head back, their mouths parted for a moment and Tessa felt the change. There was a pull that she didn't know was possible. She let out a small noise between a gasp and a moan. He went still and pulled away.

"I'm sorry. I…" Tessa couldn't explain herself.

"Why are you apologising?" he laughed breathily. He stroked her cheek with the back of his hand. "Tessa…"

She suddenly loved the sound of her name. She smiled and looked up at him and received a smile in return. She felt him shiver so close to her. She nearly forgot he had readied himself for a swim in the lake. "I'll meet you in there," she said, nodding her head in the direction of the water.

He smiled again and pressed his still-smiling lips to hers quickly before she watched him run and dive into the water. He resurfaced and flicked his hair, spraying water in an arc above him.

She brought her fingers to her lips. Tessa had wanted to kiss him since they were kids, and she finally did it. She wanted more, craved it, needed it. She noticed that the tingle on her lips got stronger with his absence.

"Last day of freedom," she mumbled to herself.

Tessa removed her shoes and debated for a moment about removing her shorts. Suddenly the tightness in her belly formed a mischievous idea.

The sun was starting to set and the sky had adopted shades of purple and pink. She listened for a moment, noting no boats or cars. Even nature silenced for her to gather her nerve as she smiled wickedly across the water at Alex.

She removed her shorts and her underwear in one movement. While she stepped out of them, she removed her top and threw her discarded bra behind her. This was her last day of recklessness, her last day of freedom. After today she knew it would be stress, worry and accountability. But in that moment, she was in control. She could do what she wanted, and she was going to savour it.

Her toes hit the water, sending goosebumps shooting out of her skin at the coldness of it. It would have been warmer to dive in, submerge her head under the water and get it over with. But she wanted an entrance. The cold water tamed the tightness in her core, settling her heart, and creating a distraction from the rest of the world. She looked ahead and saw a gaped-mouthed Alex and grinned.

Options may be power, but so was this.

When she reached him, her chest was under the waterline, but he looked down anyway. She giggled and reached over, closing his mouth for him. This seemed to bring him back to the present as his gaze fixed on hers.

"Holy shit."

She laughed at that. "That's what you have to say?" She had no idea where this confidence came from. She felt like a different woman than the one talking about the future. What she did know was that she loved the feeling of it. The control. Tessa spent a lot of her life living by and through others. Her family name, her parents' money, she was even planning a future with Alex for security, but this moment was hers. She would create comfort from this fear of the unknown. At that moment, she decided that *she* would play well. She didn't need anyone.

"I have a lot that I could say, but quite frankly none of it would be very polite. You are… wow."

"Wow, indeed." She walked closer to him, eliminating the gap between them. She suddenly felt the hardness of him against her belly. "Would you still want to do this, even if we weren't talking about being partners?" She needed to know her actions weren't agreeing to anything more.

He brought his lips to hers and held her hand under the water. "I've wanted to do this before I even brought the option up." He smiled down at her. "We decided not to make anything permanent until the Draw and this doesn't change that."

She flicked her eyes away from his taking in what he was saying. Fun and freedom today, the Game would be for tomorrow. How long had he wanted her too? "You know, we don't have to do this. Is this too much?" she asked him. He was still pressing against her. She thought that the thin cotton layer between them did very little to cushion them.

"This is simultaneously too much and not enough," he laughed and put his arms around her, pinning her closer in an embrace. It pushed out the water between them and she felt the heat of his chest against her cheek. "If you're willing, I am not going to give up the opportunity to make you feel the way you deserve."

"And how exactly is that?" she managed to get out. Fates, this felt good.

He pulled back slightly and tilted her chin up for her to look at him. She watched as his eyes wandered what he could see above the surface of the water which only gave him a glimpse at the swell of her breasts.

"Like you've won every game," he said slowly, placing his hand on the small of her back. "Like your luck will never run out." Alex bent down and kissed the soft skin behind her ear and whispered, "And like with me, you will never lose."

Her lips frantically met his at that moment. She wrapped her hands around the back of his head; his hair was wet, and the water dripped down his face and found hers. She tasted the lake on his lips.

He let out a small groan when he looked down. She joined him and noticed with her arms up around his neck, she had raised her breasts from the water and they were pressed against his chest.

"Your nipples are rock solid. You must be cold. Shall we go warm you up?" He brushed his nose against hers.

The idea excited her but she needed to know. "Have you ever?"

He nodded. "Have you?"

She shook her head. She wasn't shy about this and if anything, wanted him to know everything going into this.

He looked at her gently, some of the hunger fading from his eyes and he kissed her on the forehead. "Could have fooled me," he laughed lightly. "Why don't we go back to the tent and *actually* warm up. Then we can go as slow as you want, or not go at all."

"And if I don't want to go slowly?" she mused, swirling her finger at the back of his neck.

He pulled her hands from the back of his neck and quickly twisted her around. Her lower back now felt the full length of his hardness and he wrapped their arms around her.

"Then we don't go slowly."

CHAPTER 7

Dante

Dante gingerly opened up the front door and peered inside.

"He's gone. No need to skulk around." His mother was sitting on the leather chair facing the door, so Dante opted to sit in the one across from her. He hated these chairs; they seemed so formal. He decided that when he got a house only comfortable furniture would be allowed.

"What did Dealer Avarice want? I assume he wanted to chat about making Squirt's partnership official?" He crossed his ankle over his knee in an attempt to get more comfortable, but he just made it worse.

"And what do you think of this partnership?" Opinions were always freely given in the Gamble household. Everyone was considered an adult even if they hadn't done the Draw yet. Their mum had prepared them both for the Draw by preparing them for the Game of joining society afterwards.

"I mean, I guess it makes sense. Both of them come from good, established families, they've known one another their whole lives… Fates, Alex has been coming here for Monday night dinners since his eighth year. He is essentially family already."

"Is knowledge of a person as well as their prestige all you think a partnership is made out of, Dante?"

He scratched his chin. He hadn't shaved today, he noticed. It had been a busy day with the announcement, Tessa's news, and the Dealer's visit; it was a busier than normal day for him. Luckily, he wasn't volunteering that day.

"It's practical, isn't it?" he offered.

"How romantic, Dante." His mother shook her head.

"Are you asking me about love? You may as well ask me about a unicorn. I know you loved Dad but that isn't how the Game is played anymore. You have to find and take the advantages you can, at least publicly. More and more this Game has become about money. People have already found it odd that I've spent the last of my freedom years in the Complex. They don't see the value in a community. They see value in opportunity, power and money. That is how the Game is played. When I was asked why I was doing it, I always cited networking as my response or looking to create opportunities where there weren't any. Well, none that would make profit, anyway, and that's what they care about." He dusted an invisible fluff off his pant leg.

"Why not just tell them the truth?"

"The truth? Mum." He turned and looked over his shoulder out of the window before hushing his tone. "It is all about appearances. You had a handsome Drawing gift and Dad had the luck of the Draw like every Gamble before him. Together you could make a choice and be seen as a smart pairing. In a perfect world, I would want Tessa, heck, I'd want myself to marry for love and enjoy what we do. Do things out of *passion* and *enjoyment*." He put the two words in air quotations. "But it is borderline heresy to say that these days. Let alone put any stock in. You know that. As far as the Region is concerned, I will have to try and be good and play well within the confines of the Game in front of me, as much as the Fates allow."

His mother seemed hurt by his words. "I thought I had raised you to do exactly those things. You can rely on our money and our connections, and do what you want. You both can."

"Mum, this is just the way the Game is. Those who Draw lower can do what they want without being scrutinised. Obviously, not everything. Their rank dictates the jobs they can and can't do as well as the people they associate with, but they can pursue a passion. We can't. Not without question, anyway. There aren't the same expectations for the Working-Class or Low-Borns. Sure, they *must* work, and live differently, and wouldn't ever have the same opportunity if they Drew well, but nobody cares or even looks at them. They rely on one another. They have more freedom than just a few allotted years, and Tessa didn't even get those!"

To that, his mother went silent. She had never put pressure on them to perform in any way of excellence. They were to focus on their education, but she supported their interests.

"Is this what they taught you in your education?"

"Mum. This is what life teaches. Citizens suddenly disappear for questioning the hierarchy of their cards and their value. It doesn't take a genius to figure out that if you want to live, you play by the rules of the Game." He uncrossed his legs, leaned forward across the table and took her hand. "You and Dad taught us to be kind, caring and open-minded. Some would call even *that* an act of rebellion. I would wager Dealer Avarice already does. But what you did was give me and Tess a different view. We see the whole hand for its individual parts and how it fits into a larger game. We got the best of both. So, don't be sad that we may not partner out of love. Be happy that we won't have to do it out of necessity. In time, love may follow."

Beatrice's eyes glossed over and she covered her son's hands with hers.

"I think I need to tell you more about your dad."

CHAPTER 8

Dealer Avarice

"Come in." Dealer Avarice didn't so much as look up from his immaculately manicured mahogany desk, perfectly organised with file folders, colour-coded paperweights and three matching gilded frames. One for each of his children.

"Dealer Avarice, I apologise for this interruption."

"Mr Largesse, my time is limited which makes it even more valuable than it usually is. I do not have the resources required for pleasantries. What do you want?" Dealer Avarice tolerated his assistant but did not take the focus off his work to pair with his very welcoming acknowledgement.

"I'm sor—" His assistant cleared his throat when the Dealer finally looked up in irritation. "Sir." He deepened his voice. "I have the report you asked for regarding the rebels, sir."

The Dealer waved him forward in annoyance. He took it from his assistant's hand without so much as a word or a glance. The only reason he looked up at all was because his assistant remained standing there expectantly. Dealer Avarice pinched the bridge of his nose and waved him off.

The assistant cleared his throat again. "Sir."

"Hmm?"

"As you know, my Draw is quickly approaching."

"Concise words if you will, Mr Largesse." The Dealer was already aggravated coming into his office today. This interaction was making it worse.

"I would like to work here, sir. If you would have me," his assistant said quickly as if he was ripping a cord of words out of himself.

Dealer Avarice finally put his pen down and crossed his hands atop his work. He took a deep breath before continuing.

"You don't know what you are to Draw yet, Anthony. Do you think it wise to limit your options to only a single employer?" The Dealer had done his best to coach Anthony in his tenure with him. Anthony was a Working-Class boy and wasn't as well educated in these matters. "What if you were to Draw too low? I must admit, you have been a reliable and valuable asset to me for your freedom years. The Cassino Region only allows their political employees to come from an Elite Draw, as you well know."

"Yes, I do understand that, Dealer. I only intended—"

"Your interest is noted." The Dealer cut him off, getting bored of this conversation. He made his tone firm with finality, and it worked.

"Thank you, Dealer." Anthony retreated quickly, clearly understanding that he had overstayed his welcome.

Once the door was closed, Dealer Avarice stopped what he was working on and put it neatly away into a suitable file folder under a red paperweight. He picked up the Rebellion Report that he had placed to the side.

He regarded it, stood up from behind his desk and paced the far wall while reading through it. The reports were always important to him. He believed he had a good handle on the information, but the last few weeks had proven that there was more than he was able to control.

He ran his fingers along the bookshelf, landing on a tome with green binding. He pulled it out and opened it on his desk, still standing and leaning over it. He unfolded a few pages to reveal a map of the Region. The centre hosted the Elite village and then in rings showed the other placements of the citizens, the Working-Class and then the Low-Borns on the edge of the Region. The Region backed onto a forest to the south-west past where the Voided went. Every so often, the Dealers would organise a clear-out of their temporary structures. He knew this was a hub of the rebellion, but luckily, they had not been able to organise well enough against the Political Elite.

However, today's report concerned him. As had the past few that had come in.

A knock at the door caused a pause. "Who is it?"

"Dealer Prudence."

He immediately relaxed. He trusted his fellow Dealer entirely. There were things that she knew that his own partner did not. "Come in, Dealer."

After taking in the scene in front of her, she closed the door and locked it. She strode forward and noted the concern on his face. "What troubles you, Raymond?" She was the only person, due to equal rank, that was socially allowed to call him his forename. However, she never did so in public.

He handed her the report without hesitation, hoping she would see the same thing he did.

"Recruitment age: twenty-five to twenty-nine." She looked up at him. "I don't understand. This is the same as it has been."

"Exactly the problem, Jeanette. They continue to target those in their freedom years. However, look lower down. Working breakdown."

He watched as the realisation hit her. She whispered, "Volunteer." She rounded the desk to look at the map next to him. "We know this information may not be fully accurate…"

"It is, Jeanette. I wouldn't be handed this without proper vetting. They're coming after the Elite, and they've got one." The Working-Class usually worked through their freedom years. They weren't able to afford to live otherwise. Typically, once a Working-Class or Low-Born came of age their families encouraged them to start making money. Only the Elite could afford to volunteer. "I wasn't as concerned when I saw 'unemployed' because that could be Low-Born or Voided, but you and I both know that the Elite are the most dangerous. They are educated and connected. They could be one of us."

The thought of an Elite rebellion terrified him. They had squashed it for this long, but with the tracking system, they had eliminated the threat. However, the true rebels became wise. Only adults who had Drawn could be tracked. They could not discreetly know who had been recruited until they entered the Game. After that, if the mentality had changed in these Elite children, the damage would already be done and could spread. The educated, the well-connected, those with resources, who could not simply be bought, were the most dangerous to the Region.

"What are you thinking?" Jeanette asked, watching the gears turn in his mind.

"How prepared are your children?"

"Raymond?"

"How prepared? Do they need the time? I know my Alexander doesn't." This wasn't a challenge or an insult to her. He was aware of his strict parenting method. He needed to know he wasn't going to create a problem for his fellow Dealer and her children.

She straightened, putting on her political persona. "I have prepared my children. They may not like it, but they are ready for anything the Fates throw at them."

"We need to get a better hold on this, Jeanette. Before they get to our children with their liberal ideology. The longer they are able to recruit, the worse this may get for our entire way of life." He started to fold up his map and insert it back into the tome. He took out a small pebble in the size and shape of a coin from a hidden compartment and ran it through his fingers. A reminder of how this all started.

"What are you suggesting?"

He gripped his fist around the artifact and slammed it against his desk. He ignored the startled look he saw in Dealer Prudence. "I'm not suggesting anything. Get the broadcasters." He placed everything back where it was and closed the book. The Dealer ran his fingers over the embossment on the cover.

"We Draw tomorrow."

CHAPTER 9

Tessa

In the heat of the moment, Tessa hadn't appreciated just how bare she was as she got shallower and more of her wet skin met the cool evening. A slight breeze blew as they waded to her waist. She sunk back down into the water and laughed. "I didn't think this through."

Alex laughed along with her and left the water, the chill not seeming to affect him. He walked past her clothing and stepped over her discarded bra. At first, she was worried that he was just going to walk away and leave her there, but he bent down and collected his own doffed shirt.

He stood back up and turned towards her, raising it towards her in an offering. She smiled and he took that as acceptance as he met her at the water's edge. She stood from the water and took him in, eyes resting on the way the fabric of his boxers was tented by his hardness.

"Like what you see?" he laughed, breaking her stare.

She was embarrassed but not enough to become shy because she recognised that his eyes wandered just as much as hers did. "No less than you liking what you see, no doubt." She watched as the tented fabric twitched with his movement. She was filled with a strange sense of pride at the impact of her flirtation.

She walked towards him, collected the shirt from his hand, and donned it. This seemed to shift his attention back to what she said as she raised an eyebrow awaiting a response.

He cleared his throat. "Yes, well... um, yes." His hand swiped through his hair again, causing it to stand up due to its dampness.

She had never seen him like this before. He was usually so confident and in control of his emotions. She realised that she, herself, had caused the interruption in his mental clarity and relished in it. The shirt hugged her curves and ended just past the apex of her thighs. She liked her curves, especially her hips. She knew how to dress them but hadn't expected a man's shirt to illicit such a reaction. She didn't interrupt his staring any further as she bent down to collect her clothing that was spread about.

"We should probably get back to the tent now, don't you think?" Her voice was husky and gruff; she enjoyed this feeling.

"It is getting dark." He swallowed hard and she laughed inwardly at his apparent lack of discipline.

"Wouldn't want to get lost heading to a place we could go blindfolded," she joked, walking past him. She didn't hear it clearly, but she swore she heard him repeat her final word under his breath.

How different she felt compared to this morning when she had heard the announcement. She had felt so lost, sheepish, unprepared. She feared her lack of control, the absence of options. All she needed to do was harness that vulnerability. Tessa decided then and there that believing in herself and relying on her confidence could get her exactly what she wanted. With, or without Alex.

But at that moment, it was Alex that she wanted.

When they got back to the tent, she intentionally bent over slowly to unzip the entrance of the tent. She hinged at her hips to allow him an unobstructed view. She heard him drop something, a couple of thuds that she imagined were shoes and she grinned to herself. There was a pride that she hadn't felt before; this was proof that there was more to life than the Game.

She sunk to her knees and looked over her shoulder at him before crawling into the tent.

"Fates alive," he cursed. Then he followed her quickly into the tent.

She sat on her feet, knees splayed in front of her, allowing him a gap to get closer. "You should probably zip the door up." She didn't allow herself to laugh, but she was amused at how the simple things had slipped his mind.

He followed her orders, but the zipper caught a few times with the speed and force he was putting into it. She broke into a laugh at this, and he joined her, swearing at the zipper for its uncooperative nature.

He finally got it closed and knelt between her knees. "Now that I have fully embarrassed myself," he breathed an airy laugh, "shall we get ourselves warmed up?"

Tessa smiled and stuck a finger in the waistband of his boxers, pulling away and releasing, providing a wet smack against his hips. "I hear bare-body heat is the quickest way to reduce the chances of hypothermia."

"Oh well, we wouldn't want that now, would we?" he mused and leaned back, peeling off the wet fabric before discarding it near the door. He normally would have corrected her, citing some piece of information that made him more correct than her. But she grinned knowing he didn't want to be superior right now. Also taking note that he *did* know how to choose his battles.

She only had a couple of weeks left to harness this power within herself. She wanted to grow into this sexuality and use it to empower her and her confidence. She was never going to use sex as a weapon or tool to buy her way in, that wasn't her. But she was invincible and had been since her nudity at the beach. She was invincible because she *chose* to be. At her most bare, she somehow lit a fire of self-belief in herself.

She looked down and there was no longer any barrier between them. The only thing between their bodies was the length of him. She locked eyes with him and saw the same hunger she felt in her core.

She ran her fingertips up his thighs and grinned. "Game on."

CHAPTER 10

Dante

He sat there ready and attentive as his mother started speaking. He could tell that she didn't know where to start so allowed her the space to decide. She was never one to be lost for words; she was the leader of this family. Even when his dad was around, their mum ran the roost.

Just as she started getting somewhere, the broadcaster played its usual attention tone.

"Oh, for Fates' sake! Two in one day?" Dante asked.

His mother stood up and went towards the broadcaster, seemingly relieved at the distraction. He heard Dealer Avarice's voice and took notice. It wasn't usual that Senior Dealers gave announcements themselves so this was likely not good news. He stood up and creaked as he removed himself from the uncomfortable chair. It took him a few steps to correct his gait from the stiffness, but he made his way beside his mum.

"Citizens of Cassino, as you are all aware, the Fates decided that due to the declining population, all members of the age groups twenty-five, twenty-six, twenty-seven, twenty-eight, twenty-nine, and of course, thirty, will be required to Draw.

This ceremony of adulthood and entrance into the Game has been pushed forward."

"What?" Dante asked nobody in particular and his mother swiftly shushed him.

"The Draw will now take place tomorrow. The seventh hour, of the seventh day, of the seventh month. All Draws will, as tradition states, be performed in alphabetical order. This is regardless of your age group. Failure to attend the Draw will result in Voided placement, indefinitely."

Dante watched the colour drain from his mum's face.

He was old enough to remember why.

Dealer Avarice continued, "I wish you all the luck of the Draw. Play well, Cassino."

The broadcaster went black and silent for a moment before repeating. Without Tessa, this announcement would continue into the night.

"Mum, I—"

"Go get your sister." She spoke to Dante, but her eyes stayed on the screen. She hugged herself and Dante wondered if she was about to cry.

"Are you okay? Can I—"

She sighed. "For once, Dante, don't ask questions. I want to speak to you both at the same time. Your sister now has only a single night, outside of working hours, to gather her resolve for the morning. Fates!" She cursed and Dante instinctively wrapped his arms around her.

"Dealer Avarice." She used the same tone as if using his name to swear. "Nothing in this world is by chance, Dante. I need you to know that. Decisions such as these are made by those who simultaneously play and are in charge of the Game."

He swallowed hard. Opinions were freely given in the Gamble home, but he was still afraid of words such as these. Even if he did agree with them. "Mum, we need to be careful. I know this is stressful—"

"Just go and get your sister. She is likely in the usual spot at the lake. There is much we all need to discuss. Bring your flashlight, it will be dark. Do not return without her."

He unwrapped his arms from his mother and nodded his head. His mum needed the space, he could tell. The drive would also give him time to think about this change. As he collected his coat and opened the door he heard his mother, loudly enough to hear from the broadcasting screen where she still stood.

"This was very risky, Raymond. Very risky, indeed."

CHAPTER 11

Tessa

The two words seemed to ignite something in Alex. He shook and reached towards her. He stroked her sides, down the sides of her spread thighs, ending at her knees where they hit the sleeping mat and his hands roamed back up again. He stared at her body in amazement and she drank it in.

"Do you want this?" Alex asked with a shake in his voice. She felt as though it was a loaded question, potentially meaning more than just the present moment. They had agreed, though, that they would have today without the worry of tomorrow.

She didn't know what the coming weeks would bring or where their Draw would take them. What Tessa did know was that she wanted the satisfaction her body was looking for.

She moved her hand from his thigh and gently grazed her fingertips on the tip of his shaft. She watched her actions, noting how it gravitated towards her touch like a puppet to a string. The sides of her lips curved wickedly when she finally answered his question, "Yes. I want this." Though she didn't look up from what she was doing. Tessa was exploring, feeling how hardness could also be soft as she gripped the base, earning a sharp inhale from Alex. She wanted more validation.

She slid her hand slowly from the base to the tip without changing her grip. Tessa repeated that motion, experimenting with her hold and using his open-mouthed groans as encouragement.

"I like playing with you," she grinned, looking up at his face for the first time since touching him. He attempted to grin in return, but she quickened her strokes, wanting to watch his face. She got the satisfaction she was looking for when his mouth gaped, and his head tilted back.

He slid his hand around to the inside of her thighs. She recoiled at the touch at first; it was far more sensitive than when she experimented with herself. He paused, not moving his hand, and looked at her. She simply nodded and brought herself back towards his touch.

She could feel the slickness and heat against his hands as he rubbed; she had never wanted anything this badly before. He plunged his fingers inside her and she let out a light squeak. It was all she could manage.

The intrusion was uncomfortable at first; his fingers were larger and moved at a foreign pace, desperate in their movements. He curved his fingers, finding a spot she never had before. She moaned and ground her hips towards him.

"I like playing with you, too," he breathed, stroking the inside of her as she rocked in appreciation.

They moved closer, and faster but Tessa wanted more. She shoved him back, separating them and he fell on his back. The tent shook in response and his eyes were wide with surprise. She didn't allow him to say anything before she took him in her mouth. She wanted to be full of him, full of that moment, everywhere.

She listened to his groans, taking the guidance to do what he liked. She flicked her tongue along the ridge of his tip and took him until he hit her throat. He seemed to especially like it when she would lick from the bottom to the top while looking him in the eyes. The pride she took in his pleasure was unparalleled. Making him feel good, made her feel amazing.

"Come sit on my face," he managed through his teeth. Her chest clenched at the husk of his tone.

"Sit on your face?" She didn't think that would be very comfortable.

He laughed lightly and sat up. He brought his mouth to hers and kissed her gently but passionately. "With moves like that, I forgot... anyway." He shook his head and stroked his hand through his hair. She wanted to twist her fingers in his dark locks. "I'll lie down and I want you to straddle my face. Knees on either side of my head." He kissed her again before lying down as promised.

She was confused but did as instructed. She climbed up his body, pausing when his erection hit her heat. They both reacted to the closeness and want of that positioning.

"Come up here," he groaned. He grabbed her ass and moved her up his body until she was in the position he wanted.

If she thought his hand on her was sensitive, this was an entirely new sensation. It tickled in a way that made her want more, *need* more.

He licked and sucked, jutting his tongue inside her with every pass over her clit. She was moaning loudly, feeling the freedom they came out here to have. She tried not to get angry that they had lost years of this. She wanted to enjoy tonight and make up for the lost time in euphoria.

While she was wriggling with pleasure, she felt more movement. She looked over her shoulder to see him stroking himself as Tessa rode his face. She smiled at the spell she had over him; he wanted more too. She couldn't get enough, and neither could he. When he moaned into her, she became undone.

Her moans became higher-pitched and more regular. She had to gasp for air in between her quickened breaths. She grabbed her breasts, kneading them, desperate for more. Her hips bucked against him as he latched onto her clit, taking it in his mouth as if it were the oxygen he never had.

She let out a final cry as her body convulsed. She shivered with the aftershock.

He went to continue, lapping up the dampness that had released. It was too much; she was far too sensitive to continue and dismounted.

"You taste… incredible." He was out of breath, and he ran his hands through his hair. He searched her face. "How are you feeling?"

She smiled. "That was so much but also not enough. I want to keep going, but—"

"You don't have to explain anything to me. I'm glad you won," he said with a wink that made her flush even more.

"I'm sorry you didn't… you know." She looked down. His hardness was fading.

He took her head in his hands. "Don't. This isn't about that. We don't always have to finish. Trust me, I won just as much as you did." He laughed. "You have no idea how long I have been wanting to do that." He leaned his forehead against hers.

This movement somehow felt even more intimate than what they had just done, as had his admission. Had he imagined them like this? Why had he never said? Her thoughts were interrupted when she heard a noise outside the tent.

Her window was still unzipped, and she saw a light moving outside. Alex saw the same thing she did.

"You wait here," he instructed her with a clenched jaw. He put his damp boxers back on and unzipped the tent, going outside.

Tessa looked down at her naked body and felt as though she could move mountains. She took a quick inventory of the tent before deciding that she wasn't going to let him treat her like someone to be protected. She was strong, and she was powerful in her own right.

She donned her underwear and his T-shirt and followed him into the night.

CHAPTER 12

Dante

Dante got out of his truck and saw the Avarice motorbike parked at the head of the trail. He sighed in relief that they were at the usual spot and he wouldn't have to somehow track his sister in the woods at night.

Turning on his flashlight, he illuminated the path ahead of him. He didn't have to go very far and knew the way like the back of his hand but a noise in the distance made him slow.

"Well, shit," he cursed to himself. His mum had sent him to interrupt their little sex-fest camping trip. Fantastic. He cleared his throat as loudly as possible, hoping to catch their attention. When his sister grew louder, he let out a frustrated sigh and scraped his hand down his face. He looked back at the trail that headed towards the car. He couldn't go home without Tessa, but he sure as hell didn't want to stay there.

"Tessa!" he hiss-whispered towards the general direction of the tent. "Pssst! Tess!" But she didn't let up.

He saw light shine on the trees and looked back to see a pair of headlights headed for the top of the trail.

"Oh, for Fates' sake!" He ran towards the cars, hoping

to intercept anyone attempting to enter the forest during his sister's… well, he didn't want anyone surprising her, that's for sure.

"Mr Gamble." Dealer Avarice was walking away from his car but kept his door open, allowing the car lights to illuminate the unofficial parking area. "This is a strange place to find you on the eve of your Draw."

Dante was winded from sprinting up and wasn't exactly thrilled to find that it was Dealer Avarice he needed to keep away from that tent. "Yes, Dealer. It is quite late, but my mother sent me to retrieve Tessa. They are… camping out tonight."

Right on cue, Tessa had cut through the silence of the night, and though it sounded distant, it was unmistakable. Dante grimaced in response.

Dealer Avarice looked over Dante's shoulder at the path "Yes… camping." He let out a disappointed sigh.

Dante did his best to cough loudly as his sister reached a crescendo. This awarded him an eyebrow from the Dealer. "Something in my throat," he lied poorly.

"It would seem so." Dealer Avarice caught on to the lie. "I would like to ask you something, Mr Gamble."

Dante hated speaking with the Dealers but any distraction at that moment was welcomed.

"Of course, Dealer."

"How are you feeling about the Draw tomorrow?" The Dealer kept his voice level and plain.

Dante shrugged. "I feel as well prepared as I can be for not knowing what the Fates have planned for my future."

"Are you suggesting preparations are pointless?" The Dealer was attempting to lead Dante in a certain direction and Dante knew it. He noticed the tension between the Dealer and his mum before he had left earlier.

"Without knowing all of the facts, I believe it is impossible to prepare fully. When a hand gets dealt in any game, when dominos are chosen, and when dice are rolled, there are always several different possibilities. Only one of which will happen at any given moment. The Fates will decide what gets Drawn and I will play well with the card I am dealt."

"And your feeling towards the Fates?" Dealer Avarice challenged.

Dante took a step back. This was not an innocent question. He thought back to what his mother had said before he left, wondering if it could be true that the Dealers were the ones really in charge of the Game.

"I don't know if I have any feelings towards the Fates," Dante finally said after a pause. "They exist as I exist. In the moments of their decisions, sure I may feel lucky or that they are unjust. Ultimately, thoughts and feelings don't matter so much as using anything, everything, to one's advantage."

A small grin tugged the sides of the Dealer's lips. "You would do well to remind your sister of such wisdom before the Draw."

"Of course," Dante agreed with a slight bow of his head. This was a well-packed statement by the Dealer. Why would Tessa need to be reminded about the fundamentals of playing the Game? Unless he was speaking of Alex.

Alex.

Dante listened for a moment and recognised that the forest had resumed its normal volume and activity level. He turned his flashlight back on.

"It may be worth me getting them on my own?" Dante offered, silently pleading the Dealer wouldn't come.

"Nonsense. It is dark." With that, the Dealer closed his car door. The only light being offered was the sliver of moon and the light from Dante's flashlight.

Dante turned his back to the Dealer and started walking. He slowed his pace, wanting to give the couple as much time as possible to right themselves.

He waved his flashlight ahead of him on the trail, hitting the distance as far as it could reach until it finally hit the tent. He stepped on a pile of twigs, likely gathered for a fire that was never lit. The cracks echoed through the trees as the twigs broke underfoot.

He faked his surprise when he brought the light to his feet. This was the only warning he could give them, the only time he could buy his sister. She owed him one.

"Mr Gamble, it would be wise to mind your feet in the dark." Dante felt the frustration in the air between them.

"Yes, of course, Dealer," he replied, louder than necessary. Dante relaxed when he heard the zipper of the tent. *Thank the Fates.*

"Alex!" Dante greeted him loudly and warmly, though he noted the absence of his clothing.

"Alexander, I have come to take you home." Dealer Avarice was less fuzzy with his greeting. A man who gets straight to the point.

"Home? Father, Dante, why are you both here, together?" Alex was right to be confused. This was an odd pairing to be out in the forest at night.

Tessa now exited the tent, and Dante was relieved that she had more clothes on than Alex, but not by much. He looked at the Dealer to attempt to gauge a reaction; he was stoic as always.

"Dante, Dealer Avarice, what's going on?" Tessa asked cautiously. "Is it Mum?"

Dante stepped forward, immediately reassuring her. "Mum is fine. She just sent me to come and get you. Dealer Avarice had the same idea to collect Alex."

Alex and Tessa looked at one another. Dante figured a wordless conversation passed through them. Maybe they did love one another.

"Why?" Alex asked his father.

"I believe when you took the motorcycle to come out here it was to spend your last day of freedom speaking with Miss

Gamble about your futures. From what I heard, and what I see, those conversations went well and are fully resolved. There is no need for you to remain out here with Miss Gamble."

Dante's fists clenched at the rudeness of the Dealer, but there was little he could do. He looked at his sister and was grateful for the dark to mask the emotion that coated her face.

"Father, I don't think—" Alex started standing up for himself and Tessa, a rare and bold move. Dante was impressed.

"What you think is not suitable. You have already proven tonight to have had a lapse in judgement." Dealer Avarice was firm.

Dante's teeth ground together. His sister was not a lapse in judgement or a slight on his son's moral character. If anything, the Avarice name was.

Alex stood up taller and Dante noticed he looked as confident as one could in wet boxers. "It was not a lapse in judgement." Dante was surprised at the courage of Alex standing up to his father, also a Dealer. He wasn't sure which came first in their relationship. "As stated before, we decided to spend our last bit of freedom together. One day before the last few weeks of preparation."

Dante noticed how impressed Tessa was at this as well. He did this for her. She also was likely terrified for him. This public display of disobedience to his father wouldn't go unpunished.

"Tess." Dante gripped her elbow and said quietly, "I'll explain on the way. Get your things, please. We will go home now and collect the equipment another time."

She nodded. "We can come back tomorrow with your truck." Dante winced at this, knowing Dealer Avarice wouldn't give up the chance to be an ace-grade piece of shit.

"Won't you both be a little busy tomorrow, Mr Gamble?" Dealer Avarice's smirk cut through the dark. "You are all expected at the hall no later than 06:45 for your Draw tomorrow."

"Tomorrow?" Tessa asked Dante.

"Tomorrow!" Alex demanded, striding up to his father, though losing a bit of the air of confidence he previously had. "What did you do?"

"Oh, my dear boy, I did nothing. As we all know, the Fates decided. Now, say goodbye. We are leaving." Without so much as another word or beat, Dealer Avarice walked the path in the dark towards the cars.

Tessa, Dante, and Alex all looked at one another. Dante suddenly felt the weight of his presence and decided to closely inspect a nearby tree while he waited for his sister.

"No matter what this means, or what happens tomorrow, I am glad we had tonight," Alex whispered to Tessa. Dante appreciated that at least now they were trying to be quiet.

"I know," Tessa replied simply and Dante noted the sadness in her tone.

They both entered the tent and exited wearing what Dante had seen them in earlier. Alex disappeared into the darkness before Dante led his sister with the flashlight.

"Tomorrow?" Tessa confirmed to Dante.

He nodded his head. "They made the announcement this evening. Mum sent me to come and get you."

When she opened the passenger side of the car, she paused before she entered. "When Dealer Avarice said 'heard'?"

Dante sighed and jumped behind the wheel. "Look, Squirt. I don't want to talk to you about this, really, I don't. But I will say that you were doing very little to keep your... activities to yourself."

"Fates," she cursed to herself as he turned on the ignition.

"Pretty sure you said that a few times, too..." Dante said loud enough for her to hear and chanced a joking smile in her direction.

She looked at him and punched him square in the shoulder which only made his laugh bubble over. This seemed to break the tension between them.

"Now, let's get you home. It is going to be a long night."

CHAPTER 13

Alex

Alex and his father sat in silence for the duration of the car ride home. He had never stood up to his father like that before today.

He didn't bother asking about the motorcycle. The way his father spoke to him back at the tent told him enough about keeping his mouth shut. The Dealer hadn't even mentioned getting the motorcycle home when they walked past it, which emphasised how angry his father was. Alex figured that, like the tent, the bike would be there tomorrow.

Tomorrow.

His father parked the car in the designated spot and turned off the ignition. They continued to sit there awkwardly. He wasn't accustomed to this, being the favourite child and only son, so Alex decided to attempt to break the tension.

"Did you mean it when you said the Draw was tomorrow?"

"The Draw is tomorrow," the Dealer replied curtly. Alex knew when he was speaking to his father and when he was speaking to the Dealer. In that moment, it was the latter. "You will listen to the entire announcement on the broadcaster."

"Father, if this is about Tess…" He had never had a problem with Tessa before. His father also knew he was sexually active already. Alex didn't understand what he had done wrong.

"Miss Gamble served her purpose tonight, I'm sure. Though I do implore you to explore your options past tomorrow."

"Served her purpose?" Alex should have known better than to be defensive of Tessa. This is what had got him into this situation to begin with. "Father, that wasn't what I was after. She is the person I know best in this world. She is a person I can trust. She is the person I want to—"

"And what do you know about trust, boy? You have yet to have anything of substance on the line to truly test who you can trust. On the base of want," his father took a breath and Alex noticed the shift from Dealer Avarice to a friendlier father figure, "freedom years are a good time to satisfy yourself and eliminate any potential distractions to your future. Past tomorrow you will meet more people outside your age group. Your mother and I met at the Draw when she went to watch your uncle."

"I don't need to meet anyone else, Father. I want her. She isn't just some 'urge to satisfy' as you so crudely put it. She is brilliant, kind, confident and makes me feel more at peace than anyone else."

To that, his father grimaced. "Alexander, I do not want you to feel peace. That will breed complacency. You need someone who will help steer your fate alongside theirs, play the Game, and play it well. I want you to find someone who fuels the fire inside of you. I want you to get someone that encourages you to work harder than you have ever worked before."

"What if I don't want to care about the Game nearly as much as I care about her?" Alex snapped it out but immediately regretted saying it. He was not an adult yet. Had he just kept these opinions to himself, he and Tessa could officially become partners without anyone's approval. Alex made the mistake of showing his father the only card of value in his hand. A card his father did not want him to play.

He took a deep breath and faced his father, slightly turning in his seat. "What I mean to say is that I do not value the Game without her nearly as strongly as the Game with her. Strategically, she comes from a good family who have always had the luck of the Draw with them."

"You will listen. You have *one* last night of advice. Narrowing your options, no matter what they are, makes you less powerful. Having such an obvious loyalty and direction makes you weak. Actions have consequences, boy. Luck runs out, and I have a strong feeling Tessa will not find luck in her Draw."

Alex was taken aback by that. "What are you saying?" His teeth ground together.

"Stay away from her. You are an Avarice, not a Gamble. Tomorrow, I expect you to start acting like one. The social skills you have learned under that roof will serve you well. However, to be successful in the Game, especially as an Elite, one requires ruthlessness. You will be required to make the calculated decision-making that this family is known for. You know how the Gamble family operates; you can align yourself all you want with her goals and aspirations. However, I will *not* support a partnership with someone so ill-prepared for their Draw."

"Is that her fault?" Alex asked in a demanding tone. "The Fates decided to eliminate years of freedom and preparation from her life!"

"As they did with yours. Tessa Gamble will sink tomorrow. Mark my words, boy. You get to decide: swim without her, or sink with her."

Without another word, the Dealer left the car. He closed the door behind him leaving Alex in darkness.

Alex wanted to scream, but he couldn't. The best option he had to get Tessa still, was to Draw well and be with her without a care of what others had to say. That day, Alex found a piece of fight in him. A small glimmer of defiance that he could nurture and grow to make a life of his own outside the Avarice name.

"I will have Tessa," he promised himself. "I have to do anything I can to make that happen."

With this oath, his Game was set.

CHAPTER 14

Tessa

She swore Dante to secrecy about the events that happened at the lake. He rolled his eyes and agreed but Tessa was serious. She didn't need everybody to know about her and Alex.

"It isn't like I'm just going to run in yelling about it, Squirt. I will say that you owe me one. I'll cash that favour in some other time." He laughed but she knew he was serious.

"Mum, are you okay?" When they entered the house, Tessa saw that her mum had been waiting for her. This in itself was not unusual, but the gloss in her eyes was.

"After. We will talk after." Her mum gestured towards the broadcaster and the family moved at once to the acknowledgement pad.

Tessa really couldn't be bothered with paying attention. She was too caught up in her thoughts about everything. She felt lost again but with an undercurrent of knowledge that she was going to be fine. She supposed that it was an improvement. Having some sense of stability was better than feeling lost without that, wasn't it?

She didn't notice that the broadcast had stopped until Dante moved from her side and stepped down from the pad. "I just don't understand."

"What part?" their mother asked, following him off the pad. Though Dante didn't have a sense of direction after stepping off, it was clear their mother did. They opted to follow her.

"Any of it. Why push it forward? Why eliminate preparation time and freedom years? Why make the Voiding indefinite?"

Their mum had led them to the dining room. This was the unofficial meeting space of the family. They had been having heart-to-hearts and hard conversations there Tessa's whole life. At that moment, there were two binders on the table, each one displaying the name of one of the Gamble children. She assumed her mum had organised the chairs already, Tessa and Dante on one side, their mum on the other.

"I think a lot of people are asking those questions, Dante. Most wouldn't admit it though, mostly out of fear." Their mum sat and gestured to the chairs in front of them.

Tessa took their mum's cue to sit down in her usual seat, lowering herself in the chair behind her named binder. She opened it and quickly flipped through the pages. Her languages professor would have told her this document had 'flack value' because it would make a satisfying sound if dropped at height onto a table. She opted not to experiment with this.

She noticed the cover page listed her full name, birth number, age group and a future date. She assumed by the year that this was meant to be the date of her Draw.

"Dante, will you sit down, please?" their mum gently requested.

Tessa looked up and noticed Dante hovering behind his seat, gripping it with both hands.

"I think I would rather stand, for now, please." He sounded shaky and weak. It was the first time Tessa thought he had taken anything seriously. Normally he would have flipped the chair around, sitting on it backwards or made some sort of joke. Instead, he pleaded for understanding.

She watched as he stared down at his binder and wondered for the first time how Dante must be feeling about this. Though she had years of her life uprooted, he still lost some time.

Their mum took a look at her children, almost in appraisal, and set her jaw. Tessa knew that they weren't just going to be talking to their mother tonight but to Mrs Gamble: the matriarch of a well-established Elite family.

"As you both know, your Draw is tomorrow. This, you will have been told and will continue to be told, is the most important day of your lives. It is the day when you are considered an adult in society, or as we call it, the Game, and no longer a dependent of your family."

Tessa opened up her book again to see a graph which led to a very substantial financial figure. She slammed the binder shut. "Mum."

Beatrice Gamble raised her hand. Tessa stopped and clamped her mouth closed.

"Your dad and I both believed that your Draw is *an* important day in your life. We also believed that there was no singular day that was more important than the other." She took a breath. "Starting tomorrow, the rest of your life will be a game and you will be players. Every single person out there is an ally or an enemy. Everyone in attendance tomorrow will be watching you." She glanced up at the clock and Tessa found she chased her line of sight. "Eight hours from now, your Draw will commence. Until every single person has Drawn, nobody will be dismissed. Your Game starts the moment you register and become a Recipient of the Draw.

"You should also know that this will be the first time in your lives where you will be on equal footing to those around you. Within the time frame between your registry and your Draw, every Recipient is equal in rank and standing. Be aware of how you school your emotions and reactions. Low-Borns, Working-Class and Elite alike will all be together in a single space."

Tessa had never interacted with anyone else from a different class to her. Their education, residential zones and even stores were all separated. She hadn't worked or volunteered outside the Elite village, so she had very little experience with others.

"Now, as Tessa has seen already, and as you will see, Dante, your dad and I, and the family before us have all played well. We have used this culmination of generational wealth for your benefit in the Game. In these documents, you will know everything each other has, and everything available to you depending on your Draw."

"So, we have to Draw well to get any of this?" Dante asked, not understanding the pages in front of him. Tessa was confused as well; these were all wagers from a betting office paired with account information.

"Not any." Their mum shook her head. "Your dad and I are more aware than others how Fates can change the course of our lives. We have been preparing, on your behalf, for any eventuality."

"Are?" Tessa asked, ears perking up.

"I'm sorry?"

"You said you both *are* aware…" Tessa didn't get to know her dad. She lost him before she was able to create any lasting memories with him.

"Tessa. It has been a trying day and will be even longer should we focus on things like tenses." Her mum looked pointedly at her, and Tessa shrunk in her seat a bit.

"Sorry, Mum, I guess I just wish he were here for our Draw."

Dante placed a hand on her shoulder and squeezed. "Let's just hear Mum out, Squirt." He pulled out his chair and finally sat down at the table. "Though I would like to have my questions answered."

Mrs Gamble sat back in her seat and looked between her children. She folded her hands and put them on the table in front of her. "How much do you know about the rebellion?"

CHAPTER 15

Tessa

Tessa was taken aback at the casual nature of her mother's question, but she was even more surprised at the tone her brother used in his response.

"Likely about as much as they taught us in our education, but who knows how much of that is actually true?"

"Dante!" Tessa warned. "We were taught that the rebels are a group of rogue Voideds, Low-Borns and Working-Class who Drew poorly. They blame the rank the Fates gave them in their Draw, blaming them for being unable to play the Game with any success. Due to their bitterness, they take it out on the Elite and use any means to advance their agenda."

"And that agenda is?" their mum turned to Dante.

"We were taught that their agenda is to uproot the Drawing system. We were taught that they don't like structure or authority, that they are essentially anarchists."

"They *are* anarchists," Tessa corrected. She wasn't sure why Dante was beating around the bush about any of this. Their education was very clear, though he had spent more time outside the gates than she had. Maybe he was jaded.

"What are you taught about what Cassino does to remedy the situation?"

Tessa noticed Dante's hesitation in answering the question. He glanced over at her and decided to give a very even and level response.

"We are *taught*," Dante emphasised the word and caught Tessa off guard but she didn't let that show, "that if a rebel is found guilty of being a leader, they are eliminated from the Game publicly. If a rebel is found guilty but isn't a leader, they have the option to be eliminated or to be Voided of position with the potential to Draw at a later date from a reduced deck. They will never have the chance to become an Elite in fear of repeated disloyalty to the Region."

Their mother considered this for a moment and looked between her children.

"As you both know, I am responsible for research and reporting to the Dealers regarding different issues within the Region. My most recent projects have involved the rebellion and their recruitment." She paused and Tessa felt her mum was waiting for a reaction, but she wasn't going to give one. "Their recruitment has become quite active in the past several weeks." She took a breath. "What I am telling you now is strictly classified. I could get fired for telling you what you already know."

"Mum, we're family. No matter what, okay?" Dante said smiling at his mother, but Tessa was struggling with this conversation. She allowed herself a curt nod in agreement.

"My research shows that the recruitment is targeted towards those in their late freedom years." Her mother sounded cautious to Tessa, and she had a right to be.

"So, the Dealers want to make us adults earlier? Punishing us for the rebels and those who decide to join them seems hardly fair. This doesn't make any sense." Tessa sat back in her chair and crossed her arms in a huff. She was sure there had to be a better reason. They were told the Fates decided this, and she had to believe that.

"When you Draw, you become an adult, as you both know. However, you first need to register your rank with things like your birth number and name. In this process, they will prick your finger. This, they will tell you, is to gather health information about you."

"But there's more," Dante said more as a statement than a question.

Their mother nodded and smiled lightly. "Oh, my darling boy, there is always more. In the finger-prick, you are also fitted with a tracker. This is used to ensure you are in your correct social areas and to watch for movement within Cassino. Your tracker is unable to monitor movement past the border of the Region."

Tessa was stunned. "So they know when and where you leave?"

"Yes, my clever girl."

"Why do all of this, though? They could just tell us about the tracking and the rebellion. We could all work together that way," Tessa said, almost hurt at the new information and invasion of privacy.

"And incite panic and distrust, Squirt? No way. By telling the Region publicly that there's a problem at all shows a sign of weakness."

Tessa felt the charge in his voice and felt the air shift. This was a loaded conversation about more than just their Drawing gifts.

Their mother seemed to sense the same thing so she stepped in. "What we know is that we cannot change this. We can, however, play with it." She gestured to the binders, bringing their attention back, though Tessa still felt the friction. "I made some calls, and you will be able to receive your trust after the Draw concludes. This is your Draw gift from me and your dad.

This is the start of your life and everything past this must be earned within your Draw." She was gesturing to the graphs, but Tessa still didn't quite understand what they meant.

"You made bets on our Draw?" Dante flipped through his book. "Two to five, six to nine, ten, each face card, and the ace. Why?"

"It was the only way to ensure you both had a promising outcome. No matter what, we've lost a lot of money because we took bets on every card you could Draw. This amount here," she gestured again, "is guaranteed. This is exactly half of my own Drawing gift. One half to each of you."

Tessa couldn't quite process what her mum had just said. She flipped through the binder again and understood the contents now that they were explained. She hadn't heard of anybody playing so selflessly. Her mother hadn't used her Drawing gift at all but instead she had saved it for her future children. Not only that, but they put their wealth on the line. There weren't any strings attached and there were even solutions should the luck of the Draw not be with them.

"Thank you," Tessa choked out.

"But, why?" Dante asked. "Why do all of this for us with absolutely no benefit for yourself? Actually, at a great detriment to yourself. We barely have to play at all with these figures."

"Dante. Tessa. There is more than one definition of winning. When I partnered with your father, I didn't do it for opportunity. I did it because we both felt and thought the same way and had similar priorities. We had one another, then we had the two of you and all we wanted was to be a family. We wanted to have friends, allow you to be kids, have fun and take chances. What would we have got with the money to be bigger winners? We have a nice enough car and a big enough house, we took vacations and had good jobs. What more could you want or need?

"Tomorrow you will start to learn what real privilege looks like. You have no idea how fortunate you both are to be in this position. To be happy with where you are and what you have. I also want you to know, that even if you do Draw poorly, you won't ever lose my love. You will always have a friend and ally in me. No matter what, we are always family."

Tessa had a hard time processing her feelings. She wanted to argue that there was a use to wanting more. Having motivation and ambition was important, but she was conflicted with her gratitude. She was always thankful for her life and her family. Tessa was worried that she agreed with her mother's sentiments which went directly against the Game.

What would she do if she weren't actively playing? Would time with Alex and maybe a family be enough for her? Suddenly another, more troublesome, option was presented to her. One that could bring her a lot of grief if she didn't play it well.

"How did you get away with this?" Dante asked in an awe-filled whisper. "To go so long without playing…"

"We were playing, Dante. Every bet in those binders is a play in the Game. Every holiday, each day we go to work, everything we do is playing. The Gamble name makes it easy to maintain an identity. As a well-established family, nobody looks at us to do any more than we already are doing."

"Why maintain anything if you are still playing the Game?" Tessa asked. Only the guilty hide.

"I will say this to both of you: play the Game for what *you* want. Not what others want, or what you think you *should* want. You can live modestly and still play a game. Play for happiness. Play for peace. You should play for what truly matters to you. Tessa, I'm sorry you didn't get very long to decide what that is. Unlike many other parents once their children Draw, you will always have me to talk to. Just know that any advice I give either of you is simply that: advice. The decisions are yours starting tomorrow including the consequences that go with them."

Tessa wasn't sure if that really answered her question, but she felt nervous about this answer and decided not to pry.

"Why wouldn't everyone do this? Why aren't we taught that playing for comfort is an option?" Dante asked and Tessa sensed a little waver in his voice.

Their mother offered a sad smirk. "Because most people play to win. Whatever the cost."

CHAPTER 16

Tessa

Tessa barely slept that night. She was mulling over the conversation she had with her family. Would Alex play in any other way than to win? To succeed? Be the Avarice son of his parents' dreams?

Then if he wouldn't, she wondered if she would, if she *could.* It seemed wrong. It went against everything she was taught success and victory were.

She hadn't even done anything to prepare, yet she would walk into that Draw completely ready to enter the Game and become an adult. That was in every physical way. She was still too unsure herself.

She heard a knock on her door and welcomed her visitor to enter.

"You're up early, Squirt." Dante strode easily across the room with two mugs in hand. He handed one over to her.

She accepted the tea and joked, "I think 'up late' is probably more accurate." It was still too hot to drink but she allowed the warmth to relax her hands. Tessa breathed the earthy scent in as if it would cleanse her of her nerves.

Dante sat on the end of her bed. "I've been the same. What do you think about what Mum said last night? Playing for happiness…"

She answered honestly and spoke into her mug, "I don't know how to feel about it. It sounds wrong but it feels… right? I mean we had always prioritised one another anyway and this house is far more of a home than the Avarice house. Something just keeps gnawing at me like it isn't what we should be doing. All our life to be instructed to contribute and play a certain way to have Mum hand us a binder and change it all."

"Squirt, Mum didn't do that to tell us what to do. She did it to give us options. Nobody is stopping you from taking all that money and investing it or even pooling it with Avarice and owning the Region like the heir and heiress you are," he joked.

"I know." Though she heard her own insecurity. She felt like every decision for the rest of her life needed to be made right then and there. Even his joke about Alex set her further on edge. They could be great and do great things and maybe they should. But maybe that wasn't what she wanted.

"People will be watching today. They will listen and observe everything we do. It likely isn't wise to tell anyone what Mum told us last night. Even Alex," Dante warned lightly and she suddenly knew why he was in there.

"If it is, in fact, playing, is it so wrong to do it and talk about it?" This was where her hesitation truly lived. If you weren't willing to do it with someone watching you, was it truly innocent?

He sighed. "I just think if this has been fuelled by the rebels like Mum says, it is probably within our best interest to stick to the status quo, even if only for show. Besides, do you think Alex will still want to partner with you if you told him this? Do you know if he would just run off to his dad?"

"He wouldn't." She didn't like what he was suggesting, but she wondered about it herself. She said it firmly enough for him to get the idea that she didn't want to talk down that road. "Anyways. We should probably get ready to be adults today."

She offered him a weak grin and in response he tussled her hair. "We'll have a couple of weeks left to live here with Mum before we are expected to move out. I just wanted to say that I'll miss you, Squirt." She noticed his eyes started to gloss over.

She wrapped him in a hug. "Oh, don't get sappy on me now, Dante! You'll see me loads. Age groups don't matter anymore now that we will all be playing in the Game. We could even get a place together?" If she wasn't going to pair with Alex, she sure didn't want to be alone so soon.

"Squirt, I love that idea! How do you think Loverboy would handle that arrangement, though?"

"I don't even know if *Loverboy* will still want me after today. He may not even be allowed to have me. If I Draw anything less than a ten, most of our family and friends would shun me." She gave a sad laugh, but it was the truth. Drawing a ten wasn't an Elite rank but it was just below it. It was close enough that if you still had ties to family and friends, you'd likely still get invited to family events and hold decent jobs.

"Then are they truly your friends?" Dante asked cautiously. "Let's let tomorrow live there. Today we Draw, tonight we party." He plastered a smile on his face and Tessa knew it was fake. She offered an equally cheesy grin in return that made him laugh.

As Dante got up and headed towards the door Tessa called after him. "Dante!"

He paused in the doorway and waited.

"Whatever happens today—"

He smiled. "We'll always be family. Play well, little sister." Then he left, closing the door behind him.

They would enter the hall together later. They would Draw as the older brother and younger sister, and exit as a rank. They were going to be two separate adults playing the Game.

Another knock at the door followed by the door slowly opening revealed her mother's face poking through. When she saw that Tessa was up, she entered fully.

Her mother wore a flowy blue skirt and a tight white top. Tessa couldn't remember the last time she saw her mother wear make-up. She smiled to herself; it was nice to see the life in her mum.

"I won't keep you long, I just wanted to make sure you were okay?" Her mum stood awkwardly at the end of the bed with her hands clasped in front of her. Tessa wasn't sure if the distance was for her benefit or her mother's.

Tessa reached her arms wide, and her mother came in for an embrace.

"I just didn't expect to lose both of you so soon."

Tessa knew what that really meant. With her dad gone and the two of them Drawing today, in a couple of weeks, her mum would be alone in this big house.

"You won't get rid of me that easily, Mum! Dante and I are both crap at cooking." She laughed and stroked her mum's back.

"You are both welcome any time. Breakfast, lunch *and* dinner." Her mother laughed but Tessa heard that it was through tears and sniffles.

Tessa was starting to tear up as well. "Thank you, Mum. For everything."

She let go of her mother and reached for the box of tissues on her bedside table. She offered one to her mother before taking one herself.

Her mother wiped her nose. "You know, Tess, with everything going on I forgot to ask how your trip to the lake was with Alex?"

Tessa froze. "Did Dante say anything?"

Her mother flinched at her panic. "No? Should he have?"

Tessa became immediately embarrassed and a flush rose to her cheeks. "No! No. It was… nice."

Thankfully her mother ignored her obvious awkwardness. "Did you speak more about playing together?"

"I think last night may have changed my mind and feelings about a few things. Though it is still an option."

Her mum nodded in understanding. "Just please don't rush anything. Don't let him force you to do things you don't want to do. Gameplay or otherwise."

Tessa wanted this conversation over. "I won't, Mum."

"Good girl. Now, I wanted to give you this." She held out a necklace for Tessa. "I wore it to my Draw, and I did fairly well; a jack of clubs. I want you to have it."

Tessa took the necklace and placed it over her hand. It was a locket in the shape of a spade. She popped it open, and it was engraved: *Bet on yourself.*

"Your father had it engraved for me one year. I was furious." She laughed at the memory. "I'm now glad he did it. You can have a piece of both of us, always."

Tessa realised she was crying again when she attempted to ask her mother for help to put it on. Her mother took the necklace and Tessa shifted so her back faced her mum. She made quick work of doing the clasp and putting Tessa's hair back in place.

Her mother cupped her face in her hands and kissed Tessa's forehead. "Beautiful."

They sat there for a moment like this. Tessa was so grateful that she had a mum, not just a mother. It was unlikely Alex would get such personal moments with either of his parents that morning.

"Get ready, my little love. It is a big day ahead."

With that, her mum left the room and Tessa felt like she took the air with her. There was an air of security and sureness around her mother that she was terrified to lose. What was she going to do without her?

Tessa finally rose from her bed and opened her wardrobe. *They will be watching* she repeated in her mind.

Reaching to the back was a dress with the tags still on. "A day of firsts," she mumbled to herself.

She ripped the tags off. She remembered how bold and brave she felt the night before. Alex hadn't given her that power. She had given it to herself.

If her body made her bold, she would use it as a tool. She was determined to believe in herself. She believed she could do anything, *be* anything. "I am powerful, and I am in control," she reminded herself.

And control, Tessa thought, would eliminate any weakness that remained.

CHAPTER 17

Tessa

They thought they would arrive early to give themselves plenty of time.

"Seems like everyone else had the same idea," Dante observed, straightening his tie uncomfortably.

"Hmm," was all Tessa had given in return, not paying any real attention. She was scanning the crowd looking for Alex. He was the real reason she had suggested that they go early.

"Both of you look at me." Their mum took their chins in her hand. "No matter what happens in there, everything will be okay. I am so proud of who you have both become and I know your dad would be too." She brought both of them in for a collective hug. When she pulled back, she gripped their shoulders. "Now go in there, head held high, and be a Gamble." She patted where her hands had just been and wiped a rogue tear running down her cheek. "Take care of each other and I will see you after your Draw. May the luck of the Draw be with you both."

Tessa watched her mother walk away towards the spectators' entrance.

"Come on, Squirt. I'll be with you the whole time."

They both turned and walked towards the disorganised mess that was unfolding in front of them. Tessa turned to her brother. "Are you still going to call me Squirt, even after today?"

He placed his arms around her shoulder. "Squirt, the day I stop calling you that is the day I die."

She grinned at that and continued forward, still held by her brother. She appreciated the stability he gave her.

Some tables were set across the exterior length of the building, each with a letter range posted to the front. Several clumps of people were forming and stretched from these tables across the adjacent field.

"I know they said they wanted to make up for smaller numbers, but this is definitely more than they bargained for," Tessa said while trying to see where to go.

"If what Mum said was true, it had nothing to do with numbers and everything to do with control."

"Is that such a bad thing?" Tessa challenged his tone. "Look how disorganised this is. Imagine if life was like this. We need someone in charge."

"You're right, but this chaos was caused by the very people who are trying to maintain their own control." He gestured towards what appeared to be a sibling pair like themselves. "He's in my age group but he didn't know what line to join so just joined any one. He is meant to be over there in the A-C but he's in with the M-N crowd."

Tessa wasn't sure why, but she felt the need to defend the Region. "Does that not say more about him than it does about whoever organised this?"

Dante shook his head and rubbed his chin. "People are as easily led as they are led astray. Decisions were made last minute and that has this as a consequence." He gestured to the mob around them. "People are confused, stressed and worried. Those are all the direct result of the Dealers and the Fates. The control they try to grasp through desperation caused this. I know it is less, but I have been coaching and leading people for all of my freedom years. So, I know how quickly even the most well-planned event can fall into disorder."

They approached the front of their table where he continued to speak in a hushed tone. Tessa had a hard time hearing him over the noises around her.

"Sometimes the very thing you think is best is the very thing that will work against you."

She gave him a side glance. "This is sounding very anti-establishment, Brother."

"Pointing out the faults in a system doesn't mean we are working against it. We just want to improve it."

"We?" Tessa asked just as she was called forward to register for her Draw.

She gave her birth number and her name and was handed a number. The person at the desk gestured for her to go inside.

She waited for her brother, and they entered the building together.

"Damn, if I thought it was wild outside…" Dante laughed.

He was right. Aside from the numbers being taped on the floor, it seemed like there was no order at all inside. When they were outside, they had the benefit of space, something that was severely lacking in this herding pen.

People were standing on their numbers and Tessa realised that she barely recognised anyone. Dante greeted some people while they were on the hunt for their number, but Tessa opted to keep to herself.

"Remember, Squirt, everyone is watching. You also look nice which won't help you blend into the crowd." He said it as a low warning before greeting another person. She grinned at them this time, heeding his coated advice.

Tessa knew she looked amazing. This dress was her armour today. Her dress was very fitted and lacked fabric in all of the right places. It had a high turtleneck, but her shoulders were exposed as was the majority of her back. There was a sheer material across her midsection which she was sure was going to help her keep cool in a packed hall with the heat of the summer. Other than these small details, her body did the work. She was curvy and the red dress clung to her as if she were dipped in the material.

"Let's play well, then." She took his arm and squared her shoulders. His arm naturally took an angled pose and he put his hand on her arm. "To our numbers, if you will, Mr Gamble."

He smiled and played along, nodding his head in a single bow. "Miss Gamble." He led them into the centre of the tightly packed group.

They were so focused on the numbers on the floor, looking through feet and pooled dress material, that Tessa walked right into someone. She looked up to apologise.

"Anthony! Are you on your number or searching?" Clearly Dante knew this Anthony person.

"I am on mine! You'll be down that way. I set this all up so perfectly and they made a right mess of it all."

Dante chuckled politely and teased, "Careful, Largesse. That's your employer you're talking about."

Tessa figured these two were quite close.

"Who are you telling? Who do you think was called out of his bed on the eve of their Draw to stick some numbers down and set up some chairs? That is the only reason I knew where my number was at all." He looked to Tessa, and she didn't miss the scan he made down her body.

"Anthony Largesse," he said, offering his hand.

"Tessa Gamble." She accepted putting her hand in his. She went for a shake, but he tilted her hand, leaned down and kissed her knuckles. Based on how warm she felt, she figured she likely turned the colour of her dress.

"What is your number, Tessa Gamble?"

She enjoyed the way he said her name. She told him her

number and he angled his arm just as Dante had. "Largesse Express, if you would like?"

She smiled and took his arm. Dante's groan in the background wasn't lost on her.

Anthony and Tessa walked ahead, and he bent towards her ear and spoke to her in a low voice. "Tessa, I know that we just met but I feel as though I must give you a warning."

She looked up at Anthony and carefully monitored her expression. Everyone was watching. "Warn me? Anthony, if you are about to tell me something shocking that my brother has done—"

"No, unfortunately, nothing as fun as that. Though I do have stories should you wish to hear them another time."

She gave a light, polite laugh in response to try and mask her nervousness.

"I have overheard some conversations as of late." He paused.

She wasn't sure if he was waiting for a reaction, so she just said, "Oh?"

"If I were you, Miss Gamble, I would choose a card that is not obviously meant for you."

She blanched. "What? What does—"

"There are bigger things in play today than you likely know. Don't take the obvious card."

She was stunned and couldn't form a proper question. She just stuttered until Anthony came to an abrupt halt.

"Here we are!" His tone changed back to his false, jovial tour-guide role. "Take your place, Gamble siblings. I will see you both at the after-party." He looked to Tessa, took her hand and kissed it again. "Play well." Then he walked away towards his number where they had found him.

Dante looked down at his sister. "What was all that about? Seemed like a very intense conversation."

She ignored his question and asked her own. "What does Anthony do for the Dealers?"

He seemed a bit confused but answered anyway. "He is Dealer Avarice's assistant. Why?"

"No reason," she replied simply.

As if it were perfectly timed, all of the curtains surrounding the Draw Recipients flew into the rafters above. Tessa spun on her spot, taking in the change in the room. It looked like the hall was made into an arena. The seating was in a semicircle all facing the stage in front of them. There were chairs in front of them at ground level.

"Tess!" Dante whispered loudly and poked her back to face her forward again. They were moving. Neatly, as if instructed, the Draw Recipients walked in order, snaking through the line of numbers, stretching out like an accordion before Tessa.

As she started moving, she scanned the crowd for any sign of her mother until the voice in her head reminded her that everyone would be watching.

She faced forward and attempted to remain focused on what was in front of her. The seats looked padded, with alternate colouring on their upholstery matching the Region's emblem. Up on the stage sat a simple poker table covered in green felt. Two chairs were sat on opposite sides and a single deck of cards was within the box in the middle. Tessa could see this on the large screen above her head. Luckily her attentions were brought back to her surrounding area as the snaking slowed, forcing her to pay more attention. She and Dante finally had their turn to take their seats.

"Next row, please," some official in an usher's vest said to Tessa.

She watched as Dante lowered himself into the last seat of that row. They were going to be separated the whole time.

Dante mouthed *play well* and she understood. The Game had started. She turned in the row behind him, making her way to the very opposite end. She skimmed her hand on the padded chairs; black, red, black, red, black… green.

She looked around quickly, noting that she couldn't see any other green chairs. Behind her, red, behind that one, black. This ruled out the difference being caused by being at the end of the row. Surely it was a coincidence. This was suddenly a large group so maybe they had run out of chairs.

"Welcome, one and all, to this all-important Ranking Ceremony," a disembodied voice boomed through the hall. "Welcome to this year's Recipients. This is the most important day of your entire life."

CHAPTER 18

Tessa

The loud voice boomed around them. Nobody was onstage and Tessa thought perhaps it was a pre-recording.

"Spectators, please observe quietly and do not exit from your seats until all Draws are complete. Draw Recipients, congratulations on maturing to adulthood. Today, you are equals, living the rank of your parents and guardians. Tomorrow, you join society as determined by the rank that will shortly be given to you by the Fates. Your freedom years are hereby over. Once your Draw is completed, you will exit the stage following the line on the floor to register your new rank and complete your health checks. The Dealer will now show you the process that is to be completed. May the luck of the Draw be with you. Play well."

An awkward applause started around her, and she couldn't help but join in. She thought it was strange to applaud something that she couldn't see.

Dealers Avarice and Prudence entered the stage together. The sight of Alex's father made her more nervous than usual today.

Dealer Prudence walked up behind the podium and

tapped the mic, echoing a banging sound throughout the hall. "Recipients, please watch the demonstration closely and listen to the rules carefully." She picked up the microphone and sat across from Dealer Avarice at the poker table. She shuffled the deck of cards after removing the box and plastic wrapping. After she had shuffled, she presented the deck to Dealer Avarice. "Once your Dealer shuffles, you will cut the deck wherever you like."

Dealer Avarice cut the deck.

"The Dealer will now collect the card from the top of the stack." She flipped it and there was an audible gasp from the crowd, then the screen zoomed in on it.

"What is your Draw?" She asked Dealer Avarice, more of a statement than a question.

"The six of spades," he replied. A poor Draw. Life-changing for the Low-Borns but seeing an Elite, *the* Elite Draw so low, was sobering. It reminded her, and likely everyone else in the room, how much rode on the card you were dealt.

Dealer Prudence continued her explanation. "Once you acknowledge what you see, your Dealer will also acknowledge to confirm for everyone in attendance. This is, indeed, the six of spades."

The card was flipped back over and the deck was reshuffled.

"Once a card is Drawn, the Draw is final. As we confirm your rank, a record is being made of your Draw for the archives. The card, and corresponding rank, will always return to the deck, and the deck will be reshuffled on the spot. This means that it will always be shuffled twice before you cut and Draw."

Tessa had heard the rules before. They were taught the ranking process in their education. They were also taught about what each card meant in terms of social standing, including what each rank permitted in the Game.

Her mind flashed back to her earliest years of education. Tessa's class would play a game called 'Yes, and—'. The first person in line would state the rules, rights and privileges of a two and it would continue down the line with each person representing the next rank. They would repeat what the person ahead of them said, everyone in the class would yell "Yes, and—" in unison, then they would continue with the growth of their respective rank. Three, four, five, et cetera until they reached the ace. Each rank had the rules, rights and privileges of every rank ahead of it, *and* more. The higher the rank, the more rights and privileges one had. And has.

"Once you have Drawn, proceed on the line of the floor backstage to be processed."

The Dealers stood up and Dealer Prudence handed Alex's father the microphone.

"This series of events will be the same for each one of you today. However, due to the large number of Recipients today, and the needs of the Region, the Fates have elected to add to what could be Drawn."

Murmurs filled the hall. Bets could have been taken and strategies could have been made based on the odds of a fifty-two-card deck. Some even went as far as to attempt to calculate the probabilities based on their position in the alphabet. The first person would have the freshest deck. Pairs would be more likely and a true mix, less likely.

She was also surprised that he made mention of the size of the age group when he was the one who expanded on the group this year.

Dealer Avarice raised his hands and the room went silent at the well-known command for attention. "Who are we to question the Fates?"

The room was silent but the tension was building. Recipients were restless in their seats and they hadn't even started the Draw yet.

"Now, we have added another card to the deck." He held up a blank card but in every other way it was identical to the others.

"This card will Void the Drawer of their position, indefinitely."

The murmurs rose into a louder chaos. Tessa heard people shouting from the arena seats around her. She wanted to turn to look but wanted to appear at ease and indifferent. A good player adapts, and not a single person could have seen this coming. It then dawned on Tessa that *nobody* could have seen this coming. Including her parents. They took a bet on every single possibility except this one. Tessa gripped either side of her chair in an attempt to ground herself.

"What do they mean by indefinitely?" the girl behind her asked someone she couldn't see.

"An undefined amount of time," a boy answered.

"Yes, smartass, I know what the word means. How can someone live so long without a role or a place? The worst part would be not knowing if you'll ever re-enter the Game."

Tessa turned around. "The worst part would be losing literally everything and not having any opportunity to get any of it back."

"How do you live if you don't play? Has anyone actually been Voided before?" the boy asked Tessa.

She paused for a moment, deciding whether or not she wanted to answer.

"My dad," Tessa said quietly before turning around.

Dealer Avarice raised his hands again and after a little longer, gained the silence he was after.

"Both Dealer Prudence and I have children participating in this Draw. I will be attending to all but my son's Drawing. We will then switch out to avoid any speculation."

Usually, the Dealer that does the Draw stays the whole time, but Tessa remembered an incident that happened years ago that she was taught in her education. It was the reason there were two Dealers.

"We will begin," voiced Dealer Prudence from her position at the podium.

"Abigail Able."

Tessa watched intently. The letter G was comfortably late in the alphabet. She couldn't imagine being the first to Draw, especially if Abigail had lost some of her freedom years as well.

She cut the deck near the bottom. Not what Tessa would have done. Based on the archival data that they studied in Elite education, the first few Draws were more successful when Drawn from the top of the deck. Perhaps Abigail wasn't taught this in her education.

"What is your card?" Dealer Avarice took the same bored-statement tone Dealer Prudence had.

Abigail gulped and looked like she was about to cry. "The three of hearts."

"That is, indeed, the three of hearts." And when Abigail didn't immediately rise from her seat, Dealer Avarice pointed to the doorway for processing.

"You only shuffled once!" Dante's voice rang through the crowd as if he were on the microphone himself. Tessa's head snapped in his direction. What was he doing?

"Dealer Prudence said that before each Draw, the deck would be shuffled twice. You didn't reshuffle when she sat down!" Dante continued and the crowd went deathly silent.

Abigail looked like she wanted the stage to swallow her whole as she looked back and forth between a standing Dante and a very displeased-looking Dealer Avarice.

"It is also said that once a Draw is done it is final." Dealer Avarice somehow managed to keep his tone level, but Tessa thought his neck was so tight that it might explode.

"So, a rule is a rule for us, and not for you?" Dante yelled back in return. Tessa wanted to grab him by the scruff of his neck. This was very dangerous territory for him to be walking on. He clearly must have known this girl to make such a scene in front of everyone.

"Mr Gamble, though I appreciate your concern for your fellow Recipient, she had the opportunity to correct me before stating her card. Unless she wishes to Void her position, she will accept her Draw." The threat was for Abigail but Dealer Avarice still stared Dante down.

Dante sat back down slowly. He couldn't do anything with the finality of Dealer Avarice's voice.

Abigail burst into tears and ran off the stage.

Pointedly, Dealer Avarice shuffled the cards loudly and for far longer than necessary. This would throw off probabilities of the alphabetically early.

Tessa decided to pay less attention to the Drawing and more attention to the rest of the room. She could practically see the steam coming from her brother's ears. The blank card likely ruined the comfort he had walking into this as well. Still, she was surprised at how poorly he had regulated his emotions.

She scanned the audience. As the Draws progressed, she could easily point out their corresponding families based on their reaction. A mixture of tears, silent clapping and smiles showed Tessa that this was life and livelihood for the majority of the Region. A farming family Drawing an Elite card would create the opportunity for more land and more livestock, which could create generational wealth and better prospects for the future if handled correctly.

Tessa had heard of families who had put too much stock and pressure on their new connections and opportunities in the Game. In their education, they called this the Icarus Illness. Families, old allies and anyone else could turn on one another in the pursuit to better their position in life.

"Alexander Avarice."

At Alex's name, Tessa felt like she was going to be sick. She looked up to watch him. They had agreed to go through the Game together no matter what, and she needed to support him. Her breath caught when the screen showed his face. He looked awful. He was wearing a nice suit along with his family tie, likely gifted by his father like Tessa's necklace from her mum but he looked sickeningly tired.

His hair was a disaster. He had been combing his hand nervously through his hair after putting gel in it. She knew him better than anyone and she knew that he was not okay.

Elite children, especially from well-established families, have a lot of pressure on them going into their Draw. Where Low-Borns and Working-Class have a lot to gain, the Elite can only maintain or drop in rank.

Sometimes the most powerful position you can be in is one where you have nothing to lose.

She watched him cut on the screen. If she had a guess, she would say he cut almost exactly in the middle.

"What is your card?" Dealer Prudence said.

Tessa's stomach dropped when she saw the card on the screen.

Alex cleared his throat. "The nine of diamonds." He sounded broken.

"That is, indeed, the nine of diamonds." Dealer Prudence got up and allowed Dealer Avarice to retake his place.

Alex passed his father on the stage and he looked up pleadingly.

His father completely ignored him.

CHAPTER 19

Tessa

Tessa scanned the audience for his mother. She would be absolutely devastated at this news.

"Well, I bet he wasn't expecting that." The girl behind her spoke again, almost in a laugh.

"It isn't a bad card," the boy beside the girl returned to her.

"That is the worst card in generations of the family." Tessa turned to give them a warning glare.

The girl behind her didn't look phased at all. "Maybe that's a good thing. You Elite crop could learn a thing or two about the real world."

"And what about the world do we not already know?" Tessa challenged, shocked at the boldness of this girl. Tessa had to remember that they were all equal in this room until they Drew.

The girl scoffed. "Everything. This Game to you is life for us. The food on the table to a roof over our heads, it all needs to be won in this twisted Game of chance. Don't think we don't know who you are, Gamble. Oh, don't look so surprised. There are only so many families that own just about everything around here. Look around, most of us probably rent a property or work in a company you don't even know you own."

Tessa thought this just sounded like the Game. This purple-haired girl didn't understand that this system was built exactly to function this way. "What, so you're upset that other people and families play better than you?"

"You can't possibly play a game you have no pieces in." She was speaking to Tessa as if she were a child. "I'm willing to wager that your Draw gift is more than I will make in my entire life. Avarice isn't completely wasted. Most of us hope for a nine. There are great prospects in the Working-Class. Though I do anticipate that his Dealer-daddy will step in and make sure he never sees any limitations the nine would give the rest of us."

"You know *nothing* of Alex and his family," Tessa nearly growled back at her.

"Then I look forward to watching him scrape by for everything he needs like the rest of us. Maybe with his precious boy in a lower class, Dealer Avarice will finally pay attention to the non-Elite."

Tessa didn't understand what the Working-Class girl was complaining about. The Elite running their businesses gave them *jobs*. It was a cog just like everything else to keep the Region running. Tessa's parents both worked. It wasn't like the Elite sat around and did nothing. She was going to defend the Dealer when another announcement cut off her thoughts.

"We will take a short recess before proceeding," Dealer Prudence said before she got up from behind the podium. Dealer Avarice left the stage after pausing to allow her to leave first.

Tessa stood up to stretch her legs when suddenly Anthony was beside her. "I gave Avarice the same warning I gave you." He was speaking quickly under his breath. "You know things are bad when the Dealer is willing to mess up the prospects of his favoured kid."

"Dealer Avarice did this?" Tessa said far too loudly.

"Keep your voice down!" he hissed. "Listen, I don't know much but doesn't it seem a bit odd that the same families all Draw face cards generation after generation? Luck doesn't exist."

"But the Fates," argued Tessa. She couldn't believe what she was hearing.

"Look, believe what you want to believe. I wish I could be as idealist as you, believing that everything is fair and equal and rules are always adhered to, but I'm not. Avarice owns the betting house your future assets are in."

"How the hell—" Tessa started. She had no idea who this guy was but he knew too much about her.

"I told you to keep your voice down! Fates," he cursed. "Look, I don't have the time to get into this. Trust me or don't."

"How can I even heed your warning?"

"Play well, Miss Gamble." Then he left.

She stood there staring at him as he walked away.

"If I didn't know any better, I would say he had a thing for you. Good thing, too. Tough for Avarice to pull a nine. Must have shocked him." Dante strolled down the nearly empty row to get to Tessa. She didn't realise how far they had got through the Recipients.

"What colour is your chair?" Tessa blurted out, her mind still racing, trying to solve this riddle that could impact everything.

Dante looked towards where he was sitting. "Um, black, I think? Why?"

Tessa wordlessly stepped away from her chair so he could see it.

"Oh well, that's interesting! Avarice had a green chair, too. Not like the township to break their patterns but with so many people they must have run out of red and black chairs."

"Who set up the chairs?" Tessa spoke quickly. She needed to solve this and do it quickly. She had no idea how long the recess would be.

"Squirt, what's going on? What is with all of the weird questions?"

"Do you know?" Tessa urged through Dante's confusion.

"Largesse did, I think. He said as much earlier, remember? He's their bitch, basically." He laughed but it was fake; Tessa could tell he was still concerned. "Anyways, I have to get back to my seat. We're very soon. My row is nearly empty." He gestured to the row he walked through to get to her. "Everything will be okay, Squirt. May the luck of the Draw be with you."

All Tessa could do was nod to him in thanks. He took the hint and walked back down his row to the opposite side of the seating.

Her mind wouldn't keep still. How did Anthony know so much? In an instant, all of what she had been taught about the Region ran through her head, followed by the discussion with her mum. If Dealer Avarice owned the betting house... he wouldn't set her up to be Voided to avoid the losses of a Draw, would he? She realised she was still standing so forced her legs to bend and she took her seat.

A nine couldn't possibly provide for a Voided...

"The recess is concluded." Dealer Prudence's voice ripped through the chatter of the hall and this was followed by a quiet, interrupted only by the sound of scraping chairs and light coughing as everyone readjusted.

"Ursula Gains."

Tessa was stunned at the surname. She hadn't been paying enough attention. They were already at 'G'. She looked down towards her brother who had his eyes closed. He was likely breathing into a state of calm. Tessa took the opportunity to scan the crowd once again for her mum. It was impossible to find a singular person in a sea of what was likely hundreds.

Shuffle, cut, Draw. Shuffle, cut, Draw.

"Dante Gamble."

The air in Tessa's lungs raced out of her in a single whoosh as her brother rose and took his place on the stage. Only when he was sitting did she realise she wasn't breathing. She forced herself to inhale deeply.

Dealer Avarice mumbled something to Dante and he smiled and laughed something in return.

He cut, very, *very* close to the top.

"What is your card?"

Tessa could have seen the card on the screen above had she not had her eyes glued to her brother in front of her. She felt as though the room froze in place, her heart pumping in her ears the only thing telling her that she was in that room and that this wasn't a dream.

"The king of clubs."

"That is, indeed, the king of clubs."

Tessa's smile hurt her cheeks it was so wide. She wanted to stand up and scream in elation at her brother's Draw. With a king, he could become a Dealer.

"Tessa Gamble."

Fuck.

Tessa was so concentrated on Dante's Draw that she completely forgot she was next. Perhaps that was one silver lining of her not sitting right beside him. She didn't have the physical reminder of her place in the order.

She took a deep breath and rose, climbing each of the stairs carefully. The very last thing she wanted to do was trip up them in front of so many people.

She risked a look down at the Recipients and empty chairs below. Only two green chairs. However, she didn't have time to think about it when she finally caught sight of her mum in the crowd. Tessa immediately felt more relaxed but her mum didn't wave. She gave a single nod.

Tessa knew that nod carried weight. She didn't know why or what she was trying to say, but she needed to decode it quickly.

She sat down in the open seat and the Dealer shuffled the deck quickly when suddenly, like a vision, she was in her sixth-year education room.

Her old professor was standing at the board. "There are two green zero pockets in roulette. There is an additional chance that your wager or bet will be void and effectively doubles all likelihood that the bets will lose money."

She was shaken back to reality when Dealer Avarice presented the deck. "Miss Gamble?"

She cut somewhere near the middle. This was very uncalculated; she wasn't thinking straight at all. Tessa shook her head and saw a movement in the cards. It was very slight, but her mind was brought back to Anthony: *'Don't take the card that is obviously meant for you'*.

Who did she trust? What did she believe in?

"Wait!" she said before the Dealer Drew.

"You've already cut the deck, Miss Gamble," Dealer Avarice said impatiently.

She straightened her posture in her chair. "Yes, but I want the top card from the top stack. Not the bottom." Tessa heard audible gasps from around the room but didn't turn. She refused to let her eyes leave those cards. She clarified. "Dealer Prudence explained that the Dealer will Draw from the top of the stack. She did not specify that it was required to be the bottom."

She held her breath. This was the only thing she could think of to not take the card she was meant to Draw. She had no idea if this would work or what she was doing. Tessa felt like she was out of her own body. She felt like she was moving at 100 miles per hour, and the rest of the room was in slow motion.

Tessa allowed her peripheral to notice the Dealer's movements. He had turned to Dealer Prudence. At that moment, she knew she had him.

"The Gambles do know how to pay attention to the rules, don't they?" Dealer Prudence said. It wasn't directly into the microphone, but it was picked up anyway.

"So it would seem," Dealer Avarice grimaced before taking the top card and presenting it to her.

Once again, she heard gasps around the room followed by mumbles. She just slouched into her chair in relief.

"What is your card?"

"The ace of spades."

That's when all hell broke loose.

CHAPTER 20

Tessa

"Show us the real card!" someone from the spectators' area called.

This was followed by other yelling. People were standing, hitting the walls, stomping their feet, as well as other collective loudness that Tessa couldn't sift through.

She looked towards her mum in the crowd and she gave another nod. Calmness and resolute in a sea of otherwise chaos. What in the world was happening? What had she done?

Dealer Avarice stood and raised his hands leaving the two separate stacks and her ace face up on the table.

To her surprise, nobody listened to the command for attention. Dealer Prudence joined him at the top of the stairs and raised her hands. Still, the spectators and Recipients were all up in arms. They were calling for answers, for justice.

Tessa sat there in her seat and thought about the words her brother had used before the Draw: that people were confused. They were worried, stressed and concerned. This process remained unchanged since the very start of the Region's history and suddenly it was flipped on its head in the last twenty-four hours. Tessa had just added to that confusion.

The Dealer had been caught dealing without a double shuffle, and now Tessa used the rules to take a card she knew wasn't for her. She took a moment to analyse the events that had unfolded. She had decided that they weren't mad at her. They were mad at the situation, at the Fates, at *him*.

Tessa reached across the table and grabbed the card at the top of the bottom stack. The card she should have got.

The crowd went painfully silent.

The Dealers both lowered their hands and turned towards where the crowd was looking. They thought the victory of that silence was theirs, only to find a gir... *woman,* deprived of her freedom years, bending the rules to her will due to their failed specificity, holding up a card behind them.

It was blank.

***

Dealer Avarice closed the distance between them in a few stomping strides. "How *dare* you deal from the deck?" He snatched the card from her hand and raised it in the air. "The Fates wanted Miss Gamble to draw the blank card! They wanted her position Voided."

"The Fates provided me the wisdom to pick the card that was *destined* for me." Tessa was loud enough for everyone in the room to hear her without the amplification of a microphone.

Dealer Avarice turned to face her. She saw the flicker of hatred before it smoothed to the usual stoic disposition.

Tessa turned to face the audience. She wasn't sure where her gall had come from but she couldn't back down now. This was her first play in the Game and it was a very public one.

Tessa continued. "We put our trust and faith into the Fates. This is *the* critical foundation of our society." Everyone was listening to her but she had no idea where she was going with this. "I felt a special gravity towards the top card. However, there is no possible cut that would make that Draw possible. Remembering the rules as outlined to all of us at the start of the ceremony, I simply wanted to allow the Fates to give me the direction they chose."

Dealer Avarice walked next to her and demanded her attention. "You undermine me like this, girl? You honestly expect all of these people, desperate for Elite blood, to allow you to walk out of here without that blank card?"

She took the challenge for what it was. She addressed the crowd but spoke as if she were speaking to the Dealer. "You introduced the blank card today, and today alone. With that introduction, it is no longer a standard deck of cards as was written into the founding of the Region. That was Dealer infiltration of the process that outlines the Region's hierarchy, opportunity and overall economy of this land!" Fates alive, that felt good. She needed that. Though she knew there was no way she was getting out of this one unscathed, she figured she was already this far. "Just as it was Dealer infiltration not to double shuffle in the first Draw with Miss Able."

An audible gasp came from Dealer Prudence this time but Dealer Avarice's jaw was getting more and more clenched.

Tessa continued, "It is unnatural for someone to be without a position in this society. You rid your people of opportunity and hope and expect what in return? They will only rely on the charity and goodwill of others. Which you, sir, do not have." She recoiled from that one herself. That was personal.

"What do you wish for us to do then, Miss Gamble?" Dealer Avarice asked between clenched teeth.

"Eliminate this card," Tessa said, ripping the card into several small pieces before throwing them in the air like confetti, "and honour the ace that the Fates provided."

This was a public act of defiance, she knew it. She was going against the Dealers, but she didn't go against the Fates. This was the most important thing to her. They were the ones written into the Region's very way of life.

She knew he would have something up his sleeve, but she was playing offensively for now.

Tessa scanned the crowd to see if she had them onside but her eyes landed on Anthony who had a wicked grin plastered to his face. She wondered if this was what he had in mind. The rest of the Recipients looked terrified. She wasn't sure if this was all for her or them.

"You expect to be able to twist the rules, vandalise a piece of the Draw, insult me and get exactly what you want? To become the highest ranked individual in the Region?" Dealer Avarice demanded of her.

"I expect you to uphold the will of the Fates. Not to further your own interests."

He paused at that and the whole room was sucked of its oxygen. Nobody knew how to react. Regardless of how you felt about the Dealers, you didn't question them, let alone so publicly.

Tessa, though, had just learned that there was a certain level of protection public conversations had that private ones did not.

She took a deep breath. She had to offer something up. She wasn't leaving here without some form of public whipping. Better that she was in charge of the act.

Tessa addressed the crowd. "Dealer Avarice interrupted a camping trip where his son and I were coupling." She straightened her dress. "The easiest way to be rid of me was to Void my position." It was a believable narrative, anyway.

"That is speculation!" The Dealer's immediate defensiveness criminalised him immediately and she saw the shift in the audience.

"He rigged it!" a spectator shouted.

"It's *always* rigged!" A Recipient this time.

She clutched the necklace that sat on her chest: *bet on yourself.*

Tessa raised her hands and the hall fell silent. Dealer Avarice stared at her in a combination of anger, awe and disbelief.

She decided not to give him an opening to speak in the silence she herself created. She addressed the hall. "The ace has always been a card of opportunity. It allows the Recipient the freedom to pursue any risk, bet, investment, et cetera. It is the highest and most powerful rank in the deck. However, we all know, that in any game, an ace is flexible. It can represent the highest or lowest number in value.

"Therefore, it is only right to assume that, in addition to allowing the Recipient to be the highest rank, it also allows them to be at the bottom of the Low-Born class, below the station of a two. This effectively Voids them of position while still having a role in today's society."

Tessa had no idea what the hell she was doing, but with the payout she would get from the bet her parents made, she would be fine even in the Low-Born rank.

"Ask me what my card is," she demanded.

Dealer Avarice looked to the crowd. The Recipients and spectators were the ones who were really in charge of this exchange and its outcome, but they probably didn't know it.

"What is your card?" Dealer Prudence stepped forward when Dealer Avarice wouldn't.

"The *low* ace of spades."

The crowd went silent. She felt the shift of unease as she made her choice. There wasn't a 'one' rank; nobody in the history of the Region had ever opted to lower the most powerful rank in the deck. It was more unknown, more change and they didn't like it.

Dealer Prudence looked to Dealer Avarice who shook his head slightly. "That is, indeed, the ace of spades."

Without defining it, Dealer Prudence had given Tessa the full potential of her rank.

Tessa could have cried. She let out the breath that she didn't realise she was holding. Her knees wanted to give out below her. She had thrown herself on the sword. She risked her entire future. She took the bet, and she won. It felt good.

She had offered up all of her options as a sacrifice. She essentially eliminated her options just to be gifted them back in seven words. Tessa stood on her own. She made her own future and bettered the odds of others in the process. The feeling of pride consumed her.

"Thank you," Tessa whispered to Dealer Prudence.

Dealer Prudence leaned in closer and whispered back, "I didn't do this for you. I did this for me." She retreated towards the podium.

"Dylan Gamer."

Tessa caught one last glance at Dealer Avarice before exiting the stage and though she knew she had won this round, she knew that there were many more to come.

CHAPTER 21

Tessa

"What the actual fuck was that, Squirt?" Dante greeted her backstage at registration.

"Hello to you too, Dante." She rolled her eyes. She was still too high from the power-filled adrenaline rush to allow him to deflate her ego.

"No, no, no. You don't get to pretend like *that* didn't just happen."

She sighed. "It is a bigger story than one I would want to explain here. Though maybe you should get off your high horse since you started sullying the Gamble name by shouting after the first Draw."

Dante just laughed at that, a man with no worries, ranked a king. "Dealer Avarice is going to have an aneurysm by the end of the day."

The woman behind the desk cleared her throat. "Name, birth number and card verification, please."

Tessa provided her details and held out her hand ready for the finger prick.

The woman looked between the two siblings. "Play well."

Tessa looked at her hand, confused. "Aren't you going to…" Intentionally, she eyed the lancets that were positioned on the table and the sharps box beside it.

"I said, play well."

Dante took Tessa by the arm and practically dragged her down the hallway into a room similar to the holding pen they lined up in before the Draw.

"I don't understand, did she poke you?" she asked him.

He shook his head. "She did the same thing to me, just told me to play well. That was when you lit the beacon of rebellion on that stage."

"I didn't!" she protested defensively. "I'm not. Look, Anthony warned me and he was right."

"Largesse put you up to this? I'll kill him myself."

Tessa clearly didn't understand their relationship very well.

"If it weren't for him, I would have Drawn a blank. I don't know how, but he knows things, Dante. Things he really shouldn't know. I don't know what's happening but it doesn't feel good."

"Tessa?" a familiar voice sheepishly asked behind her.

She turned around and saw an even worse version of Alex than she thought she saw on stage. He had been crying. By looking at some other people in the room, he wasn't the only one.

"Oh, Alex." She went to comfort him but he just stepped away.

"What did you Draw, Tessa?" He wasn't looking at her.

She tried reaching out for him again. "Alex, it really doesn't matter."

He shifted away again. "Just, please, tell me."

She sighed. They had to have this conversation at some point. "Ace of spades."

He looked at her, horrified. "But he said you'd sink."

She assumed that wasn't meant for her ears.

Dante stepped forward now. "Who said?"

Alex stared at the ground and his voice sounded like it was being dragged over gravel as he spoke. "Maybe my nine was meant for you and I should have got the ace."

Dante and Tessa both looked at one another before turning back to Alex. Tessa clasped her hands in front of her to keep from reaching out again. "Alex, what are you talking about? You are so much earlier in the alphabet. A nine isn't so bad. There's a lot we—"

"We!" Alex barked in a harsh laugh.

Dante stepped closer in reaction to Alex's tone towards Tessa. "Avarice, take the day. A lot has happened and emotions are high." He was stern. Tessa might have outranked him as an ace, but he was still protective of her.

Alex turned his anger towards Dante now. "What did *you* Draw, Gamble?"

Dante sighed. "That isn't important."

"Isn't important? Dante Gamble, you cannot tell me that the Draw is unimportant. Today we have been ranked and sorted. The haves and the have-nots. Guess what I am now!" Alex was yelling and he spread his arms wide dramatically. He was making a scene and noticed he had an audience. He turned to them. "The fall of a great family. That's what you all wanted, isn't it?" he demanded of the crowd.

Tessa had had enough. "Alex! Shut. Up." She had never seen this side of him before. It had to be a play. There was no other explanation for it. "As Dante said, a lot has happened today. With me being an ace alongside your father's connections and family name we can more than make up for a nine. As I said, it truly isn't a bad card."

"*I* was meant to be the hero here, Tess. I can't have a partner so much higher in rank than I am. What, so I can ride your coattails just like I've ridden my father's all these years?"

She tried to plead with him. "Alex, it has never been about

that." She attempted to connect with him again and he pulled away. His immaturity frustrated her. "What is it you want then? Did you want me to Draw poorly? Draw the blank?"

"Well, it would have been better than this! I could have taken care of us, Tess. I could have taken care of *you*, provided for *you*."

She was insulted to learn that her value to him as a partner was as a damsel, not an equal. "I don't need that, Alex. I never have."

"You know, when your dad became Voided you looked up to your brother in so many ways. You adore him and turn to him whenever you need anything. I wanted that, Tess. I wanted to be that person for you."

She recoiled at the mention of her dad. They didn't speak about it unless Tessa brought it up; that was always the unwritten rule. "So, you're telling me that the only reason you wish to be with me is to keep me as a pet?"

"No! Not at all, Tess. I care for you and want to take care *of* you. I can't do that when you're so high above me."

She sighed loudly. "Alex, I don't care about—"

"I do, okay? I do!" He yelled in her face and Dante stepped between them, forcing Alex back. Even though Alex was always younger, they were roughly the same height but Dante was broader after all his hours in the Activities Complex. She watched as Alex realised how he had been acting and gave Tessa an apologetic glance.

"Well, well, well, there she is. That was a bold move back there. I know I said a bunch of crap in there, but we don't need a martyr." It was the girl who was sitting behind Tessa in the Draw. She must have Drawn if she was through into this pen. "Veronica Haggle." She extended her hand. "You know, they didn't end up replacing the blank card after that little stunt you pulled. I loved the theatrics, by the way. They didn't even pick up the torn-up bits you threw. I was tempted to get a piece for you to keep." She laughed.

Tessa turned to her, thankful for the distraction from Alex. "Thanks, Veronica. I didn't mean to be a martyr, and I *really* didn't want to become one. I don't actually know what I wanted. I just felt that something was going on."

Veronica looked uninterested in what Tessa had to say. "I still can't believe *you're* banging *him*. Look at you! No offence, Avarice, but if this dress speaks for the body underneath, it is screaming to be seen."

Alex just glared at Tessa. "How does... whoever the hell this is, know about that?"

"Veronica, as I said." Then she turned to Tessa. "I thought Loverboy would be in on the coup."

"Coup?" Tessa, Alex and Dante all asked in unison.

"Oh, Gamble. You didn't think your little show ended when you walked off the stage, did you? Who knew one of the Fates-damned Elites would finally be the one to rock the boat."

When Tessa opened her mouth to speak, a very large boom rang out. It shook the floor beneath their feet and Tessa felt the vibrations in her chest. She looked to Dante who she found looking at Veronica.

Anthony ran into the room suddenly. "Change of plans. We're going, now."

The Recipients started running out of the side-access doors.

"But wait!" Tessa turned back to face the door that would lead them back into the hall. There were so many people in there. Her *mum* was in there. She didn't care that she would need to fight the current, she couldn't just leave.

"Fucking Fates, Tessa, just go!" Anthony grabbed her and started pulling her through the crowd.

"Wait. Dante? Dante!" She called out for him, trying to yank her arm free of Anthony's grip.

"He's a big boy, he can handle himself."

Anthony continued to drag her through the doors and out into the field where they registered as Recipients earlier. There was another large bang. She didn't know if this blast was larger than the first, but she knew that people were screaming and running everywhere. She couldn't believe what she was seeing.

"Did you get pricked?" Anthony asked, grabbing Tessa's face.

"What?" Tessa was too overwhelmed to properly process what he had said.

"Yes or no, Gamble."

"No."

Tessa saw the relief on his face. "Good, you have to come with me."

"What about Dante?" She finally was able to rip her arm from his grip this time.

People were shoving past them as they ran from the hall. Their shoulders got hit several times by people passing. They didn't care about Tessa or Anthony; they cared about getting out of there.

"He knows where he's going. Or feel free to take the blame for all of this?" Anthony gestured towards the growing mass of smoke billowing from the building. Her shock at his words gave him enough of a pause to get a grip of her hand. "You trusted me once. Let me get you safe and then we can talk, okay?" He looked up and she followed his gaze, landing on security officers looking through the crowd. "We have to go."

She didn't argue or put up a fight, though she didn't know exactly what she was running to, or where, or with whom. She had just met this Anthony character. There were so many unanswered questions she had on her mind.

The one thing that she did know: Anthony's was not the hand she was expecting to be holding at the end of the day.

CHAPTER 22

Dealer Avarice

The Dealers, as well as other political staff, were all raced away from the scene to the Dealer Compound. Once safely in his office, Dealer Avarice needed answers. He needed *her*.

"Did you find her?" he barked at the officer who had just entered the room.

"Not yet, Dealer Avarice."

"You tell your entire patrol that they will not see their homes until she is delivered to me, understood?"

The officer gave a nod followed by a salute and exited the Dealer's office.

"Father, there is no way that Tessa is behind this." Alexander was sitting nervously on a chair in the corner of the room. Dealer Avarice had neglected to speak with him since his low rank of nine was Drawn. "She is loyal to a fault."

"Loyal to whom, exactly, Alexander? She dared to accuse me in front of my people. She even dared to address them herself!" Dealer Avarice very rarely allowed his emotions to seep into his tone, but his pride was hurt. An Avarice was nothing without their pride.

There were knocks at the door.

"Enter," Dealer Avarice bid the person on the other side of the door but still looked at his son.

"Dealer Avarice, the report regarding the explosion in the hall…"

In very few quick strides, the Dealer snatched the papers wordlessly out of the secretary's hands. His assistant wasn't brought in with the rest of the employees. Raymond Avarice assumed that he was doing his own independent work.

"What does this mean? How could there be no evidence to support foul play?" He was angry. He wanted Tessa to be the enemy, because, to him, she was. Though he couldn't do much for just disliking someone. He needed a reason to find her guilty and make an example of her.

"Sir? We thought you would be thrilled." The secretary seemed to take a step back when they said this.

"Thrilled? Almost being killed is meant to have me filled with joy?"

"There are no fatalities, sir. There are only minor injuries. There is not a single citizen that is even in critical care."

"Secretary Betts, though I appreciate your optimism in this report, I highly doubt this is coincidental. Today of all days." The Dealer rounded his desk and put the report on a bare space on the mahogany surface. He would go through it in more detail later.

"A faulty boiler, sir. That was the situation. The second blast was caused by poorly stored goods that caught from the first fire as it spread."

To Dealer Avarice's frustration, Alexander chimed in. "Who is responsible for the maintenance and proper storage of the goods in question?"

The secretary fell silent and looked to Dealer Avarice, who waved them to proceed with little interest.

"Budget cuts and the rerouting of resources recently have left certain gaps in the operations of public buildings and services. We found that the most recent inspection was not done, nor the time before that. There is also currently no singular person who is responsible for the acceptance or storage of any goods in the hall."

Dealer Avarice and Dealer Prudence had rerouted the resources for the rebel cause. Raymond pressed the tips of his fingers into his desk thinking of the ramifications of this. The Working-Class who lost their jobs would know it came from them, but perhaps he could twist the narrative.

"How can that be possible? Father?" Alexander asked turning to him.

"Leave us, Secretary."

With a nod, they left.

Once the door clipped shut Dealer Avarice addressed his son without looking at him. "Not that you will ever know the responsibility of leading given your Draw today, but there are many complicated decisions that must be made. You should also know and remember that you are now a nine. Anyone above your station is no longer required to acknowledge your existence, let alone answer questions regarding conversations you shouldn't be in the room for. The only reason you *are* here is because you are my son and there was a possible attack at the hall. Past today, you will no longer be welcome on the Dealer Compound. Even my cleaners are ranked a ten or above."

Alexander took that in. He had been spoiled with the privilege of his name his entire life. Treated with respect and fear due to who his father was.

"You didn't ask those questions because you knew, didn't you? You probably even fired them yourself."

Dealer Avarice scoffed at Alexander's feeble attempt to rattle him. "I have people who do that for me, Alexander." He finally looked up at his son. "We didn't go over any options below a jack, did we? There is much you should learn, but not from me.

There is opportunity in a nine ranking, should you be clever. Though nowhere of great importance." He picked up a picture frame that had a photograph of a pressed-shirted Alex.

"It really is a pity, you know, that you chose her. Don't deny it. I saw it in your eyes the moment I gave you the ultimatum. Now that the whole Region knows that you've slept together, you may as well make it official." Dealer Avarice said this as a test. He didn't want his son running off with someone so troublesome.

He watched as Alex slowly got up from his seat and stood on the other side of the desk from him. "Did you do this, Father? Did you give me the nine and give Tess the blank?"

"Well, my boy, this *is* all a game. Offensive, defensive, players and pawns. Your decisions and actions had consequences, Alexander. I didn't deal your card and Miss Gamble chose her ace. Interesting how things can go exactly right, but still end up perfectly wrong. We do play on, don't we?" He gave his son a nod. "You are dismissed." The Dealer could tell his son was angry and he had a right to be. But he gave that nine for a reason and he wanted to see Alexander play his role.

As he stepped over the threshold, the Dealer finalised the conversation. "You know the rules now. No more than two weeks until you are out of the house. See that our paths don't cross."

The Dealer then picked up the frame and dropped it from standing height into the bin.

That was his hardest sacrifice, his only son, but it was the only way to get what he wanted.

CHAPTER 23

Tessa

Tessa got out of the car and stepped onto the soggy grass. She noticed that it wasn't the only car there, and there was enough disturbance to the ground to tell her that more cars had parked there not long ago.

"I am not following you into those woods until you start talking." Tessa crossed her arms and leaned against his car. Her hard exterior was challenged by her feet slowly sliding out from underneath her in the mud.

Anthony looked down at her feet and scanned her body up until he met her eyes and smirked.

"Alright, Gamble, three questions. Then we get you inside, deal?"

"Inside?" She looked around and all she could see was this clearing surrounded by a densely packed forest of trees. She couldn't even see any paths or well-worn areas of grass that could suggest they would go anywhere.

"Yes, inside. Two more questions. I hope they are better than that one." He crossed his arms and she was sure it was in mimicry of her.

She scowled. "Why did you bring me here?"

"Because it's safer than a building that just blew up. One more question."

Fates. She wasn't very good at this. She had to treat this like a game.

"Why have you taken a sudden interest in my position in the Region?" She wanted to know why he warned her without knowing her, why he made sure to save her instead of anyone else. They had just met today; this had to be a play.

He grinned and held out his arm. After rolling her eyes, she accepted. "Ever the gentleman." They started walking across the clearing and when they had crossed about halfway Tessa stopped. "You didn't answer my question."

He looked at her and smiled wickedly. "I said three questions and you asked three. I never said you would get three answers."

She tried to catch her reaction before her mouth popped open but she couldn't.

He reached over and gently closed it and spoke to her still holding her chin. "Word of advice, always listen carefully. I know you can do that because of your performance during your Draw today. Don't ever make any deals you aren't sure you can win." He looked down at her mouth and gave an arrogant smirk before letting go of her chin. "You can call me Tony, by the way."

She noticed that her feet had hit something hard. Her low wedge heel gave a 'clunk' under her. She hid her curiosity but stopped on that spot.

"Good instincts, Gamble. Also, good job keeping your question internalised. Oftentimes, the greatest value of information you will get is through observation. Asking fewer or no questions at all allows people to speak freely. Information is a tool." He put his hand in his pocket. "Brace yourself."

She had no idea what he meant by that when suddenly she was falling.

"Fucking, *fuck*, Anthony!" Tessa had no idea where she was or how far she fell, but she landed on her side on a large blue mat and it was much firmer than it should have been. She looked over at Anthony who had gracefully landed in a superhero pose and swiped his auburn hair from his face.

"I said to brace yourself," he said as if that were enough warning.

"Why am I following you, anyway? Are you taking me to some dungeon to kill me?" Tessa had to admit to herself that following a stranger into the woods was probably not the smartest thing she had ever done. She heard laughter come from behind her and she scrambled to her knees.

"You always have a way with the dramatics, Squirt."

"Dante." She breathed with relief at the sight of him.

"What's the count?" Anthony turned very seriously to Dante.

"Zero, thank fuck. What the hell was that back there, Largesse?"

Anthony shrugged. "Let's just call it a show of force."

Tessa turned to Anthony. "That was *you*?" She then turned back to her brother. "Dante, please, what is going on?"

Dante looked at Anthony and they had a wordless conversation that ended with Anthony nodding.

"Squirt, I will tell you everything, I promise. Let's just get changed and meet in The Circle."

Tessa was about to ask another question when Veronica landed on the mat. She did it as elegantly as Anthony did and stepped off the mat moments before another person did the same. "Changed, you say? I like Tessa dressed as she is. Perhaps less clothing. What do you think, Gamble? Need some help?"

Tessa just rolled her eyes at Veronica's offer. "Not that kind of help, anyway. I also don't have anything to change into."

"Come with me," Anthony said already moving and Tessa followed behind after getting an approval nod from her brother.

They walked out of the darkly lit entrance room and entered what she assumed was The Circle Dante had mentioned. It was a rounded room, like a large dome. It was windowless and Tessa couldn't see any doors but the one they entered through, but it had lots of picnic-style tables in it.

"Welcome, Tessa Gamble, to the rebellion."

CHAPTER 24

Tessa

Tessa nervously walked across the floor, tapping her foot down before she committed to a step. The surprise entrance made her feel uneasy about any potential trapdoors.

Anthony laughed. "Calm down, there are no more doors in the floor." He said it as if it was the most obvious thing.

She looked at him. "Of course not. How absurd would that be?"

He gestured towards the people on the far end of The Circle congregating around different tables. "All of these people are part of the rebellion. They want justice for the Low-Borns and Working-Class."

"So, my brother…"

He nodded. "…is one of our newest recruits. We tend not to recruit from the Elite but after years of volunteering and doing what he could for us, I took him in."

"*You* did?"

He smiled proudly. "I'm kind of in charge around here."

She unknowingly trusted and fell into the lair of the leader of the rebellion. She also just learned her brother was a rebel. She could barely take it all in.

"People are staring," she observed.

"Maybe they haven't seen someone look so beautiful before." He smiled down at her and then scanned down her dress again. Her cheeks filled with heat at the attention. "Let's get you changed. I have an office you can use."

Tessa took another look around the room while they walked and still couldn't spot any doors. They made their way through the tables. Tessa noted who was likely to have been at their Draw by how some people seemed to be cleaner than others.

They reached the end of the room and Tessa hid her curiosity again as they stood in front of the brickwork wall.

Anthony pushed on a brick and it popped out, exposing a doorknob beneath. He looked over at her and smirked. "No need to brace yourself for this one, it works just like a normal door." The door swung into the new space and Tessa allowed her eyes to adjust to the dimmer room.

It was a small room, a strange, rounded shape with a poker table in the middle. Other than a few sparsely packed bookshelves and a single trunk, there wasn't much else to take in.

He walked past her and closed the door behind her, normal in appearance from the inside. "Not what you were expecting?"

"I guess when you said it was an office, I had a different picture in my head, yes."

He opened the truck and reached inside, pulling out a baggy shirt and a pair of sweatpants. "Sorry these aren't nearly as fashionable as what you are currently wearing, but these are probably more comfortable."

She took the clothes from him and he immediately turned around to face the shelves. "You know, when I got dressed this morning this dress was meant to be my armour."

"Expecting a battle, then?" he asked, his voice peaking up in curiosity. She smiled to herself to get him questioning for once.

"Isn't every game a battle of sorts?" she countered.

"A very cynical view." He laughed. "Though you aren't wrong." He toned his voice down to be gentler. "Can I turn around now?"

She flushed again with embarrassment; the whole time they were talking she couldn't undo the buttons on the back of her collar. They were always so much easier to button up than they were to undo. "Um, I'm actually having a bit of trouble with my buttons."

He turned slowly to make sure she was still covered and then stepped behind her. "I didn't expect to be undressing you so soon." She could practically feel the arrogant smirk burning into the back of her head.

She loved and hated it. It lit something inside her that she didn't know could exist. She held her hair to the side and placed her hand on her chest so the whole dress wouldn't fall to the floor once undone and coyly said, "Neither did I." She wasn't going to allow him to feel like he was in charge.

She felt his hands pause when she made her remark and she was proud of herself. He undid the few buttons with ease and released the fabric. The collar fell forward loosely above where her hand was, leaving her back, neck and shoulders bare for him.

"Is this enough?" She noticed a level of husk in his voice that wasn't there before.

"For now." She looked over her shoulder and smiled. There was the smirk she felt burning into her and she loved the sight of it.

He crossed the room to continue his false examination of his nearly empty shelf. "Everything changes today, Gamble. Now that you've joined—"

"Whoa, whoa, whoa," she interrupted. "I haven't joined anything."

She saw him urge to spin but didn't. She finished dressing and gave him approval to turn around.

He turned to face her and gestured towards the table. He waited for her to sit before he took his own seat. He took a moment to study her but she was the one who broke the silence first.

"What do you want with me?"

"Here are the facts, Gamble."

"Tess, please."

He took a breath. "Okay, Tess. I want to do nothing more than protect you."

What was with these men wanting to protect or save her all the time? It was getting annoying. "I don't need protection."

"Really? You make a big scene like that, make a fool out of a Dealer, get the best possible rank after toying with the rules, blow up the place, and don't expect anyone to come for you?"

"I didn't blow anything up!" she protested, but the rest was all factual and there were hundreds of people to witness it.

"That isn't what it looks like. I also doubt Dealer Avarice will invite you over for tea to have a civilised discussion about it all."

She paused at that. "So, you want me to join your rebellion? Then what?"

"I don't *want* anything. You have entered the safe house and you know who the leader of the rebellion is. Not only that, but you can identify other members of it." He rose from his chair but Tessa remained sitting. "Like it or not, Tess, you're in this now."

She crossed her arms. "You don't get to decide any of that. I was led to some pit in the middle of the woods and that is hardly a binding agreement."

"I decide a great deal of things. You also wouldn't want to put your brother at risk, would you?"

That got her up. "Is that a threat?"

He walked over and grabbed her hands. "No, Tess. I don't want anything to happen to either of you. Your knowledge and apparent lack of interest put him at risk."

There was something in the way he said her name, the cadence when he spoke of her brother, that made her trust him.

"I won't tell a soul. However, I still cannot join something I know nothing about. Lacking information is a weakness, you said so yourself."

He looked into her eyes with fierce intensity. "I need you to know that if you put this, any of it, any person involved, in jeopardy, I can no longer guarantee your safety."

Though it was gently delivered, Tessa recognised the promising threat that it was. "You saved me from whatever that was back there. You warned me and Alex about the Draw. For those reasons, you have my word. I will listen and observe and make a decision for myself."

"Ah, yes, Alex." He dropped her hands. "He didn't take my advice. He trusted too much in his father and the system. Which was to be expected, after all. You were the one that surprised me. The Elite have a lot more to lose in the fight for equality."

"It was a test?" Tessa gasped.

"Not in the way you are thinking. The planting was going to happen, that much I knew. As I said earlier, information is power. I am the assistant to Dealer Avarice. I overhear a lot of things I likely shouldn't. I also read and process some sensitive things on his behalf. My access to him and his information is what has got us this far. Getting you or Alex to join us, to trust us, is helpful to our cause."

Tessa couldn't believe what she was hearing. The cards *were* planted. She gathered as much but that meant the Dealer gave Alex a nine. Her entire world had been flipped upside down and she didn't know what to do with that information.

"Don't you have so much to lose from this? You hold a good job, and from that job I can gather that you are part of a good family."

"Yes, but Tess, that's all I'll ever be: *good*." He shook his head at the thought of it. "I've given your brother permission to teach you what he knows. For any real change to happen, we need our people to be *great*. We need people who can change the Game to make it fairer for everyone playing. Not just for those who have unlimited access to money."

She took a moment to let that sink in. They needed people at the top to change the way things worked. She could get on board with that; Tessa had already done that much at the Draw on her own. Though she didn't feel like being a tool. "Now, you want me to become great?"

He smiled at her. "You already are."

CHAPTER 25

Tessa

"I want you to lie low for a little while, Squirt," Dante said as they began their steep climb up near-vertical stairs. She realised she must have fallen pretty far considering how many steps there were to conquer.

"Lie low? According to Anthony, I hold no cards at all and yet I am the most powerful player in a game, *the* Game I didn't know existed."

"That's privilege, Squirt."

She sighed loudly. "I don't see how I can be both the enemy and the hero, Dante. How can I, by simply existing, be the problem while being simultaneously responsible for the solution?"

He was in much better shape than she was. He spoke as if there were no stairs at all. "When you get a good hand in poker, do you trade it with the person who is about to lose all their money?"

Tessa raised her eyebrows, surprised at the question. "Of course not."

"Right. People like us, who come from good families and have good prospects use them for our own gain. We can see a problem we can fix and afford the consequences of that solution, yet we still want more."

"That's the Game, Dante. That's called winning." Tessa wasn't understanding. She could get why Veronica was bitter about the Elite, but this was her brother. He had the same situation she did.

"It isn't a game when the person who is losing can't eat," Dante said simply.

"What, so I am expected to give up my hand, my good Gameplay and all the work I've done to just throw it away?"

"Is it good Gameplay, though, Squirt? Perhaps it is just the cards you're dealt. You and I both know a bad deal ruins a game before it starts."

Tessa wasn't sure if the stairs were what was making her more agitated or this conversation. "Not necessarily. Any hand can win or lose. It just depends on how the hand is played."

"Tessa, a losing hand only wins if you're willing to take the risk on it. You might be willing to try, because to you that hand represents a new jacket or that dress you wore earlier. That other player? They would need to risk feeding their families on that poor hand to win."

Tessa heard him sigh behind her. She looked up and finally saw light up ahead around a door that she assumed was their exit. "I guess I just don't understand how this guilt is meant to help."

"Squirt, it isn't about guilt. It is about seeing a problem you have the power to solve and doing so. Did you know that the volunteer position I do at the Complex is normally a paid position?"

She stopped just in front of the door to wait for him, and when she didn't say anything, he continued.

"I chose to volunteer when the role was cut."

"Why was it cut?" asked Tessa curiously, but also out of breath from the climb.

"The powers that be – oh, sorry – the Fates, decided that the funding for kids and youth to participate in after-education activities was a waste of resources."

Tessa wasn't surprised by his answer; funding needed to be reallocated every year. "I'm sure the money went somewhere useful."

To that, Dante scoffed. "Oh yes, everyone who works in the Dealer Compound enjoyed their second pay increase this annum, I'm sure." He caught up to her after pacing himself on the steps and held the handle. "I saw a problem and had the means to solve it, so I did. Not only did I volunteer but I asked Mum for a forward on my Draw gift to get them new sporting equipment."

"And she agreed?"

He laughed and nodded. "Squirt, she paid for it all herself anonymously so suspicion didn't fall onto me. A young man in his freedom years, preparing to enter the Game, doing things with no chance of return? It doesn't look good." He sighed. "I came to love those kids and those families. I got to know them: their names and their hobbies. They are *people* just like us, Squirt. I didn't even do much, I just gave them dodgeball or soccer a couple of times a week."

She thought back to the conversation they had the night before the Draw. Was her mum a rebel too? "How much did that cost?"

Dante groaned at her. "You aren't focusing on what matters." He finally opened the door and they found themselves in the forest. They stepped out of what appeared to be an old broken-down hunting cabin. Tessa followed Dante's lead as he led her through the trees.

"Squirt, they can't change any of this. They simply don't have the means to. Trying has put them even more at risk and they only get even more trouble than they already have as a result. If we, the new generation of high-ranking adults, try, we can break the cycle. There won't be another Draw for years since they pushed the ranking for so many. Now is the time for the shift."

Tessa paused to take in what he said. He wasn't speaking of anarchy; he was speaking of change. The same change she wanted on that stage when she felt wronged or in danger of losing her future. Perhaps they felt the same way. "And what about people like us?"

He shrugged. They had made it to Dante's truck and he opened his driver-side door. "I, for one, am willing to be a bit less rich so my local transport driver, or grocer, or cleaner can live without worry of losing their homes."

Tessa entered her side of the truck and stared at her hands on her lap. "Why was nobody told about the cuts?"

"Why would they tell us? It was the *Fates*' decision, after all." He nearly spat.

Tessa couldn't bring her next question above a whisper. "Do people really worry about losing their homes?"

He looked at her until she lifted her face to meet his gaze. "That and then some, Squirt." He turned the key and the car fired into life. "Let's go for a drive."

CHAPTER 26

Tessa

Dante slowed to a stop outside a single-level residence in the Working-Class zone of Cassino. Tessa had, of course, driven through the zone before but she had never spent any time in it; she never needed to.

"See this house? A family of five lives here," Dante said, pointing at the building they were in front of. It was red brick with a few old wooden steps leading up to the door. There was a hanging basket swaying beside the faded-blue front door.

"Seems small for five…" Tessa observed. This entire home would likely fit in the Gamble living room.

Dante shrugged. "It has three bedrooms. The young boys share a room."

Tessa was stunned and turned to her brother. "They don't even have their own rooms?"

He shook his head. "This is how most people live, Squirt. This family is actually very lucky. They own this home and pay a mortgage instead of rent. They hope one day they will own it outright."

She nodded, smiling at this family's success. "At least they were able to create generational wealth using the Game."

Dante seemed almost insulted at her joy. "Tessa, there is absolutely no guarantee that they will be able to keep affording payments. Every few years their payments go up by a per cent or two."

Tessa was aware of how mortgages worked. "Seems right. They will likely get that in income increase every year anyways."

"Is two per cent always equal? If you make fifty dollars and get a two per cent increase, but owe a hundred dollars and that increases by two per cent…"

"Then it's a bad move," Tessa laughed before seeing how serious Dante's face was.

"What choice do these people have, Squirt? I told you before, these people are *lucky*. Rent would be even higher because people like us own the property and make them pay the mortgage *and* give us some profit. You also already said that it is too small for their needs. You also haven't considered if one of the parents loses their job due to cuts or otherwise."

Tessa was not a fan of how this conversation was making her feel and she lashed out. "What's the solution then, Dante?"

He took a breath before lowering his tone and continuing. "I didn't bring you here to argue with you. I came here to show you what is the best-case success story for these people. This is a family doing the absolute best they can and it still isn't enough. That is because they are not allowed to truly be secure let alone flourish.

"Think of that poker game I asked you about. You alone in your twenty-seventh year have more liquid assets than the five people in this house will likely ever have combined throughout their entire lives. Yet, you would consider that their singular dollar has the same value as yours."

She was taken aback by that. "Of course I would. You wouldn't? A dollar is a dollar."

He took another deep breath and Tessa was frustrated that he kept doing that, as if she was the problem in the conversation.

It wasn't her fault she was in the position she was in. She was educated just the same as the rest of the Region by going every weekday to classes. Everything in her life was dictated by the situation of her birth. Dante was in the same position she was in but was acting as if he was better than her.

"What would you do with a dollar, Squirt?" He finally broke the silence after some time.

"I don't know. Save it?"

He smirked. "So, you are assuming you already have food, shelter and time to save?"

Tessa looked at him questioningly; she didn't understand.

"The things you take for granted are the exact things that plague the minds of this family and people like them every single day."

"I couldn't help be born a Gamble," Tessa snapped defensively at her brother.

"You know what, Squirt? You're right. You couldn't. But neither could these people help that they weren't born a Gamble or any Elite family. What the rebellion wants is what you want, I know it. You proved it at the Draw. You want fairness, a bridging of the gaps between our worlds. Listen, times are changing. If the Elite don't change—"

"What, Dante? They'll blow us up?"

He raised his hands in surrender. "I must admit I had no idea what Largesse was thinking there. The whole point of getting people like me and you on their side is so they don't have to play with violence."

"Play?" Tessa nearly yelled at her brother. "Lives could have been lost today and for what? A demonstration of force or whatever the *fuck* he said!"

"Lives are lost every single day with this problem too, Tessa. Literal starvation, having no shelter, hopelessness, feeling like there is no way out other than death."

"Our Game doesn't murder people!" Tessa screamed in denial.

"It does, Tessa! It. Does. Sure, a big bang or two is a lot more obvious than slowly strangling the population through pollution, the cost of living and a general lack of resources. Guess where it all stems from, Squirt? Us. People like us. Our greed! The people, *these* people, the workforce, the people *actually* keeping the Region running? They are not the enemy."

"And we are, Dante? Is that what you want me to admit? I do understand what you are saying. These people deserve better but how can we do that wit—"

"Without fucking our lot over like we've fucked theirs since the dawn of time? You can't, not really. Change is hard and uncomfortable and the rules of this Game are hard-lined. However, the Elite are the only ones who can pick and choose from the rules to suit our needs. Incentives, tax breaks, not even to mention all of the plays that require buy-ins that are higher than they can ever dream of getting into.

"I don't need all the millions that are in my bank account right now. Neither do you. With proper investing and saving, we could live our entire lives on a fraction of that and still live more comfortably and lavishly than these people who work their whole lives, far harder than any Gamble has *ever* had to."

She swallowed hard. There was so much uncomfortable truth to what he was saying. After a certain amount of money, it didn't matter anymore. It was all about the status, the bragging rights, the power.

"Tessa, nobody wants to make us 'not rich'."

"Oh no, *nobody* wants that." She shot him a look.

He laughed. "Okay, maybe some want that. But this is all about levelling out the playing field. Making the difference between us much closer than it currently is. Giving them opportunity, life and *hope*. We could teach future generations of the Elite that being born into a good family shouldn't be a place of complacency, but a place of action."

Tessa nodded with what he said. Fairness was a perspective taught to her in education, but surrounded by people just like her because of where she lived. How could she be taught that she was superior and to pity those in a situation the Elite created for them? So many impossible rules, unrealistic expectations and caveats.

She thought back to her economics and business growth classes. Every single good thing or action to increase revenue had a consequence that she never had to bear. None of the Elite did. They safeguarded themselves through the downfall of someone else.

For someone to win, others had to lose.

"What can I do?" Tessa looked up at her brother, her eyes itching with tears.

He smiled at her and took a large exhale. "I'm glad you asked, Squirt." He ignited the car again and drove off still smiling to himself.

CHAPTER 27

Alex

Alex walked into his house to find his mother and sisters sitting in the reception room waiting for him. He was dreading this conversation.

"Mother, I'm sorry."

His sister, Louise, answered for her instead. "So are we, Alexander." She looked to the other two women on the chairs and continued to address Alex. "As you know, you have two weeks to set yourself up. As your sister, I offer that you rent my property from me and Laura has arranged some paid work to get you on your feet."

Alex was shocked. He didn't want this. He was an Avarice and it seemed that they wanted nothing to do with him. "I will find my own way, but I appreciate the offer."

His mother sighed and finally addressed him. "Legally we are required to provide for you for a further two weeks." His mother wasn't even looking at him. "That is the bare minimum. However, as you are my son, if you take your sister's offer and leave the house with immediate effect, you may keep your things and a percentage of what your Draw gift would have been."

His mouth opened in surprise. "You would take my belongings?"

"They are not yours, Alexander. They are ours, as this house and the family are. Your sister is offering you a lower monthly payment than she would give someone in your situation and it is one of her nicer properties in a good Working-Class area. Laura is setting you up with a job with a lot of growth potential."

He was hurt when he turned to his sister. "You want to make money off housing me? I'm your brother."

"You are a nine," Louise corrected.

His other sister, Laura, stepped in. "The only reason I am even able to get you such a good job with your rank is because I know the owner."

Louise side-glanced her. "If you call 'sleeping with', knowing…"

"Louise! That is quite enough," their mother scolded and shook her head. "Alexander, there is an image that this family must maintain. If you aren't succeeding, regardless of your rank, you will hurt this family more than you already have."

He recoiled at that and settled his emotions by running his hand through his hair. How could he have hurt them? It was his own father that gave him this card and ultimately created this situation. His father effectively kicked him out of his own family and somehow, Alex was the one to blame for it.

"It wasn't my fault, Mother."

"It never is anyone's fault, is it? Those Low-Born and Working-Class always blame us for their problems but celebrate the chance to become one of us," Louise noted while absent-mindedly smoothing her skirt.

Laura laughed. "You could take the weekly gamble if you want. Put some more money in Father's pockets at the chance to rejoin the ranks."

"Don't you dare," his mother warned. "If you are seen attempting to better your hand you will show you have contempt for the Fates. Take the deal, Alexander. Please, for me." His mother finally looked up at him and he could have sworn she had been crying.

He cleared his throat. "I take it negotiation is out of the question."

Louise balked. "Like you are in any position to? No. You should be grateful, little brother."

He looked again to his mother who was now looking out of the window. He wanted a moment alone with her but he knew well enough that his sisters were there to keep that from happening. He took a deep breath before admitting defeat. "I've never paid rent before."

"Welcome to the land of 'have to', little brother. We put boxes in your room; pack them and load them into my car. I will take you to the apartment. You can follow on the bike."

His head snapped to his mother. "I get to keep the bike?"

Louise muttered under her breath, "We were just as surprised as you are." She got up out of her seat with a groan. "But Father had already given it to you and registered your name to it before the Draw. If I were you, I would sell it. It is the only true asset that you have."

He took her movement as a hint that the conversation was over. He took one last glance towards his mother whose eyes were closed.

He left the room to go up the stairs and pack up his old life.

***

In a single day, Alex had lost everything. He had lost his rank and his status, he pushed Tessa away, and now his own family was going to use him for passive income.

Almost as soon as the door was closed behind him, a very light knock sounded against it. This was immediately followed by the door opening. He didn't even have a right to a bit of privacy.

"Father will be home soon and he wanted you out before he got back." Laura walked into his bedroom and closed the door behind her.

Alex had just walked into the room. He hadn't begun packing yet and felt betrayed by his whole family. He wondered if they knew what he had done.

"Is this all his doing?" Alex asked, gesturing to the boxes in his room.

"Some would say this was your own doing," she replied, picking a baseball off his shelf and tossing it between her hands.

He was confused by that answer. "What would *you* say?"

"I would say that you should have taken the warning when it was presented to you like Tessa Gamble did."

He froze in place, halfway through placing a sweater in his box. "How did you know?"

"Oh, little brother. I have some pennies in every pot. The difference between you and that Gamble girl is that she took the bait."

"Bait?" he asked, turning towards her.

She just laughed. "Everyone always uses all these card analogies in reference to the Game. It's life, so it is far more complicated than that. Some situations are cards, sure, but others are chess, some might be tic-tac-toe…"

"What are you getting at?" he demanded.

"Easy there, Nine. I'm on your side, for now. Here." Laura threw the baseball in the box he was packing and handed him an envelope. "There's your first few months of rent. Louise may have lowered the price for you but she is still going to suck you dry."

He looked down at the envelope but didn't open it. "Why are you doing this? What are you hoping to gain?" Alex figured it was a play; it had to be.

"It isn't what I hope to gain, it's what I don't want to lose." Her face softened and she knelt beside him. "This rent money is seconds of my time in value. In this job of yours? Likely weeks or months. You're worth a few seconds of my time, Alex. You must remember, especially now that you aren't an Elite, that every single game must have a winner. But you don't have to win. All you have to do in life, in the Game, is break even."

He nodded and tried to hold back tears. He and Laura were always the closest siblings. Before she moved out, they were best friends.

"Thank you, Laura."

She laughed and stood back up. "Don't thank me just yet. *Actually* use this money for your rent. Do whatever else you want to do with what you earn but don't spend more than you have."

"Laura, I know better than to go into credit."

"You say that now. Just, listen to me, alright? Also, get your head out of your ass and talk to Tessa. She's an absolute idiot for the show she put on at the Draw, but she's also the most bad-ass person I've ever seen because of it. If she can go toe to toe with Father like that, she's worth having on your side."

He narrowed his eyes in suspicion. "Are you saying this because you want her on *your* side?"

She clutched her chest dramatically. "You wound me, Brother! I would never." She laughed, just like they used to. "Let's get these boxes packed and in Louise's car before Father gets home. Also, hide the envelope. If anyone asks, I am embarrassed to be your sister."

Alex was shocked at that. "Ouch, Lau. Now who's wounding whom?"

She shrugged and dumped a drawer of random contents into a box with no grace. "Do you want help or to be coddled?"

"Both?" he asked, hoping for the best.

She dumped another drawer into the box making Alex wince when he heard a smash.

"If you want to be coddled, I am not the one for you." She picked up her box and left the room.

Alex took in the last sight of his room. This was always his space. He laughed, cried, did homework, even had sex for the first time all in this room. He knew when he left the room that he would no longer have a family. He had Laura, but not publicly. At least she was an ally to him.

He thought back to his conversation with Tessa and realised how selfish he had been and how greatly he underestimated her. She did what he couldn't and for that, she was better than him.

He picked up his box, faced his room and sighed.

"Goodbye, old friend."

CHAPTER 28

Tessa

"Mum!" Dante yelled as soon as they crossed through the doorway.

"Dante?" she yelled back down from upstairs and they heard her cross the length of the upstairs above them. "Are you okay? I was so worried." She paused halfway down the stairs when she saw Tessa and she clapped her hand over her mouth. "Tessa, you're okay. I was so worried. I thought they may have…"

"We went to the safe house." Dante interrupted her train of thought.

"She knows about the safe house?" Tessa thought that nothing could surprise her anymore but she was wrong.

Their mum finished her descent and hugged both of her children separately and then together. She released but held both of their faces as she had before the Draw. "Come." She took Tessa's hand. "I need to speak to you both about so many things, especially before you go and speak to Dealer Avarice."

"You want her to go to the Dealer?" Dante sounded outraged.

"Only guilty people run, Dante. She is also an ace, meaning

she is technically higher ranked than he is. Though, Tessa, he is still a Dealer. You will need to tread lightly and play well."

Tessa was just as surprised to hear this. She thought she would come home and readjust to this new world that had just opened up to her. "He has connections, Mum. Power, money, people; I'm just me."

She released Tessa's hand. "If you were at the safe house, it isn't just you anymore."

"I haven't joined the rebellion yet. I am sworn to secrecy, but I just want to learn more before I do." She looked to her mother who sat down at the dining room table. "Are you a member of the rebellion, Mum?"

She paused a moment. "Let's just say, I used to be. Now I just write reports of very well-curated information to provide the Dealers. Each report is approved by the rebellion leader before submission. It keeps me active enough to not be considered a threat to the cause and if any questions are asked regarding my knowledge, I am merely an investigative reporter."

"So, you're like a double agent?" Tessa asked.

Her mother shook her head. "No, I have no loyalties to the rebellion or Raymond and his leadership. I also couldn't risk too much seeing as I was alone to raise both of you."

Tessa didn't think she knew Dealer Avarice's forename before now. She and Dante both sat down at the table. She noticed she was still in Anthony's clothes but didn't care. The support of the seat felt too good. She didn't want to leave it.

"Now, with your Draw gifts combined with the fact that you both Drew high cards you're both incredibly comfortable. This was exactly what your dad and I wanted." She smiled at that and Tessa smiled in return. "I recommend you both buy a property in this same area for you to live in. This is so people don't ask questions about you coming back to see your widow mother too often. You don't have to invest with this level of money, but you could if you'd like. Though I will warn you that things are quite unsettled at the moment, so I would protect your principle. Your bets were done through a betting office—"

"That Dealer Avarice owns," Tessa finished.

Her mum looked between her and Dante with confusion. "Yes. How did you come to know this?"

"Anthony." Tessa then questioned whether or not to tell her about the warning and his knowledge about her future. *Information is power.* "He had warned me about getting funds out before Dealer Avarice did something with them." She lied to her mother. Tessa felt awful about doing it but her mum had apparently also hidden things from her.

Her mum nodded. "He's the Dealer's assistant. I wouldn't be surprised if he heard something. I do think that would be a good idea. Cash out and go to another bank."

"Are funds not protected?" Dante asked.

"They are, but investments aren't. There is a loophole for everything."

Tessa stared down at the table trying to think of her next move. "I'll give him the option. The last thing he will want is to lose that amount of money from his banks. He'd want to keep our money internal. It is in his interest to transfer it from his betting house straight to his holdings."

"This is a lot of money to risk, Tessa," Dante interjected.

"But if we both pull all of our funds it would not only look suspicious but might impact rates for others in his banks. He wants my money more than I do. He won't lose us if he can help it."

Dante and her mum both looked at her and one another. He sighed. "Do you want me to go with you?"

Tessa shook her head. "I want to go alone. I started this and this is my Game so I need to see this through. If you're okay with it, I'll add that we are a package deal."

He nodded slowly.

Her mother nodded too. "Before you go, I need to tell you both some uncomfortable truths. He may use some of these things against you and I don't want you to get caught off guard."

Tessa looked at Dante and then at her mother with concern before agreeing.

"It's about your dad."

CHAPTER 29

Alex

"Home sweet home." Louise dropped the box she was carrying onto the floor. "Here are your keys. I'd rather you not change anything since I recently remodelled. I guess you can paint if you want but it needs to be in keeping."

"Okay." That was all Alex could say. The apartment looked like it had never been lived in before. It was cold and colourless with very sleek furniture and shiny accents.

"I'll let you get settled in. I'll also give you this month's rent for free, but next month I expect your first and last."

Alex turned to his sister. "Can't I just pay you now and then pay singularly each month instead?"

She laughed. "Don't look a gift horse in the mouth, Brother. It is also all furnished." She gestured to the open-layout kitchen-living-dining room they were standing in. "If there is anything wrong with anything here when you move out, you'll pay for it. Rips, tears, stains, wearing in…"

"Wearing in?" Alex laughed incredulously, not believing what he was hearing. "You mean using the furniture at all?"

She shrugged. "It is all part of my investment. I bought it

new and it is to be maintained as such. You should be happy it is furnished for you. You don't have anything so you'd have to get it all yourself otherwise."

He muttered under his breath, "I'd rather that than owe you for using the bed."

She looked insulted at that. "Look, I get that this is an adjustment. Renters need properties to rent so here we are. We give you the opportunity to stay in a property that you can't afford on your own."

"You're talking to the guy who was taught the same things you were, Louise. I am likely paying more than your monthly mortgage payments."

She scoffed. "As if I have a mortgage." She then left and closed the door without saying goodbye.

He couldn't help but think of how far he had fallen so quickly. To his name, he had what was once a single week's allowance, rent for a few months and a couple of boxes with whatever his sister dumped inside.

He didn't allow himself to wallow in self-pity though. He sat down with his notebook and started running numbers.

Not nearly enough for a down payment anywhere decent, not enough to invest to make a quick return while having his principle protected. He sat back in frustration. He didn't even know the banking options for a nine. He sat back up and realised he had accidentally smudged some ink into the flat-pack table. He attempted to wipe it off but made it worse. He laughed at himself. His sister would likely charge him a couple of hundred dollars for what was probably a twenty-dollar table.

He laughed and continued to laugh until he broke into a sob. He wanted nothing more than to see Tessa in that moment. He wanted to hold her and apologise for being such an ass. Alex wanted to be the ever-winning bet for her, someone she could always count on, and there he was, sobbing on the floor over some pen on a table.

He wiped his face and threw the pen onto his notebook on the table.

If it was Tessa he wanted, it was Tessa he was getting.

CHAPTER 30

Tessa

Tessa was greeted on her way to the Dealer Compound. It seemed as though people were out and looking for her. She thought they were doing a terrible job considering she had been at her home for the past while.

She was escorted through the property and straight into Dealer Avarice's office. That suited her perfectly as that was where she was headed anyway.

"I was wondering when you would come to see me, Miss Gamble," he said, looking out of the window with his back facing her.

"Truthfully, I didn't have much of an option once that burly man saw me." She had a game to play. This was the second round of what she started at the Draw.

"We had no idea where you were, Miss Gamble. As the highest-ranking Draw of the group today, and the highest-ranked individual in the Region, we were naturally concerned for your well-being."

It seemed as though she wasn't the only one playing.

"How kind of you. I was seeing my mum after I found my brother. We ran from the explosions, you see."

He was still facing the window but she saw him stiffen. "Oh yes, terrible thing, that. How coincidental that it happened after your little tirade."

She grinned to herself and sat down in the seat across from his desk without invitation. She had to keep power, and he had the home-field advantage. "Would we call 'playing the Game set out for me to do my absolute best to succeed above all others' a tirade?"

He turned from the window after she intentionally scraped the floor with her chair. He elected to say nothing and sat in his seat behind his desk.

"I would call your little speech regarding my son and my supposed views of you a tirade, yes. Then after Dealer Prudence graciously gave you the full power of your new rank, others saw it fit to choose the other card as well."

She picked at the arm of her seat and feigned apathy. "Sounds like the rules to the Draw weren't clear enough. Not enough to control the outcome, anyway." She threw the challenge out there not expecting he would bite, but he did.

"Miss Gamble, I will tell you what you want to hear and what you already seem to know. Most ranks, especially those for established families, are predetermined. Adding a potential second option when they don't know that they are being set up to succeed is and was… consequential."

She smirked at him. "You mean the way it is intended to be? Where people have a say in their futures and can follow what the Fates want from them? Not what *you* want from them?"

His jaw tightened but he kept his voice level. "We curate the future generations based on their potential and familial merit. Every so often a Low-Born or Working-Class can get lucky as not every Draw is predetermined, or we fix the Draw to provide hope. It is a powerful thing, Tessa."

"Miss Gamble, please." As the higher ranked of the two, she had the opportunity to be addressed with formality, regardless of his position.

He merely grinned. He seemed to respect that move. "Miss Gamble," he said with a nod. "Now, some of our greatest potential candidates for leadership and opportunity no longer have the means to do so, and that rests entirely upon you."

She stared at him, trying to determine what he was wanting from her. "Who are you to say who the best candidate is?"

He ignored the question. "Did you know, Miss Gamble, that when a Low-Born wins the weekly Draw, the winnings are usually all spent within the calendar year? Very little comes back and cycles through the economy as a return or future investment. Very few of them even know what compound interest is," he said with a laugh. "Wealth breeds wealth, Miss Gamble. Wealth knows how to manage it, manipulate it."

"And you don't think this can be taught?" Tessa challenged lightly.

"Oh, of course it can be. We teach it to our Elite children from a young age, but if everyone has access to that knowledge, everyone has access to power."

There it was.

"You don't think earning that power would produce better long-term outcomes?"

"You know, you sound just like your father." He tilted his head to the side and seemed to be studying her. But she was ready thanks to her mum. He continued when she didn't react. "He was willing to jeopardise his own children's and grandchildren's futures for the lesser. For the weaker, the meagre. You see, Miss Gamble, there has to be tiers or this won't work. People need order and need to be controlled. They think they want the power, but they don't know the weight of it or what to do with it once they have it. Not every game needs to be played and the best chance of survival is to simply play none. But that isn't how the Game works." He got up from his desk. "They say comparison is the thief of joy, but comparison is the entire foundation of the Game. You want better, more, and it is never enough."

She was done with his self-fulfilling crap. "Why give Alex the nine?"

"He wanted something I didn't want him to have. You weren't wrong to think I planted the blank for you, Miss Gamble. Though I would never admit that to anyone else. I was right, too. You are your father's daughter. A traitor to the Elite."

"I am not a rebel," Tessa clarified.

"Perhaps not in name, but in spirit you are. I needed to crush the potential in that. I needed you to be nowhere near my son. He wanted you. We discussed it last night after I picked him up during your... activities. You must have given him *quite* the show."

"That's enough." She gave a stern tone. As an ace, he should have known better than to speak to her like that, Dealer or not. His belief system was based on the ranks, and she now ranked above him, above everyone.

Her breath caught lightly when she realised that this made her a threat.

He seemed to brush off her tone and answered her question, not noticing the changing in her breathing. "A ranking of nine is humble, yes. It is at the top of the Working-Class for most jobs and with enough hard work, it will bring him opportunity. He knew it was a punishment but I was hoping he would see the card I planted for you and consider himself lucky. Your brother was one of those that we scouted for leadership which is why we gave him the rank required of a Dealer. Even after his little stunt."

"Speaking of my brother, we both want to ensure our Drawing bets have been finalised." She looked up at him and picked lightly at the arm of the chair she was seated in.

A slight grin played at the corners of his mouth. "And if they have not yet been finalised?"

"I would suggest you do so with considerable speed, Dealer." She looked down at the studs below her hand, pressing them as if they were buttons. "We will withdraw all goods, services, funds, investments, bonds and the like made in the Gamble name from all banks and businesses that you own and transfer it elsewhere."

Though his face itself didn't change, she watched the numbers run through his head.

"You can't."

"I assure you we can and we will. We Gambles are a team. I wonder just how much money you would lose as a result?" She tapped her chin in dramatic ponder.

"I don't think you wonder anything, Miss Gamble," he said cordially.

"You're right, Raymond, I don't." The name felt tart when she said it but the twitch of his chin was all that she needed for it to be sweet.

Red dress be damned, she didn't need her body to be confident. She had a mind, a brilliant one at that.

"I'd like to finalise it now, if you will. I would like to see the numbers go into my account so I can invest quickly, in your bank, of course." She nodded to him to urge his promptness.

His smile in return was more of a baring of teeth but he pushed a button on his desk.

Tessa attempted to hide her surprise and glee as Anthony entered the room. What a game this had turned out to be.

"Mr Largesse, I would like you to personally finalise Drawing bets made by the Gamble siblings within the next hour."

"Of course, sir." He gave a nod to the Dealer and turned to Tessa. "Shall I do any investing on your behalf, Miss Gamble?"

She wanted to grin from ear to ear at this version of him but fought it. "No thank you, Mr Largesse. I will handle my own accounts," she said pointedly. "Though, with the permission of Dealer Avarice of course, I would like you to look at the logistics of transferring funds to another bank." She knew full well how to do such a simple thing and that it was possible. She just wanted to show Dealer Avarice that it didn't all have to stay there.

"Oh, Miss Gamble, that won't be necessary. It is quite easily done and for aces there are no transfer fees."

She clapped her hands together in fake enthusiasm. "Excellent, thank you…"

He smirked at her. His eyes twinkled a bit at this little theatrical game that they were playing. "Anthony, miss."

"Ah, yes, thank you, Anthony." He walked away but just before he closed the door she called after him, making him pause. "Largesse, that's a Working-Class name, isn't it?"

"Yes, it is, Miss Gamble. We have worked our way from Low-Born to Working-Class proudly."

"And what, may I ask, was your recent Draw? I believe I saw you in the Recipients' line."

He smirked at her again. "A jack of hearts, miss."

She smiled genuinely. "The luck of the Draw was with you, indeed."

He nodded then continued his exit, carefully closing the door behind him.

She turned to Dealer Avarice. "Was his card planted, too?"

He pressed his fingertips together in front of him. "He Drew what was required in order for me to keep him close."

She took that in. She wondered if he knew or even suspected. Perhaps he was just loyal and the Dealer appreciated it. Either way, it was interesting information.

"I think I'd quite like to be a Dealer one day," Tessa said, playing with the Dealer, dangling a toy just waiting for him to pounce.

"You command attention well, Miss Gamble, but I do fear that you are too governed by your feelings."

"I did have a few years of figuring that out taken away from me." She wanted to make him aware that she did not forget how early this was in her life.

"So I recall," he said with no inflection. "May I offer a word of advice? Or rather, an observation?" She gestured with her hands for him to continue so he did. "Keep your cards closer to your chest. Revealing the ones that you care about to the wrong sort is dangerous."

"The love for my brother?" She wasn't sure how she would hide that, especially if they did end up living together.

"And my son. Having conditions to any deal makes an offer weaker. I was willing to sever a limb from my family for my end goal."

She finally got out of her seat. "That says more about you than you would care to admit." She made her way to the door.

"I openly admitted that my ambitions are selfish. What you see is what you get. I also have not lied to you."

She paused at that. "Are you suggesting that someone else has?" She looked over her shoulder to see a very relaxed Dealer.

"I'm saying that just because we are not allies does not mean we must be enemies."

She opened the door towards herself. "I'll keep that in mind."

CHAPTER 31

Alex

"Avarice." Dante opened the door and blocked the entrance with his body. Alex wasn't sure if this was the usual false rivalry or the very deserved defensiveness of an older brother towards someone who was an ass to his sister.

"Gamble."

They stood there for a moment until they both cracked a smile and impacted with a hug.

Dante leaned against the doorway. "Come with your tail between your legs from earlier? You made a right ass of yourself."

Alex looked down at the welcome mat. He knew he had messed up. That was why he was there. "I really did. I don't need her to forgive me. I just have to apologise."

"You just missed her," Beatrice called over Dante's shoulder. "She went to go and see your father."

He was stunned at this. He would have thought his father would be the last person she wanted to see, besides him, of course. "Why?"

"Kill him," Dante said seriously.

"What?" Alex exhaled in shock. He believed him.

"Dante!" Beatrice scolded her son.

"Would you both calm down? I was obviously joking. She went to go and clear her name."

Alex didn't understand. "Why would she have to clear her name?"

Dante looked at him like he was the dumbest person in the Region. "You know, the big 'kaboom' thing that happened?"

Alex shook his head. "That was a faulty boiler. I was there when my father got the report."

Dante looked back at his mum and back towards Alex. "You should probably come in."

CHAPTER 32

Tessa

Tessa walked out of the Compound and turned along the trail towards the Elite village. It was late, and the darkness of night was finally breaking through the light of the day. Since it was the summer, the days were longer, but today had felt like an eternity to Tessa.

As she passed the line of topiaries, she saw Anthony leaning against his car. She thought he had no right to look so good just being… normal.

"I think it was pretty bold of you to show up to a meeting with the Dealer wearing baggy sweatpants and a T-shirt," he laughed.

She smiled too. "Well, Mr Largesse, did you finalise my bets as promised?" She put on a very formal accent. A striking contrast to the way she was dressed.

"I did and you're fucking rich, by the way. You and your brother both are."

She looked around at the calm of the evening. "You said earlier that the blast was a show of force. Why is nobody reacting?"

He shrugged. "Can't be seen panicking, can they? Look, nobody died or was even really injured. It was perfectly done."

She looked at him. "*If* I join, I want there to be an end to the violence."

He took her hand and kissed it like when they first met. "I love that you think you have any sort of power over me."

She did. She knew she did. Not just in the way he looked at her in the dress, but in what she represented, who she was. The potential her ace gave their cause.

"Don't I?" she nearly purred towards him.

He gave the arrogant smirk. "I can probably be convinced." Anthony took a few steps backwards and opened the passenger-side door. "Get in, Gamble."

She laughed at him. "The last time I went with you, I fell down a hole and climbed Everest to get back."

He chuckled. "I know Dante took you on a little drive earlier, but I want to take you on a better one."

She was done for the day. There was nothing he or his smirk could do to convince her otherwise. "As much as I love sightseeing, and really, I do, I should go home."

"I'll drop you off. Just let me show you what you don't want to see."

She scoffed at him. "Is that meant to be inviting?"

"Listen, I literally know how much money is in your bank account right now. I know what you can do with that level of money. I just want to let you see the other side."

"I saw the other side today, Dante explained it all to me."

"I highly doubt your protective and loving big brother took you to where I want to take you."

He's playing a game, she thought to herself. He seemed to be oddly comfortable trying to force her to be a piece in this puzzle of his.

"I told you I was going home," she said sternly. Tessa couldn't let him think that he was in charge or just had her in his pocket. She walked back to the path she had come from and heard gravel shift behind her.

"Let me walk with you, at least. Please, Tess." He caught up with her but didn't stop her from walking. She looked at him and thought for a moment that maybe it wasn't a game.

"And your car?" she asked, nodding in the direction of it.

He shrugged. "Some things are more important."

Her stomach oozed inside her like warm honey but she didn't want to show him any form of weakness. She knew her mind and she was sticking to it.

"You realise we just met today, right?" she said looking forward as if she didn't feel a gravity towards him.

He stopped in place and she had to consciously drive her feet to keep moving. She would not comfort him; she would not let him be the victim of a situation he created by not listening.

"Someone recently told me to keep what's close to me close to my chest," she called behind her.

A pause and she thought he had gone until he yelled after her, "Good to know you want me close to you." Then she heard the gravel move further away as he walked back to his car.

Shit. In her attempt to keep leverage over his emotions, she showed him hers. He was the rebellion leader and likely didn't get to be in that position by being completely honest.

You don't get to the top of anything without playing the Game yourself.

CHAPTER 33

Tessa

Tessa had made it to the gates of the Elite village. She looked up, noticing for the first time how intricate the ironwork was. The bars of the gate were twisted with an overlay of gilded ivy leaves.

"You know, it was likely a Low-Born who made those pretty gates."

Tessa had noticed Anthony was following her home in his car. She just didn't want to give him the attention he obviously wanted from her. Her stomach fluttered at his care for her safety, but that's likely what he wanted. She continued to look at the gate without turning around. "You're probably right."

Nobody in the Elite village had this type of talent. The Elite focused on marketable skills like languages and music. Some could even paint though it was not to be pursued in earnest.

"Ironic, isn't it? The barrier between us, fabricated and maintained by those you are trying desperately to keep out. Almost like we are keeping ourselves away from where we are not welcome."

She sighed and looked towards Anthony with feigned indifference. "Is there something you would like, Anthony?"

"For you to call me Tony?" He stepped closer and gave that smug grin that melted her insides. She didn't know how he managed to make her feel this way, but she hated that she loved it.

"Why did you follow me home, Anthony?"

The grin on his face was wiped too quickly for it to have been genuine.

"I told you, I want to keep you safe, just like I did earlier today."

She scoffed. "You saved me from yourself. Some might call that anti-heroic."

"At least it is some kind of heroic." He shrugged and stepped closer.

"Goodbye, Anthony." She dismissed him, not wanting to allow herself to get too close to him. She stepped away and opened a smaller door in the larger gate.

"Sweet dreams, Tess."

She had to turn to face him to latch the door, though she didn't have to look at him. Tessa did, anyway.

"You know, Tess, it doesn't have to be like this." He gestured to the gates. "This between us now, the Elites and the rest of us. A barricade isn't the answer."

"And a bomb is?" she challenged.

He put his hands up in surrender. "We aren't heard unless we scream. It benefits those in power, with the very power to do anything about how the majority of us live, to pretend not to hear. To pretend not to see the problems. They will also never admit that they are at fault."

Her lips pressed into a thin line. "A show of force is not a substitute for power."

"No, but it does give the impression of it. For now, it will have to do." He reached his arm through the gate and held up his palm. Inside was a token with a rough hole poked through it. "Take this, please. This will let you access the safe house.

Come and see me. We can talk everything through and come up with a plan that works for everyone. I cannot promise a lack of disturbance… I can't even promise a lack of violence." He was interrupted by Tessa shooting him a look of disbelief. "People are angry, Tess. Not slightly perturbed, or mildly annoyed, they are *angry*. Not a single creature on this planet does well being backed into a corner. Desperation can and will ignite at any time."

She went to turn and just when she thought he was done, he kept talking.

"Help guide us into doing this properly. You and Dante are the best cards we have been dealt since we started. There is only one voice we are able to use alone, but with you we have options. We don't want a rebellion. We want a revolution. However, we can do that in many different ways. That includes the use of force."

She heard the threat for what it was, she just didn't know if it was a bluff or not. Tessa didn't want the wrong call to be on her shoulders. "If I want to be in the safe house, I will go with Dante."

"Have the option, Tessa."

Options are power.

She walked back to the gate. "This is not a guarantee of anything."

She thought she saw relief on his face.

"You can return it to me at any time."

She nodded silently to him and he nodded in return. She then turned her back to him and walked away, feeling the heat of his gaze on her back.

Tessa turned the corner and once she was comfortably out of sight she ran her thumb over the token. There was some familiarity to it but she didn't know where that feeling could have possibly come from.

She continued to walk around the bend in the road. The lawns were all perfectly manicured, not a single one longer or shorter than the rest. Tessa glanced down at her feet, remembering the pavements in front of the house Dante had taken her to. That one was cracked like unintentional cobblestone. These were level, evenly spaced and whole with a dimple pattern of a repeating sun motif. She had never noticed these small things before.

She looked up and faced her house at the end of the road. There was a motorcycle in their driveway. "Alex," she whispered to herself.

Once again, simultaneously the first and last person she wanted to see.

She sighed and continued walking. Sometimes the only way out is through.

CHAPTER 34

Tessa

"Squirt!" Dante greeted her and ran out before she made it to the front step. "Before you go inside—"

"Alex is here," she finished, pointing at the motorcycle in their driveway.

He was only slightly deflated at her guessing but continued. "Yes, but apparently the bomb wasn't Largesse!"

She didn't think she heard him right. She was tired and frankly, done with the day. "What?"

Alex leaned in the doorway behind Dante. "Hey, Tess." He had been playing with his hair again which made Tessa smile. She was still angry but was immediately comforted at seeing him. Knowing he felt bad about how he had acted made her feel a bit better.

Dante spoke under his breath. "No rebel talks with Alex." Then he spoke louder. "I'll leave you both to… yeah." Then he ran up the steps and closed the door.

"Tess, please forgive me. I am so sorry."

She grinned. "Alex, I've known you our entire lives. It has been a very long day, and if we play together, it won't be the first disagreement we ever have." She didn't realise what she had said before it was already out of her mouth.

His head snapped up and he grabbed her hands. "I have nothing, Tess, if I'm honest."

"I'm sure you're being modest. Either way, we will play well. We always have."

He released one of her hands to stroke his hair again. "Tess, I can't do a whole lot of playing anymore. I got kicked out of the house, I may as well be disowned, I'm renting from my sister and I have a couple of boxes filled with random shit to my name. My biggest asset is the bike my father likely regrets gifting me."

Her mind went in circles. She knew his family was colder than hers, but to create such hardship for their son? "You're renting from Laura?"

He shook his head. "Louise. It was all very odd. Mother gave me a small bit of money to start with but Laura gave me money for rent. I just had to talk to you…"

She put her hands up in front of her and nervously chuckled. "I am still trying to wrap my head around what you just said, let alone—"

"Tess, Laura said you took some sort of bait. The warning we got."

She nodded. Anthony had told her as much. It was a genuine warning, but the rebellion wanted to create a test of their loyalties. "It was a test."

"One that I failed, then?" She watched as he tried to put the pieces together.

She needed to change the subject before she broke her word to Anthony. "Why did Laura give you money?"

"She said she has all these games moving simultaneously… I think she just pitied me now that I live with the Working-Class. I even have a job now. One that she got for me."

She nodded trying to put the information together. How

would Laura know of Anthony's plan? "Did Laura tell you about the bomb?"

He shook his head. "I was with my father when a report came through. Due to some budget cuts a boiler wasn't maintained."

So why would Anthony take credit? She would have to ask her mum if she made that report.

He interrupted her thoughts. "I know it is already dark out. But did you want to go back to the lake? Our tent is likely still set up. Unless my father broke it down when he got the bike…"

She felt like she could barely stay afloat at the moment. This was her first day of the Game and it was kicking her ass. "If I'm being honest, Alex, I just need my bed. Today has been—"

"A lot. I know, it's okay. Just so you know, I won't be allowed back in the Elite village after today without permission. I'm not Elite anymore." He sounded so sad and defeated.

He had been raised here; this was home. Even though he was just moving to a different area, he may as well have been moving to a different city. It didn't seem right.

"What does that mean for… us?" Tessa asked.

He shook his head. "I don't know. Look, Tess, I won't blame you if you don't want to—"

She interrupted that thought with a kiss. She felt him pause before he joined her movements. He held her head and she felt the apology vibrate into her lips.

She smiled and pulled away. "Even if this doesn't work out, you still have a place in my life, Alex. I know this isn't what you wanted or what either of us had planned but I can help you. Let's just not rush this, okay? Let's figure out this whole adult thing separately first."

He dropped his hands from her face. "Separately?"

"We don't have to get married to play together, Alex. We can still be there for one another and make choices together. Now that I'm an ace, I can actually still live my freedom years, just in a different way."

Frustration flashed in his eyes. "I have to work, Tess. I can't afford not to anymore. There are consequences to my actions now."

"All the more reason to try and navigate what we can before committing to something?"

He looked hurt at her words. Tessa wondered if she wanted more but she wasn't ready to stop having fun yet. Her rank gave her the time back that she had lost.

She softened. "Listen, Alex."

"No, I get it! I don't want to waste your time. Just know if the situation were reversed, I would take care of you, Tess."

Where was this coming from? "You said you didn't want me to take care of you."

He shook his head and ran both hands through his hair. She wondered if he was going to pull it out soon. "I don't know what I want, okay? I know I want you. That's the only thing that has ever made sense. I made you feel like a winner in the tent last night. I want to do that forever with you in every other aspect of the Game."

"Let me get this straight. Is it all or nothing with you? Marry you and partner up or lose you?" She felt this was unfair and unjustified. Until yesterday there was nothing other than friendship between them. Sure, Tessa always wanted it to be more, but this was too much too soon. It wasn't right of him to hold her to this.

"You'll never lose me, Tess, but I don't want to be a plaything."

"You aren't *my* plaything. You know your father; he gave you that nine." He didn't react. Did he already know? She continued, "Your fate wasn't up to the Fates at all. He punished you for the rest of your life for wanting me. If you don't believe me, ask him! I had a lovely chat with him today."

"I don't have to. I know some fishy things happened at the Draw. I just didn't believe…"

"You didn't believe what, Alex? When he said that I would sink? That he would be true to his word? You called on what you thought was a bluff without even telling me the threat he had made regarding *my* fate. You are in the position you're in because of *him*, not me; your trust in your father and the system that has always benefitted you. I took the warning and saved myself from becoming Voided, and I happened to get an ace. With that I can help you. I can help others, Alex." She passed him going up the stairs to the front door.

"Tessa…" he pleaded.

"Come back when you've figured out that this whole thing is fucked up, and for once you are on the losing side." She slammed the door and left Alex outside. That conversation was in no way what she wanted it to be. Tessa felt they had drifted further apart than before he came to the house.

***

"I take it the chat didn't go well?" Dante attempted to make light.

Tessa turned from the door to see her mum and brother staring at her from the leather chairs in the reception room. "No, Dante, it didn't." They likely heard at least the tail end of the conversation as Tessa was louder than necessary.

Her mum attempted to change the subject. "How did your meeting with Dealer Avarice go?"

There was just so much that had happened today and she felt like she was a participant in all of it. She just wanted to spectate.

She groaned loudly and Dante laughed. "That good, huh?"

Tessa threw her little token on the coffee table between them and Dante raised an eyebrow. "It looks like you had lots of conversations today."

She rubbed her eyebrows and sat on the ottoman at the

closest end of the coffee table to her. "I have. They all want to use me in their separate Games."

"Tessa, dear, you're an ace," her mother said gingerly. "You are the key to the top now."

"If they want me to play, I'll fucking play."

"Tessa!" Her mum scolded at the word choice.

She sighed. "I am going to tell you everything I've learned today and, like last night, I want to sit down and come up with a plan."

Dante looked between his mum and sister. "A plan for what?"

"A plan to change everything without becoming a pawn. My biggest strength comes not from my rank or my wealth. It's that there are men who seem to constantly underestimate me and I am sick of it. They think I am a damsel or I'm dumb and I will show them that I am neither."

"Tessa?" her mother asked, concerned.

"I refuse to allow others to determine my fate. I took my life, my Game into my own hands today when I picked that top card. In my hands, my fate will stay." The spite-fuelled confidence surged through her. She felt it more than she had at the lake, more than the dress, and more than how she felt in the hall.

Dante grinned widely. "What's first, cap-i-tain?" He gave a mock salute that made Tessa relax a bit.

"First, I change." She was still wearing Anthony's clothing. "Then we all share every piece of information we have and try to figure out what the hell is going on. Finally, we play their Game against them. We will play well and we will win."

"Oh, is that all?" Dante laughed. "Here I thought this was going to be easy, Squirt."

"Change isn't easy, someone once said." She turned to her mum. "I'm going to make Dad proud."

Her mum stood up and reached her hands out to her children who both accepted. "You already have."

CHAPTER 35

Alex

Alex allowed his agitation to fuel him. He barely got the kickstand down before heading up to his parents' front door. He had always been taught to regulate his feelings, not to show or share them. He was always expected to keep everything close to his chest, but he had been taught a lot of things.

He used the side of his fist to hit the middle of the door, causing it to rattle beneath each impact.

Not surprisingly, one of the household employees, Jacob, answered the door. "I have been notified by Dealer Avarice that you are no longer residing here. May I give him a message for you, Master Alex?"

"I would like to see my father please, Jacob." Alex had always been on good terms with Jacob. He knew the employee without the dutiful persona he saw before him.

Jacob looked behind himself, scanning the house. He stepped out and closed the door gently behind him. "You and I both know you ain't supposed to be here, Alex. You oughta be goin' home now."

"I *am* home," he said through gritted teeth.

Jacob shook his head. "You ain't never been nothing but kind to me, Alex. That's the only reason I'm getting you to leave here on your own. It's a sure awful thing that happened to you today with the family and all, but a nine's a mighty good card where I'm from. If you need any help, any help at all, you just gotta ask. Coming back here ain't the answer, Alex. With your name, you can get a good job. A decent one. Then with your fancy education and know-how, you can be comfy and happy."

"Is that enough, Jacob? Contentment?" He nearly spat the word out.

Jacob chuckled. "Well, what more d'ya need, Alex? You don't need no fancy things for a good life."

"I just… I need to find out how to get the life I had back. I deserve that much."

Jacob sighed. "I'm 'bout to tell you something you don't wanna hear, Alex. You don't deserve nothin'. That is the funny thing about you Elites. You think you're owed something but the Fates put you in the exact same place as any of us. Think of others that Drew even lower than you. Do you think they get to march up to your daddy and have a chat to him about it? Not a chance." He laughed and shook his head. "Alex, accordin' to the processes you and your folk decided on, you are below me now. But good news for you is you have some 'vantages I ain't never got because of what you were borned."

Alex scoffed. "Not exactly welcoming me to the Working-Class fold, are you? I doubt any of you will be…"

Jacob poked a finger into Alex's chest. "That's 'cause of your Fate's damned attitude. There is no 'us' and 'you' anymore. You don't just get respect on the other side of that gate, you gotta earn it. You work, you be part of the community, meet your neighbour. Not just for what they can give you, neither. Be interested in their life."

"There's no chance you will ever accept me in those ways." Alex shook his head.

"There you goes again: 'you' and 'me'." He emphasised his words by poking their respective chests.

"Is there some sort of issue here, Jacob?" Dealer Avarice opened the door and filled the doorway with his stature.

Jacob immediately straightened and dusted off his jacket, becoming the role of the employee once more. "Not at all, Dealer Avarice. I was seeing… this man off the property."

Alex noticed the word choice Jacob used to refer to him. He obviously didn't want to take the chance of agitating the Dealer with the wrong level of formality. He was still an Avarice, after all.

"No need, Jacob. However, I do appreciate the information you just shared with my son regarding his new rank. Maybe we could speak about the differences sometime soon." A statement, not a request. It was clear Jacob had not been taught to monitor his emotions as well as Alex had. He became red in the face and twisted awkwardly before nodding and skulking into the house.

After a moment of his father blocking the doorway, Alex finally got the courage to break the silence.

"Father, I would like to ask you a question regarding the Draw."

"Alexander, the Draw is final as was your mother's decision to move you out sooner."

Alex was hurt and confused. He thought his father was the harsh mastermind behind breaking the family up sooner than what was required.

"I was hoping for some enlightenment regarding the process."

His father leaned against the doorframe but it was too rigid to look relaxed. "I take it you have been speaking with Miss Gamble? I will save you the time and energy of this discussion. What she said was likely true. I cannot say for certain as I wasn't there. But, yes, the Draw is not all Fate-driven as advertised. This is for political reasons which a nine like yourself need not concern themselves with."

His whole life, his father represented the law and the rule of the Fates. He was the main teacher of his life and for this Game. He just had it verified from his father that the basis of their entire system, his entire life, was a lie.

"Don't seem too surprised, Alexander. Perfect curation of odds is impossible. Lies are necessary for control and safety."

"Tell the people, then. Tell them that you've dictated their lives, *my* life."

"Dear boy," his father sighed in frustration, "I will not repeat myself. You don't tell me what to do. You have no power in this house or inside this gate. You are a worker bee. You are in this Game and I still expect great things from you. In checkers, though all pieces are equal, some break the odds and become more powerful. I raised you to be the best. So, I advise you to do just that: be the best and win. You were never going to be able to be the best of the best with Miss Gamble on your arm. So, answer yourself this: would you rather be the biggest winner among losers or a loser among winners? Show the other classes the opportunity they don't know that they have."

Alex just stared at his father. This wasn't only punishment for Tessa, he was a pawn in his father's political strategies. A sacrifice to show what was possible to those with no hope.

"Oh, Alexander. I also heard about your little warning. You trusted me for a reason, just remember that." Alex was frozen in place as his father pulled him in for a stiff embrace. The last time his father hugged him he was just a child. "You are and always have been destined for great things. This was not done lightly and I need you to know that your trust in me was in good faith. Play well." He released Alex and entered the house without another glance.

Staring at the shut door, Alex allowed his tears to overflow. He fell to his knees on the composite decking and cried.

CHAPTER 36

Tessa

"Wait, wait, wait. So, let me get this straight." Dante interrupted Tessa and rubbed his hand over his face. "You and Alex both received the same warning that only you took. Laura Avarice considered that 'taking the bait' but Dealer Avarice planted the blank for you to get. Just as he planned the king for me and the nine for Alex. He doesn't want you to think of him as the enemy but he dragged his own kid down and admitted to it.

"You think he may know about the rebels because of him keeping an eye on his assistant. Now that assistant, Anthony, wants in your pants but you think something is going on considering the bomb wasn't actually a bomb, but a boiler. He took the credit, knowing it wasn't him and gave you the talisman even though you aren't technically part of the rebellion.

"You now think that not only these things are connected, but have to do with you? Squirt, it has been a long day. I just think everyone is doing their best to suss the other person out."

He leaned against the table in front of him. Tessa was slumped over it too, gripping a quickly chilling coffee. They were surrounded by papers and charts and she was just about spent.

"Let me see that talisman," her mother suddenly said, entering the room with a book. Dante lazily handed it over as if it were a pen and not a secret key to an underground safe house for the rebellion.

Her face paled and Tessa stood up immediately. "Mum?"

"This was your father's," she whispered.

Tessa was at her mum's side in an instant. She looked over her mother's shoulder to see a picture of her dad throwing a young Dante in the air. His necklace was on the outside of his shirt and dangling from the cord was the talisman.

"Did he give you one of these, Dante?" their mother asked.

He shook his head. "No, I think only the leaders have them."

"Dealer Prudence has one, though," their mother commented, making Tessa and Dante both snap their attention to her.

"*The* Dealer Prudence?" Tessa asked, shocked.

"I've seen it in her desk. She asked me to put the reports in her top drawer..." Her mother's thoughts took over as she looked at the photo of their dad.

"I've actually heard that she was from Low-Born upbringing and Drew well. She went back to school and got an Elite education which is why her speech is Elite too. That being said, I've never seen her at the safe house... though I have only recently joined," Dante offered.

"Is that why she gave the loophole? She's a rebel?" Tessa asked Dante and he shrugged. He couldn't answer that any more than she could.

"I think we may have got a bit sidetracked. How did he get your dad's talisman?" their mother chimed in. "Dealer Avarice took it off him when... well, when he was Voided. It is the one piece of hard evidence he has to my knowledge."

"He stole it from him then. He would have access to it, being his assistant," Dante solved triumphantly, clapping his hands together. Likely hoping he could go to bed.

Tessa shook her head. "I assume the Dealer would notice something like that going missing." She breathed slowly, trying not to panic. "Which is why he planted it on me."

Dante defended Anthony immediately. "He wouldn't do that."

"Think about it, Dante! I get the warning from him and there's an upset at the Draw which results in me getting an ace, following that there is an explosion that he is trying to have the rebellion take credit for, I go to the Dealer's office to clear my name and suddenly I have a piece of rebel memorabilia."

Dante stood up and raised his hands to soothe her. "That is a lot of speculation, Squirt. He wants you for the rebellion, remember?"

"In what role?" Tessa demanded.

It was their mum who answered softly behind them, clutching the talisman. "A martyr. Just like your dad."

Dante whirled. "If an ace isn't safe, nobody is."

A sudden knock on the door caused everyone to jump. They all looked at one another, unsure what to do. Tessa took charge. "Mum, hide the talisman. Dante, get rid of all of… this," she said, gesturing to the table covered in their theories.

They sprang into action as Tessa went to the door. She took a deep breath. "If they want me, they can have me." It was close to four in the morning. Whoever was on the other side of this wooden barrier likely wasn't here for a nice chat.

She opened the door fully in a single motion and what greeted her made her feel both relieved and terrified.

"Alex?"

He stood there, dripping with water, and continued to stand in the rain. He had very clearly been crying.

"Alex? Are you okay? It's four in the morning!"

He shook his head, then nodded, then shook his head again.

His face twisted as he began to cry again and dropped to his knees with a loud thud. He sobbed at Tessa's feet.

"Tess, everything... whoa, Avarice. What's going on, buddy?" Dante knelt to the ground beside him. Tessa was standing still holding the door, unsure of what to do.

"Squirt, help me get him inside."

She followed stiffly. It was as if her body had taken the instruction but not her mind. Tessa took one side and Dante took the other as they hoisted him up off the porch and inside the foyer. They made it to the reception room sofa and effectively dropped him onto it.

Their mum must have heard the commotion because she came in with a cup of steaming liquid. She handed it to Alex who wordlessly took it.

Dante knelt down again. "How can we help you, Alex?"

Their mum cleared her throat. "Why don't we all go to bed? Hmm? We can talk more in the morning, rested and clear-minded. Alex, honey, you can take your usual room here. It's already made up and I'll get you a couple of towels. I think a hot shower would do you a lot of good. Dante could loan you something to sleep in and wear in the morning." She nodded at Dante who nodded in return.

Alex croaked something out but they didn't hear him. He cleared his throat and wiped his face with his soaked-through sleeve. "This has always been my home more than my real home has ever been. I didn't know where else to go. I rode my bike around the village for a while but since it's past midnight, if I leave, I can't come back through the gates."

"Well, you're here now, buddy. We'll figure out the rest in the morning." Dante gave him a sad grin.

Tessa continued staring as Dante handled the situation. She was confused as to why she hurt so much seeing him like that. She wanted it to go away but he had made her so irate earlier. She was relieved to see him here but didn't want him in the spare room. She wanted the night they had taken from them. The years they had lost.

Before today, they had years of worriless nights ahead of them. Nights of fun, being reckless and young and stupid. It changed all at once and the world seemed to be working against them. She was high ranking and he wasn't, but that difference wasn't visible when they were standing in the room like this. They were both pawns in someone else's Game.

Tessa had a perfectly wrapped bundle of false hope. That was what the circumstances of her birth had awarded her. She felt useless if she couldn't play together, for one another, for good.

She didn't know at that moment if neutrality was the safest or most dangerous position to be in. She didn't know if there was another option outside of the two known views: starting everything over from scratch or keeping everything the way it had been since the start of the Region. The way of the rebels, and the way of the Elite.

One thing she did know was that there had to be something better than this. There had to be something better than lies, false hope, being used and getting your freedom stripped from you. There had to be a way of the Fates.

She decided she would be better. Do better. Or die trying.

CHAPTER 37

Tessa

Tessa woke up to a knock at her door. She had slept solidly through the night which surprised her. Her mind raced as she got ready for bed but the moment the softness and familiarity of her blankets and stuffed frog hugged her in, she fell right to sleep.

Another, quieter few knocks rang from the door and she called for the person to enter. The door slowly creaked open and Alex poked his head in and held out her favourite mug. "I brought you a tea."

She waved him in and wordlessly accepted the tea and took a sip. It was perfect; he always made her tea perfectly. She wanted to gulp it down but held her composure.

"Could I sit?" He gestured towards the foot of the bed.

She considered it for a moment, recognising that he had left the door open so the conversation likely couldn't get too involved. With the door being open, other possibilities were also off the table. Tessa nodded and took another sip of her tea.

He sat slowly, positioning himself at the very edge of her

bed. "Tess, I'm sorry. For last night, for after the Draw, just…
for everything."

"I take it you spoke to your father?"

He nodded. "I did and I guess I couldn't handle finding out
that everything I had ever been taught was a lie. Everything I've
been prepared for had been taken away from me."

She understood that. Though she came out unscathed from
the Draw, Alex had lost everything at the hand of his father.

"I bet you wish you chose the top card too, huh?" Tessa tried
to joke.

He shook his head. "This is all too messed up for 'what-ifs'.
For all I know, that would have been even worse than a nine.
You were lucky, Tess. The luck of the Draw actually *was* with
you." He sighed. "I feel like I don't know anything anymore.
He wanted me to get the nine to prove that you can win in the
Working-Class. He told me that he raised me to be the best, the
fucker."

Tessa had to stifle her laugh as her eyebrows shot up to her
forehead. Alex had always idolised his father, more out of fear
than respect. It surprised her for him to speak so ill of him.

"He could give them hope himself if he just let them play…"
Tessa offered.

Alex shook his head and laughed lightly. "Would you change
something that benefitted you so much? Would you change the
rules to a game designed for you to win every time?"

She paused, thinking back to her car ride with Dante. "I
likely wouldn't have before yesterday. But for me to win, so
many others have to lose. And it isn't even as simple as that!
They don't *just* lose and I don't *just* win. It isn't as black and
white as we ever thought or were taught. I win at their expense
but they will never win at mine."

He laughed. "Sounds rebellious."

She gave him a guilty look. "They may have already come
to me."

His shock was clear on his face. "So if you know who it is, we can stop them and stop all of this!"

"I'm not stopping anything," Tessa said sternly. She wanted to remind him that she had her own mind.

"But Tess, don't you see? They are the reason everything is so fucked up. We could have had our years together. You could have had your dad if it wasn't for them."

"Excuse me?" Tessa challenged. That was the second time he brought her father up and she didn't like that he was making a habit of it. She had just learned the truth of her dad's death yesterday; how could Alex already know?

"Shit, Tess. I know what happened, okay? Father... well, he told me."

"So, you know he killed himself after what your father did to him?"

His face went white with horror. "No! No. Tess, he disappeared, the rebels..."

"No, Alex, your father Voided his position to make an example of the rebel leadership. An Elite losing all rank and position was the same as a lower class receiving the death penalty according to your precious father."

"Well, that sounds like he got lucky then, Tess. That's what they do to rebels."

Tessa shot up from her bed, not caring that she was wearing nothing but an oversized shirt. "You're saying he deserved it then?"

He stood in defence. "Look, it was his choice to kill himself!"

The shock on his face was only outdone by the anger on hers. He evidently hadn't meant to say the words, but it was too late. The damage was done.

"Get the fuck out of my house."

He stepped towards her pleading. "Tess, I'm sor—"

She held up a finger and he stopped. "Don't you dare 'Tess' me. If you give me one more empty apology... I've given you a few chances now not to be a total fucking ass but blaming my dad for having no way out other than *death*? He was stripped of everything. His family, his job, his rank, *everything*." She was yelling at him.

Tessa was just coming to terms with this news herself. After hearing the real story yesterday, she had barely reacted. She had mourned her dad already so long ago. When she heard the new variation of his death, it seemed no different to her. Though now, it was settling in. The lies, the truths, who she was and where she came from.

He was a rebel. Fighting for something greater than himself at the risk of everything. At the risk of her. For Tessa's entire life, she had believed the public story, that he was taken by the rebels and was killed for being Elite.

According to her mother, the false version of her dad's fate was of Dealer Avarice's creation. He wanted to cultivate fear among the Elite against the rebels, so they would never join the cause themselves.

Her dad was Voided of position after a lengthy, questionable imprisonment. Once he was Voided, he was released but being Voided meant exactly that, being devoid of rank. He was released from custody, unable to rejoin their family, and the only job he could do was join the security officers, fighting against the very cause that he believed in. He would be forced into furthering the systemic gap between classes, favouring the Elite and making examples of the lower ranks.

The only thing Kenny Gamble had to his name was a bottle of pills supplied by the Region.

He took them all on the day of his release.

"Get out!" she screamed through her tears.

Suddenly Dante was between them and something snapped inside her.

"His father condemned him to die!" she yelled in Dante's face.

He took it on the chin. "I know, Squirt. I know." He attempted to reach for her but she swung around him and walked up to Alex who hadn't moved from his spot.

"Tell them, Alex, tell them Dad had a choice to make. Tell them that he deserved to lose everything," she spat out at him.

"Tessa, dear." Her mum walked forward.

"No, Mum. He needs to say it. Say that my father's life was worth the greed of the Avarice coin purse." She spun back to face Alex. "So how about it, then? Do you *honestly* think this system is worth saving? That this system is worth more than driving people to have no way out other than drugs for a small amount of respite. Do you think it is worth their numbness which drives them to do *anything* to make them feel again? A system that leads people to critical illness with no foundation to help them when that inevitably arrives? But yes, Alex, you're right. It was my dad's fault. You piece of shit."

"Tessa, that's enough," her brother scolded.

"No, she's right." Alex interrupted Dante. "I am a piece of shit."

Tessa was taken aback by this admittance.

Her silence allowed Alex to continue. "I've been distraught over a nine. I can't even begin to imagine what it would be like to lose everything. To lose you."

He stepped towards Tessa but she didn't retreat. "What hope can there be for a people who risk everything for simply voicing their opinions? I'm supposed to carry that hope on my shoulders for my father." He laughed bitterly. "Nobody gives a flying fuck about how well I do. If anything, they want to see me fail. The Elite now want to squeeze me for profit and the Low-Borns and Working-Class want to see nothing more than the Dealer's kid get fucked by the system."

She was livid at him. Her eyes overflowed with tears that she didn't wipe away. She wanted to hear more. Alex reached out for her hand and Tessa hesitantly offered it.

"I am sorry about everything. I want you to know that I am not my father. It may take me a bit to un-teach myself certain things but I am willing to listen to you, Tess. I wanted to care for you, to protect you, but I can't. I don't have to because you don't need it, you never have. I know that now and I should have known it before. What you likely want is support, and you have it in me. If that's being a rebel or—"

"I don't," she finally croaked out.

"I don't understand?" he asked, gripping her hand tighter.

She cleared her throat and wiped her face with her free hand. "I don't want to be a rebel. But I do want to make change. I want to make the change Dad tried to make but couldn't."

"How do we do that, Squirt?"

She released Alex's hand and turned to Dante.

"We play their Game and we play it well."

CHAPTER 38

Dealer Avarice

"It has been done, sir," Anthony confirmed.

"Excellent. You're sure she will be there?" Dealer Avarice said leaning back in his office chair with his fingertips pressed firmly together.

Anthony nodded. "She will join a meeting that will be called shortly. Though she has not officially joined, it will incriminate her all the same."

Dealer Avarice eyed his assistant. He never quite knew where the loyalties of Mr Largesse lay. He had been useful up to this point but had also created his fair share of trouble.

"Does she know?"

"I doubt she suspects, sir. She seems to be enamoured with me."

Dealer Avarice wasn't surprised at Tessa Gamble's change of interest. Now that his boy was a nine, he wasn't much use for an ace in the Game. That was one less thing to concern himself with.

"Consider your debts paid, Mr Largesse. You have been reliable and useful to me, more than most others in my network. It will be a shame to lose such a good assistant."

"Thank you, sir." With that, he left the Dealer in his office alone.

Dealer Avarice felt invincible at the moment. He was able to claim more than necessary for the damages to the hall, he had an idol of hope among the lower ranks, and now he was about to eliminate the one thing, one person who he couldn't control.

The Region was his, and he knew it.

CHAPTER 39

Tessa

"Largesse is going to freak out when he sees you. It's members only," Dante had warned his sister. He offered to convey the information to her after this meeting but she wasn't going to be left at home.

Tessa stepped out of Dante's truck in the clearing. She had lovingly named the entrance to the safe house the 'pit of death'. Her brother initially laughed when she said it, but he adopted the name.

"The pit of death is over here." He froze and it took Tessa a few steps to realise he had stopped.

"Are you okay, Dante?" She followed his eyeline and saw purple hair poking out of the bush. What was Veronica doing?

"Something's up," Dante said to Tessa quietly.

"Come here, quick!" Veronica whispered loudly and waved them over.

The siblings looked at one another before making their way over to a suspicious-looking Veronica. Then Tessa felt a grab. She panicked, flailed and went to scream but a hand was clasped over her mouth.

"You tryin'a get us busted, Gamble?" some boy who grabbed her had muttered.

Veronica held a finger to her lips, gesturing for them to keep quiet. She pointed into the clearing.

Tessa shrugged off her captor and followed the line of sight. Across the clearing she saw movement in the forest. She began to ask a question before Veronica slapped her on the thigh, telling her to shut up.

Tessa lowered her voice to a whisper. "Who are we looking at there?" She rubbed the spot on her thigh where she was struck, sorer than she thought a close-range smack could be.

"We don't know. But there are no scouts and the door wouldn't drop for us."

Tessa looked around behind them in the forest. There was a good number of young adults hidden. They were all at risk like this. "How do we get in then?"

"Senior members have a coin that's a key. If there's one already in the safe house the door will drop for anyone who isn't pricked."

Dante looked over to Tessa but she shook her head, knowing what he had meant. She didn't bring the talisman. She didn't even know where her mum had put it.

"So, what, we wait for Largesse, then?" Dante asked lightly.

"I don't fucking know," Veronica hissed, annoyed. "I do know that this was a full rebellion meeting without any explanation. We are all coming together and there is no way to get inside."

"You're worried about getting caught?" Tessa hadn't seen Veronica be anything but confident before then.

"Fucking, obviously, Gamble. Not all of us have the means to buy ourselves out of trouble. Some of us can't afford to get caught."

"Listen, I'm only here to help." Tessa didn't feel like getting into another argument today.

"Help?" Veronica barked a laugh. "You wouldn't even know where to start. You don't even know what's broken to fix."

"I can help! That's why we were recruited."

"*He*," Veronica pointed to Dante with her chin, "was recruited because he has already helped us. He has knowledge, he is part of our community, and has earned our respect."

Tessa recoiled at the comparison. "How can I possibly get your respect if you don't let me try? I also got the blank card removed if you recall. I'm not completely useless."

Veronica scoffed. "You did that for yourself, Gamble. Don't joke. Did we benefit? Sure. But your lot love to play hero when all you do is save yourselves."

"Look, I'm here, with you. Literally cowering behind a bush from whatever the hell is on the other side of that clearing." She gestured at the movement in the forest. "Trying to be one of you." Tessa was hurt at the accusation that her act was completely selfish. Of course, there was some truth to it. She had got her warning from a Working-Class man and she had twisted the rules to suit her needs at the time. Anger took care of the rest.

"One of us? Gamble, tell me the cost of bread. Nothing fancy, just a normal loaf of bread."

Tessa stared at her. What kind of test was this? She had no clue what bread cost. She would go to the store when she wanted to shop, choose what she wanted, and buy it.

"Well, Gamble? How about milk? Eggs?"

Tessa winced at each item listed. "I don't know."

Veronica laughed coldly. "Right, and you expect me to believe you are one of us."

"Look there!" A boy in the group beside them pointed into the clearing.

Dealer Prudence was walking towards the pit of death. The people they saw on the trail noticed her as well and went running towards her through the dense forest on the other side.

The Dealer didn't notice until it was too late, and when they got close enough Tessa recognised the uniform: security officers. They worked for the Region. They had been found.

Tessa couldn't hear the discussion between the officers and the Dealer, but she also wasn't going to risk getting any closer.

"Thank fuck it's her and not us," Veronica said under her breath.

Tessa agreed. If anyone could get out of that situation, it was a Dealer. Just as she finished that thought more security officers entered the clearing.

"I feel like we should get out of here," Tessa spoke wearily.

"So we can get chased down by those lot? Absolutely not." Veronica seemed to be speaking on behalf of her troop.

Voices were raised between the officers and the Dealer now and they were moving in closer, flipping her bag and dumping its contents.

"They're looking for something. Weapons?" Tessa questioned.

"On a Dealer?" Veronica responded in a tone that suggested it was unlikely.

They continued to watch as a female officer lifted the Dealer's hair and pulled a cord until the loop of it was at the base of the Dealer's throat.

Dante attempted to shoot up but Veronica grabbed his shoulder and slammed him down. "What the fuck do you think you're doing, Gamble? Get us all Voided?"

"We can't let them—"

"Let them, what? They won't hurt her, they wouldn't dare."

Dante nodded, but Tessa wasn't sure she was as confident as Veronica was. She watched as the officer reached to the front of the cord, and pulled it to look closer at what dangled. The officer in the back cut the cord, freeing the cord from the Dealer.

"Fuck, fuck, fuck, fuck. We have to go. Now." Veronica picked up her bag and started running through the trees. Groups of people followed her as they ran in the opposite direction from the clearing.

"What do you want to do, Tess?" Dante asked her as he looked between the situation in the clearing and Veronica's fading form.

The officer raised the cord, looking at the talisman Tessa saw dangled from it and he smiled at Dealer Prudence before kneeing her in the gut, forcing her to the ground.

Tessa let out a gasp and smacked her hand over her mouth to keep quiet but it was too late. A few officers heard her squeal and looked at one another.

"There's our answer. Let's go, Tess."

Before they could go, Tessa stood upright and in full view of the officers. She couldn't let them search the rest of the forest behind them, and they knew she was there anyway. She had to hope her ace privilege was enough.

Dante watched in horror before he stood up slowly beside her. "You'd better have a plan," he warned.

"Follow my lead," she whispered to him. She raised her voice in a jovial tone as the officers approached them. "Morning officers! My brother and I were out for a lovely walk in the woods today. Beautiful day, isn't it?"

Dante gave her a glance that said, *This is your plan?*

"State your name," one of the officers said.

"Tessa Gamble, and this is Dante Gamble. Ace and king, respectively." The Elite statistically had less trouble with law enforcement and there were no recorded crimes committed by an ace.

The officers looked at one another. "Mind tellin' us why yous were hiding in the bush, Miss Gamble?"

She knew security officers were likely a four at best. Being drafted into the service was something very few volunteered for. If you were healthy and young, it was about the only thing you could do if you were so low ranking.

"Well, we were out for a walk when we saw Dealer Prudence…" She allowed him to complete the rest of the thought and he nodded.

The other officer stepped forward. "I remember you when my lil' girl just Drew." He turned to the questioning officer. "This is the one who ripped the card!" The rest of them looked at her with raised eyebrows.

Play with confidence she thought to herself.

"It wasn't right and wasn't in line with what the Fates wanted. Nobody should be Voided of their position."

"Even them rebels, miss?" The third guard mumbled and she barely understood what he had said. She thought for a moment. They were law enforcers and were trained in harsh conditions to do so, but they were also likely Low-Born so may have been in line with the rebel cause.

She decided to keep neutral. It was working well for her so far. "Oh my!" She feigned shock. "I suppose I never thought about that. I guess I just didn't think it should have been in the deck; the blank card, I mean." She turned to the second officer; he seemed the best bet for a better conversation. "Did your daughter have the luck of the Draw with her, sir?" she asked him, both changing the subject and addressing him with formality that she didn't have to use. The officer was likely not accustomed to flattery from an Elite.

He stood up a little taller and beamed. "Drew a six, so she did. Of hearts at that. My baby girl can be a someone. She's awful clever too, so she is, miss."

She smiled at him. "A very good combination, a lucky Draw and a brain. You must be very proud."

He smiled a wide, wrinkled, full-face smile back. Tessa thought he wore happiness very well. "So I am, miss."

"Oy!" The siblings and officers turned to see Dealer Prudence well beaten and restrained. She was being pushed across the clearing.

A lump formed in Tessa's throat and Dante's eyes looked helpless.

"Best be going, miss... and mister. Enjoy your walk." He tipped his hat and the other officers followed suit. The mumbling one paused and gave her a look, spitting something out of his mouth onto the ground. He then turned and joined the rest of the officers.

"Well, that was lucky," Dante said.

"Come on, let's get out of here." Tessa's knees felt like they would crumble from under her. Those waves of confidence filled her with power at the time, but following them she felt feeble and weak. She always stood up well for others, and now that got to mean something, though she knew that she was going to have to learn to stand up for herself, first.

"Why did it matter that his daughter Drew a heart?" Tessa asked Dante. She found it odd that it was separately spoken from her rank.

They reached the car and climbed in. She was still shaking from the interaction with the officers and seeing Dealer Prudence in such a state.

Dante buckled his seat belt. "The Low-Borns and lower Working-Class put value to it. They say it says a lot about the person's character and that the Fates decide everything about the card, even the suit."

"And what does a heart mean?"

Dante shrugged. "I don't actually know if it means anything. It is just another way they sort themselves and put stock in the Fates. Those higher Working-Class call it superstition."

Tessa nodded and played with the necklace her mum gave her. She wondered if they would perceive her a certain way due to her spade.

"You'd think the lower-ranked people would want fewer boxes," Dante continued, starting the car and reversing it out of their spot in the grass. "But I guess people want any power they can get. They have little hope for a high Draw but a fine chance at a good suit, so they focus on that."

Tessa considered this for a moment. "So they have their own hierarchy in the Lower-Class in addition to the card rank?"

He swivelled his head back and forth in uncertainty. "I guess you could say so. I think it is more social and spiritual than to do with opportunity and Gameplay."

Clearly Dante didn't know the detailed answers she wanted, but she thought she might know someone who did.

CHAPTER 40

Tessa

Anthony seemed genuinely surprised to see Tessa as she waited by his car parked outside the Dealer Compound.

"Hey, Tony." She greeted him with his preferred nickname; it was the closest thing to an olive branch that she was willing to give.

"What are you doing here? Come to see the Dealer?"

She did wonder why he seemed so shocked to see her. Perhaps it was because of how she left things the last time they spoke.

"No, actually, I wanted to talk to you." She put her hands in her pockets and looked at the ground. She didn't truly feel bashful, but he didn't need to know that. "Thank you for offering to take me home and making sure I got there safely."

She looked up at him and a smirk threatened to bloom on his face. Anything that she did, she needed to make him feel like he was the hero.

His flaw was his quest for control.

"I meant it when I said I wanted to take care of you." He said it in a way that suggested that truth hurt him. She also noticed his use of past tense but didn't comment.

"I believe the wording was to keep me safe?"

The smug grin finally won the battle against his poker face. "Same thing to me."

She put a fake smile on her face but she knew it wouldn't reach her eyes. "Did you want to maybe still go for that drive?"

His grin transformed into a full smile. It took her off guard. She wasn't expecting it to be so charming with his deep laugh lines and crinkled eyes.

"This way to the chariot, Tess." He held out his arm and she grabbed the crook of the elbow like she was sure he intended.

They walked together in silence but she could feel the tension in the air between them. She didn't trust him, but she found him attractive. She found that she second-guessed herself, thinking she may have been looking too deeply into things when they were together. Anthony brought her a certain peace with his presence that Alex never could. Until yesterday, she always held her opinion and tiptoed around subjects fearing what he would think of her. Fearing his father.

Not only could she speak freely with Anthony, but she could challenge him. He seemed to enjoy her spirit.

It was entirely possible that he meant nothing but good and she had judged him based on the experiences she had with others.

Anthony opened the car door for her which made her genuinely smile. She looked up at him and locked his gaze as she entered the car and while he gently closed her door for her. Tessa released his gaze when she went down to reach for her seat belt and he made quick work of going around the front of the car and entering his side.

When he sat down, she noticed how tight his jaw was. "Are you okay?" Tessa asked him.

He turned to face her and shook his head. "You have to stop looking at me like that."

Anthony had said the words nicely but she still recoiled and looked out of the front window. "Oh, sorry."

He brought his hand over and rested it on her knee. The touch shot a pulse through her and she looked at him from the side.

"I didn't mean it like that. I really, *really*, like how you look at me. I guess I'm just confused. Why are you here? Why the change?"

She nodded and his admittance made her stomach flutter. "I just want to see a new perspective and—" She paused.

"And?" He squeezed her knee and it made her core clench.

"I just... I wanted to see you again." A half-lie.

He paused for a moment and she could feel his eyes on her. After she refused to look up at him, he broke the silence. "A nice surprise." She thought it was a strange tone but when she looked up, the charming smile from before had resurfaced.

He released her knee and put his car into gear. "Ready for a field trip?" he asked. She simply nodded before they drove away from the Dealer Compound.

CHAPTER 41

Alex

"You want to buy my apartment from me?" Louise asked in complete disbelief. "With what money?"

Alex had quit the job his sister had arranged for him and took on the coveted role of Tessa's personal assistant. He had no idea what that entailed, but he was more than happy to assist her... personally.

"I got a good job with a handsome starting bonus." That was his pay, really, but his sister didn't need to know that.

"So, you want to take one of my investment properties from me instead of getting your own place?"

He shrugged. "I don't have much of anything, as you well know. This place has furniture and all my worldly belongings in it already. The building itself is safe and it isn't too far from the Elite village."

Her eyes sent daggers at him. "You aren't welcome at the house, Alexander."

"Maybe not the Avarice house." He shrugged her arrogance off, and it felt good.

"Ah, I see. This is about your girlfriend? She still wants you even though—"

He held his hands up and she stopped. Alex hated that people, namely his family, kept lording the Draw over him. Suddenly his value and his worth were something entirely out of his control. He felt bad for the rest of the Region, the Low-Borns and Working-Class, as this was their entire reality. He wondered if that would be better, to never have had anything than to have everything and lose it all.

"Would you please sell me your apartment, Louise?"

"I will, Alexander. What kind of sister would I be if I didn't help you?"

He figured she would have been the same sister she always was, but elected not to say that out loud.

"However, I do expect fair market value for the apartment. I will get it appraised later today. If this is an advance, I assume it's all cash? I can be a little kinder to you if it is. As a moving-in gift, I will include the furniture for free."

He was genuinely surprised by that small act of kindness. "Thank you, Louise."

She shrugged. "That part is more selfish. I don't want to move it all out and move it to another unit. I also noticed that you already managed to ruin the table…"

He looked at the pen scuff he had created and made worse in an attempt to clean it. His surprise left him. There was the Louise that he knew well.

"Congratulations on the new job, by the way. What is it?" She didn't actually seem interested but he was hoping that Louise wouldn't have asked at all.

He grimaced, knowing further explanation would be required. "Personal assistant."

She laughed. "Who would hire an ex-Elite as a personal assistant? We only know how to be assisted." She paused and her eyes went wide. "Wait, is this for a Gamble?"

"Yes, okay? My network did me well."

Her eyebrow raised. "Yes, I'm sure what you were doing with Tessa Gamble was networking."

He felt the heat rise to his face and his fists curled at the sides.

"Calm down, Loverboy. Whatever works. Many people throughout history have used sex to advance their lives and careers in one way or another."

"It's not like that!" he protested.

She gave a snide grin, the same one his father would use on him as a boy, and crossed her arms. "It worked either way, didn't it?"

Just then the tone of the broadcaster sounded.

Louise groaned. "What now? I swear there's something every day now."

Alex didn't want it to repeat and was happy for the break in the conversation. He stood on the pad and waited for it to start. He expected to see his father again but when the video started it was Dealer Prudence.

He clasped his hand over his mouth at the sight of her. She was bloody, bruised and bound with rope. Her normally perfectly coiffed hair was loose and messy. She was without her Dealer jacket and all he could see was a misbuttoned shirt covered in dirt and blood.

"What the fuck?" Louise gasped behind him.

"Read it, *Dealer*," a foreign voice sternly said from off the screen. Alex didn't recognise the voice but Dealer Prudence flinched in response.

"Citizens of Cassino Region," she groaned.

"She sounds awful…" Alex said before his sister immediately shushed him.

The Dealer continued. "I regret to inform you of my immediate dismissal." Her voice was hoarse as if she had been screaming. She cleared her throat and her eyes continued to move as she read the statement that was obviously in front of her.

"I have been discovered with a relic, linking me with the rebel cause. I am to be charged without trial as I admit to my involvement." She took a deep breath.

Alex was speechless. There had to be a mistake. She was a Dealer, a leader of the Region alongside his father. Could nobody and nothing be trusted?

The Dealer broke into tears and looked up. "I was just trying to help." Just then, a gloved hand came onto the screen to grab her by the hair, forcing her to face the camera. She squeaked in pain.

"Read," the voice said sternly.

She spoke now through her tears. Alex could tell she tried to sound confident but he knew what was coming.

"Due to my involvement and guilt, I have been Voided of my position. I have been stripped of all assets, liquid and otherwise. I will also be—" She choked.

Alex could swear the entire Region was silent around him as he heard her rasping breath hitching.

She cleared her throat and lifted her chin. "I will be eliminated from the Game."

Both Alex and his sister gasped. There hadn't been an Elite execution in generations. They hadn't even executed Kenny Gamble.

The Dealer looked above the camera line again, presumably at her captors, and faced the camera again. "Play well, Cassino. Play *better.*"

There was a bang and Dealer Prudence dropped from the view of the screen and the feed immediately cut off.

Alex spun to meet his sister's equally stunned face. "Did they just kill her?"

Louise's eyes were glazed but she put a look of indifference on her face. "The rules of the Game and Region are clear." He could swear she sniffled before continuing. "She abused her position. She was a traitor to her people."

Alex stepped towards her. "You cannot honestly condone a public execution over the broadcaster? Children *must* watch that, Louise! They will have no choice but to stand on the pad and *watch*."

She squared her shoulders. "Father is now the sole Dealer of the Region. As his family, we play with his guidance. If he saw that this was fit, then the Fates must have as well." Louise was convincing herself, he knew that.

"Good thing I am no longer a member of the family, then," Alex spat at her.

He couldn't tell if her eyes were pleading or murderous but she left without another word.

He knew that nothing good would come of these actions. There was a war coming and he didn't know what side he would be on when the time came to choose.

CHAPTER 42

Tessa

Anthony had taken Tessa to an area she had never been in before and she couldn't lie, it took them a lot longer to get there than she anticipated.

"Do these people work in the Region still?" she asked.

"This is the Region still. We are still in Cassino, but this is where the Low-Borns live. My parents both grew up around here and a lot of my family and family friends are still out here. Even further out is where the Voideds build their temporary housing."

"Temporary housing?"

He nodded. "As they have no rank, they are unable to stay in the ranked zones and unless they join the security detail, have nowhere to go. They attempt to create a zone of their own and set up structures with whatever they can find. If they're lucky they'll have a tent, though anything they create is short-lived. Every few months the Region tear down what they've built."

Tessa was horrified at the thought that anybody would be subject to that. It sounded like these people needed help, not further displacement. "Why would they do that?"

Anthony glanced over at her before returning his eyes to the road ahead of them. "Their punishment is their removal from the Game. The last thing the Region wants is for them to create their own Game outside the one the leaders control."

The finality of his tone and the clench of his jaw told Tessa that the conversation was over. She wanted to believe that there was a good reason for the destruction of homes, that there was a purpose to Voiding people, but she couldn't find it within herself to believe it was the will of the Fates to do any of this to anyone.

She hugged herself and looked out of the window. The roads that they were on were incredibly bumpy and full of large holes. There were no pavements to compare to what she saw in the Elite village or outside the Working-Class home Dante had taken her to.

These buildings had no real character to them. They looked to be made of poured concrete and were rectangular in shape. They looked very robust, like they could survive a war.

"There are probably twelve or so homes in that one building," Anthony said, gesturing to one of the buildings Tessa had been looking at.

"Twelve?" She didn't mean to blanche, but she couldn't picture so many people in such a small space. She looked out of the window as they continued to drive. Tessa was doing her best to not get motion sickness with the bumpy roads. She suddenly noticed it was very grey. "Why is there no grass?"

"That would be just another thing to take care of," he replied simply as if that were answer enough. She decided not to pry, though she did want the answers to the questions her brother couldn't give to her.

"My brother mentioned earlier that the suits matter to these people. Do you know anything about that?"

He pursed his lips and looked at her, searching her face.

"Low-Borns and lower Working-Class revere the Fates," he said carefully. "They believe that if they live intentionally, the Fates will reward them. Out here, rank doesn't really matter. Cards two through to four essentially all have the same opportunities as dictated by the Elite." He looked at her from the side. "What these people can hope for is to be blessed by one of the Fates, earning their suit."

"So, the Fates each have their own suit?" Tessa knew that there were four Fates, and had seen in various depictions of them that they all carried a suit, but she thought it was simply symbolic.

He nodded. "Exactly. The Fate of Hearts is believed to fate happiness and love, for example."

He pulled into a parking lot. Tessa saw cracks form in the pavement out of which weeds were growing. The yellow lines for parking spaces were barely visible and the ones she could see weren't straight at all.

"What do these people hope for then?" She was curious about this new ranking system they had created themselves.

"Diamonds, mostly." He shrugged. "They believe the Fate of Diamonds will fate them wealth and health."

"Are there bad cards? Or suits, I guess?" Tessa asked. The first two seemed very positive.

He put his car in park and faced her. "The black suits are seen as... less desirable than the red." He said it in a looming way that told her she did not want to know what her spade meant to them. "They mainly just give them something to hope for, Tess. The courage to do what they wish. I personally think it is a self-fulfilling prophecy."

Tessa cocked her head to the side. "How do you mean?"

"Well, if you Draw a heart, you believe that you are fated love and happiness. You will then do what makes you happy, you'll find a partner, start a family, and generally be propelled into the choice of your card." He sighed. "It is yet another thing that defines people that takes their choice, their freedom, away from them. Someone with a club could be happy and find love if they chose to be, just like anyone could. But as they believe the Fate of Happiness hadn't blessed them, they won't pursue it."

"We love to limit people, don't we?" Tessa asked looking down at her hands in her lap.

He reached over to put his hand in hers and squeezed, getting her attention. Anthony gave an honest, reassuring grin. "*We* don't."

She grinned back and they stayed in that moment, frozen, holding hands and staring at one another. She felt him start to swirl his thumb on the back of her hand.

Tessa broke the eye contact. "If I can't look at you like that, then you can't look at me like that." She had to keep reminding herself in her mind that this was part of the Game. He saw her as a piece, a damsel in distress. Someone to protect and rescue.

She just couldn't help but feel drawn to him.

He laughed breathily. "Come on, then. Let's go for a stroll."

He got out of the car and beat her to open her door herself. She hesitated, looking out of the door.

Anthony saw her reservations and held out his hand. "Do you trust me?"

She watched him, unsure how to answer. No matter how she felt about him, she needed to be true to herself. She couldn't hold back like she did with Alex. "No," she laughed but took his hand anyway.

"Good," he replied with a smile and led her onward, still holding her hand.

She didn't let go; she didn't want to.

"Where are we going?" she asked, taking in the broken windows patched with wood and spray paint on the walls.

"I want you to meet my grandparents."

She stopped in her place and stared at him. Tessa never knew her grandparents. They had died well before she was born.

He stroked her hand with his thumb reassuringly. "I want you to meet people. I want you to hear their stories. I want it to help you decide if you want to join the cause or not." He pulled lightly on her hand to keep her walking. When she didn't, he sighed. "How can you help if you don't even want to see the problem?"

At that, she continued walking. She reminded herself that Dante told her this wasn't going to be comfortable. Anthony had the same point Veronica had about knowing the problem; it was always going to be easier to look away.

"Where were you today?" she asked.

He froze, clearly not expecting that question. "Working. Why?"

"You called a meeting, didn't you?"

His eyebrow raised a fraction before he regulated his face again. She recognised Gameplay when she saw it. "You *were* there?" he asked with genuine confusion.

Tessa thought the choice of question was odd. He expected her to be there, then?

"We all were, Tony. We couldn't get in the safe house though."

He straightened at this. "I gave you a key."

Was that accusation in his tone?

She became defensive. "I didn't have it on me. I didn't think I would need it considering I was going with Dante and it was a meeting *you* called."

He nodded his head at this and she felt his hand stiffen in hers. "I did call a meeting but was unable to attend."

"Well, because you couldn't attend, we all watched Dealer Prudence get arrested."

He dropped her hand. "What? Fates." He cursed and started heading back towards the car and she ran after him.

"They found her talisman, Tony."

He froze for a split second but continued walking. He opened her car door for her once again.

"Where are we going, Anthony? I thought you wanted me to see... this." She gestured out of the front window once she was sitting in her seat.

Anthony entered his side of the car and immediately started the engine. "Plans changed. Everything has changed." He swore under his breath.

She reached over and grabbed his thigh and he looked up at her. She saw the concern in his eyes. "She's a Dealer. She's going to be okay. Whatever fallout happens, we can play with it."

"We?" he asked, catching her off guard.

She didn't mean that she wanted to play together. She was surprised he had taken it that way. "I didn't mean it like that. I more meant… look. Clearly change needs to be made and with Dealer Prudence being caught, people are more likely to feel vulnerable."

He took the hand that was on his thigh and kissed it. "Does this mean you'll join the rebellion?"

She stared at him. The smug grin combined with the kiss on her hand made her want to jump his bones. Playing both sides could have its perks.

"Yes, I'll join your rebellion."

He smiled from ear to ear and cupped her face in his hands. "You have no idea what this means. Now that Dealer Prudence… now that I have you…" He sighed, unable to string a sentence together. "Can I kiss you, Tess?"

She twisted her head and kissed the palm that was on her cheek. She nodded.

He closed the distance between them and lightly pressed his lips into hers. She felt the tingle in her lips reach her core. This felt better, this felt right. It felt honest and true, easy and unforced. She couldn't trust him, but he didn't seem to mind that. Neither did she.

She pushed into him and moved her hand back to his thigh, rubbing the inside of it.

His breath caught and she used the opportunity to lick at his tongue and nibble his lower lip.

He groaned. "Careful, Gamble." But he didn't stop. He matched her passion, breaking the kiss only to graze his lips across her jaw and down her neck.

She let out a little squeak and he froze in place, nipping the spot with his teeth. "Should I take you to the safe house?" He nipped again and sucked it better. He murmured against her skin, "I do still have your dress…"

"Yes," she breathed. It was the only thing she could manage to say.

He broke away and buckled his seat belt. It fought him on the first couple of pulls until he let out a frustrated sigh and pulled it more gently. He clicked it into place and stared at Tessa. His eyes roamed her face and landed on her lips. His parted with a loud exhale before his gaze broke and he slammed his car into reverse.

Tessa could feel his need vibrate from him. She liked seeing him flustered and it reminded her of Alex unable to work the zipper on the tent. Looking over, she allowed her eyes to roam his body and paused as she saw his desire for her bulging against his trousers.

She slid her hand up his thigh and rubbed the back of her hand against it. He let out a raspy breath and she took that as encouragement to continue. He took a hand off the wheel and grabbed the inside of her thigh, pulling it apart from the other one. She felt the cold air rush between her legs.

His hand travelled quickly to the apex of her thighs. "I can feel how hot you are through your jeans." He spoke through his teeth, rubbing her dampness.

She grabbed the bulge fully and squeezed.

"Fuck," he hissed through his teeth.

His gruff, masculine tone made her rock against his hand.

She suddenly saw them come up to a line of trees. She hadn't realised how far out they were. They must have been close to the edge of the township already.

He entered the clearing bumpily, making his hand hit against her swollen clit.

Anthony drove close to the pit of death and parked haphazardly. He ran around to the passenger side door and ripped it open. He leaned down, grabbed the back of her head by her hair, and tilted her face up, quickly pressing his mouth hungrily into hers.

"We'd better get inside before I fuck you out here," he said against her lips.

She wanted to call his bluff, but she wouldn't put it against him to do exactly that. Though at this point, she wouldn't have minded anything. Tessa's mind was hazy with want. When they got to the door, he faced her, swallowing hard. Then they fell.

They hit the mat below and Anthony landed on his feet again. Tessa landed on her back that time and he took advantage of that position, crawling on top of her.

He pinned her arms over her head and sucked hard on her neck. She knew he would leave a mark but she didn't care. It felt good to be with him like that.

"Tony?"

"Hmm?" he questioned into her neck.

"I've never..."

He unlatched, giving her relief that she really didn't want. "I thought you and..."

She shook her head. "We didn't do *that.*"

He grinned in the smug way that she loved. "Let me set the standard, then?" He said it as a question; he wanted consent.

Tessa may not have trusted him, but she knew if she wanted to stop, he would do so immediately. She nodded and he scooped her up in his arms. He was stronger than Alex. There was an ease when Anthony moved with her. It made her think that maybe there really were Fates.

They crossed The Circle and it seemed larger now that it was empty. He set her down in front of the hidden door with her back to him. He grabbed her hips, hinging her into him. His hands roamed her body and ended at her throat, tilted her head back to him. She arched her back to his touch; it was electric; it was impulsive.

She moved with him as if he controlled her with a string.

"We are going to stay out here and I am going to torture you until you choose the right brick."

She loved the sound of that, but it irked her how he underestimated her once again. She had to show him that she was better and more than anyone had ever believed.

Tessa reached out, bending so her ass ground into his firmness. He pressed even harder against her and she smiled to herself.

She pressed a single brick, the correct one, and it popped out as it did before, unveiling a doorknob.

He spun her around and pushed her against the door. He pinned her arms above her head using a single hand and used his other to grip her chin. Anthony's lips brushed hers as he whispered, "Clever girl."

Her heat intensified at the compliment. She reached forward and grabbed the bulge straining against the fabric of his trousers. He awarded her a groan in response. "I would still like to be tortured, though."

His smug grin reached his eyes as he looked down her body, gaze resting on the slight dip in her shirt. "You shouldn't have won so quickly, then." He played with the seam on the collar of her shirt, fingers grazing her cleavage and she found she arched her back allowing her chest to be closer to him. He seemed to like that because his breath caught in his throat.

"I didn't realise it was a game." She had no idea whose voice that was, but she had never sounded so sultry in her life.

He brought his arm to the curve of her back, bending it towards him further. He bent down and kissed the tops of her breasts. "Oh, Tessa. Everything is a game when it comes to you."

She should have seen the threat, the warning that it was, but she was too influenced by her desires to care. If she was going to be a game, so was he.

She shoved him back and he looked surprised. She opened the door and locked eyes with him. "Come play with me then." Tessa walked backwards removing her shirt and throwing it to the side.

A groan left his lips and he bit them. She bit hers in response and that seemed to do the trick.

"Oh, I will come play, Miss Gamble. And I will play well."

He entered his office and closed the door behind him with one hand, unbuttoning his trousers with the other.

CHAPTER 43

Alex

Alex met Dante at the gate of the Elite village.

"Where's Tessa?" he asked, concerned. She and Dante had planned to go to the rebel meeting together today while he went to speak with his sister.

"She went to see Largesse."

Alex got off his bike and walked towards Dante. "Why couldn't she see him at the meeting?"

Dante sighed. "There wasn't really a meeting... but I'll explain on the way. Get in."

Without another word, Alex jumped into Dante's truck. "Is Tessa alright?" He was worried that if Dealer Prudence could get caught, Tessa most definitely wasn't safe.

"I don't know, but I am going back to the safe house and now that you know what's going on, you are too."

Alex's mouth went agape. He had just been convinced that they weren't a group of crazed Elite-killers, but he wasn't sure he was ready to face them. "I am not a rebel, Dante! I told you both I am following her lead on this and if she is neutral then—"

Dante interrupted him. "Did you see the broadcast, Avarice?

They killed her. A fucking Dealer, in front of the entire Region. They eliminated her from the Game and because Tessa isn't home, it is just on repeat in the house. Bang. Bang. Bang. Over and over again." Dante hit the steering wheel every time he mimicked the gunshot. "So, she is out there, who knows where, with the other… no, scratch that… *the* leader of the rebellion. If he gets caught, and with her…"

Alex paled at that. "Then why are we going to the safe house instead of going looking for her?"

"That's just the first place we're looking. If she or Largesse heard anything about this, they would be smart to go and seek refuge there."

"And if the officers do have her?" he asked worriedly.

Dante swallowed hard and his knuckles whitened with the tight grip on the steering wheel. "What should we do then, Avarice? There is very clearly a hunt going on and my little sister, the woman *you* said you cared for, is out there and you and I both know she is on your father's radar."

Alex allowed the air to settle from what Dante said. He resolved that if he was going in, he may as well be going in knowing everything he could. "Tell me more about this meeting-not-meeting, then."

Dante quickly summarised everything they had seen in the clearing earlier that day as well as the interactions with the officers in the forest.

By the time the story was over, they were parking up in the clearing. There were other cars there including what Alex recognised as Anthony's car. He had a special spot at the Dealer Compound for being his father's assistant. He didn't say anything, being only slightly relieved knowing that she was likely here and safe.

"This doesn't seem right…" Alex observed.

"Well, obviously, Avarice. Everyone is on fucking edge right now."

"No, not this. The talisman that Anthony gave her is what incriminated Dealer Prudence. You said they looked for it."

Dante shook his head. "There is no way Largesse wanted what happened to Dealer Prudence to happen to my sister. He is *into* her, Alex. I know you don't want to hear that and Tessa wouldn't want to admit it either, but he wouldn't just give her up like that."

Alex froze at the words. He didn't want to hear that someone else had their sights on Tessa, especially since he was no longer an Elite and didn't have much to offer her.

"Just think about it, Dante. It looks really convenient." If Dante trusted Anthony, should Alex?

Suddenly, Dante was getting out of the car. "I see Largesse is here. We need to make sure my sister is too."

Alex was behind Dante and chasing after him. "Dante! Wait, please."

"Did you not hear me? My sister—"

"Yes, the woman I love—" He paused a moment at the admittance of his feelings. He had felt that way for years, but it wasn't the time to think about that. He continued, "I heard you. Just think for two seconds. Anthony Largesse owes my father a great debt, well, his family does anyways."

Dante crossed the space between them. "What the fuck are you saying?"

They stood the same height, but Dante was always stronger and faster. Alex was intimidated by Dante when he went in his face like that, but he didn't let it show.

"Even if you liked someone, to clear your family name, what would you do, Gamble? He is now an Elite and likely owes my father even more than he did before. Then suddenly the coin my father had to prove the physical existence of a rebellion, that Anthony leads, just gets up and walks away? My father would have never let that leave the office without his say."

Dante stared at him in disbelief, slowly shaking his head. "No…"

"Why wasn't he at the meeting? Dante, he would have incriminated himself. With Dealer Prudence gone, my father is now the only Dealer in the Region. The most powerful person with nobody who can stop him. The only player in the Game that outranks him—"

"Is Tess," Dante finished.

Alex nodded his head. "We need to be careful, Dante."

Suddenly the ground gave out under Alex and with a yell, he hit a pad in a dimly lit room. Alex looked up at a grinning Dante. "What the fuck, Gamble?"

"Sorry, Avarice, should have warned you."

Alex got the impression that he wasn't sorry at all.

He followed Dante off the mat and into a large domed gathering space. It held other people, he assumed rebels. Alex was nervous but schooled his face as he was always taught to do.

A girl with purple hair and piercings came bounding up to Dante. "The boss is a little... indisposed at the moment." Then she laughed. Alex recognised her from the Draw. She was the one who first told him about Tessa's actions that day.

She then looked at Alex and grinned. She smacked him on the shoulder. "Bad first day, Loverboy."

He was confused but then Alex began to hear the echoes of a noise and Dante groaned loudly, scraping his hand over his face. He couldn't believe it but Alex knew as the moans continued to grow exactly what he was hearing.

He was hearing her.

CHAPTER 44

Tessa

After he closed the door, Tessa threw his shirt off over his head. His arms raised willingly but only for long enough to let the garment get to his wrist before he pulled it off completely.

Anthony's hands immediately fell back onto her, leading her to the table in the middle of the room. He lifted her by her ass and sat her on it. His hands slid up and unclipped her bra with no effort. She attempted to grab for the strap.

"Ah," he said, stopping her in her movements by putting his hand on her chin and tilting her so her eyes met his as he stood over her. "I'm not done playing yet."

He pressed his lips to hers gentler than he had been and laid her on her back. He cleared the chips piled on the table in a single swipe of his arm under her. They made a dramatic noise as they clamoured to the ground.

"Who needs chips, anyways?" Tessa joked in a breathy voice as Anthony's lips roamed her neck.

His voice was husky when he responded. "Anything can be won in poker, Tessa." Anthony grabbed the centre of her bra and tore it off in one movement, freeing her breasts, and he stared as they settled beneath his gaze and he grinned. "Chips." He kissed her lips and his mouth roamed down. "Cash." He kissed and licked where her neck met her shoulder. "Even beautiful women." He took her nipple into his mouth and she let out a moan as she arched into him. Her legs spread wider as he grabbed her other breast.

He moaned at her movement. She couldn't take it much longer and she reached down to take her jeans off and his free hand caught her wrist.

"Eager, are we, Miss Gamble?" Something about the way he said her name into her breast made her want him more. "I believe I already made a point that I wanted to be the one to undress you, didn't I?"

She looked up at him from under her lashes. "Yes."

He stood up then and reached for the button of her jeans. "Good girl."

Anthony slowly unzipped the front and peeled them from her hips, leaving her panties where they were. She groaned and reached for them and he grabbed her hand again.

"I won't tell you again, Miss Gamble." A warning, a threat. One that excited her.

He took her hand and brought it to his shaft. She couldn't see it from where she was but she found it was likely a similar size to Alex's but curved a bit more upward.

Her mouth salivated; she wanted him everywhere all at once.

"Fuck," he whispered and pulled away from her. She squeaked in protest and he grinned at her. "Then let me play." And went back to work, taking her jeans off.

Once they were, he kissed and rubbed his way back up her leg, making his way up her inner thigh. She could feel the ache worsening but fought the urge to rock her hips.

He thumbed circles on her clit through the lace between them. She moaned and put her head back on the table.

He kissed her entrance with the barrier between. "I can already taste you from here."

He grabbed the edge of them and slowly brought them down over her feet. She was lying there, completely naked and exposed to him on the poker table. She had taken over during her encounter with Alex, but this was different. He had control, he had her wanting him, *needing* him. And she really, *really* liked that.

His tongue lapped at her core, collecting the dampness that had been building. She had never wanted something so badly before and her moan was mixed with a whine.

"I know, baby, I know," he murmured against her. The vibrations moistened her further.

"Fuck me," she pleaded, looking down at him.

He smiled and licked slower, making her groan more. "I will, but you have to be a good girl for me first." And with that, he took her clit into his mouth and his fingers pumped into her.

She felt her wetness build as her need for him increased. Her knees splayed even further apart, willing him further. He obliged, growing wilder and firmer with his movements.

She was groaning and bucked her hips in rhythm with his cadence.

He pulled away, causing her to gasp in surprise. Anthony chuckled. "I'm coming back."

He reached into the trunk and pulled out a condom. He opened it and rolled it on as he approached. "This might hurt a little, okay? If it's too much—"

"Just fuck me, please," Tessa begged, interrupting his valiant speech. She reached for him. Pumping him was easier, though less satisfying, with it wrapped in latex.

Anthony leaned above her and chuckled lightly. "Beg me again," he demanded. One finger twirled her clit, and the other hand was slowly pumping his erection. He was tempting her, prodding her entrance.

She felt like she was going to explode if he wasn't inside her. "Please, Tony, please."

He inserted the tip and she felt herself stretch with him. "Again."

"Just fuck me, please, Anthony, I can't take this anymore."

He inserted a little more and a sharp pain caused her to wince. He paused there, waiting for her to get used to his presence inside her.

She nodded and he continued slowly. Once the pain subsided, it was exactly what she wanted it to be. She moaned and rocked her hips involuntarily. There was something so natural about the experience, so instinctual. She wanted to give in, to give up. She wanted to satisfy this newly awoken part of her.

"Can I go faster?" he asked gently, circling his thumb on her thigh.

"Yes, please, just, do it." She wanted him. However he came. She wanted to be full of him.

He thrusted to the hilt and she let out a loud cry. She had never felt anything like this before. He moved in and out and she bit her lip to try to keep her noises from echoing in the small room.

"Moan for me. Let me know that you want me. Let me know what you like. Make me fuck you harder." He sounded so dominating, so in charge. She wanted to give him exactly what he wanted.

She let go and wrapped her legs around his waist, bringing him in as far as possible with each thrust. She was moaning, groaning, saying his name like it was the song of her soul.

He was picking up the pace, groaning himself in a growl that made her want him more. That made her crave to be wanted more.

She felt the pressure; her entire body was tightening. He must have felt the difference inside her. "Come for me, don't be shy, baby."

And it was like she needed the permission. She let go and all of the tension, all of the stress left her body. All warmth gathered to where they were joined. It was as if she needed to moan to let it all out, to feel it in full, so she did.

"Fuck! Anthony." Her final cry as he pumped hard into her body. She went limp. She felt so completely relaxed but wanted more.

He slowed down, allowing her to adjust to how swollen and sensitive she was. The last time she was too sensitive to continue, but now she wanted to use that sensitivity. Tessa wanted to use it like it was a head start to feeling that completion again.

After a brief period of gentle thrusting he let out a breathy laugh. "Fuck, you are so wet, Tessa. Can I go hard again?"

She nodded eagerly and he didn't hold back. The sensation was more than she expected. It tickled in the best way. She felt wanted, needed and worshipped in the way he was being primal with his motions. With her.

He slowed to individual thrusts, exiting her nearly all the way and then slamming into her. She cried out with every thrust.

"I love the way your tits jiggle when I do this."

She watched him watching her and she grabbed her breasts and started playing with them.

"Fates. You are sensational," he groaned, watching her and speeding up his hard thrusts. He glided so easily inside her. "Beg me again."

She didn't need much prompting; she was already repeating his name over and over again. "Fuck me, Tony. Come inside me, please."

With three final thrusts, harder and faster than any that came before, she felt him twitch inside her and she gave a breathy laugh.

He pulled himself out and joined in her revelry. "Well, we could do that again." She agreed with him fully. "Though maybe not now, we do have company."

Tessa sat up and immediately faced him.

He was removing the condom but pointed up at the screen. The last time she was here she thought it was just a television, but she saw a stream of The Circle just outside the door.

She scanned the bodies she saw and felt mortified when she saw Dante and Alex sitting at one of the tables.

"Is this room soundproofed?" she asked.

"Not at all." He walked over and kissed her.

She shoved him away. "Did you do that on purpose?"

"Fuck you? Obviously. But if you were asking if it was because of an audience, the answer is no. They started coming in during but you were having such a good time. It would have been a shame to stop."

She was speechless.

"I can't lie, when I saw Avarice, I had to put on a little show." He smirked smugly.

"Is this all a game to you?" she demanded angrily.

"I told you everything is a game when it comes to you. I want you, Tess. I have wanted you and I haven't kept that a secret, have I?"

She thought back to when he flirted when they first met, and she wasn't innocent of it either.

"Clearly, you also wanted me. You almost wore out my name there. Don't look so mad. Now you don't have to keep rejecting him. You want your freedom? You can have it here, with me. A jack can live in the Elite village, I can work hard for you, we can fight for what's right together, *and* fuck. What a fantastic combination."

"He's my best friend," she said, hurt.

"And he can keep being your best friend? But I want to be the one you do *this* with. Avarice shouldn't even be in here. He isn't a rebel and shouldn't know anything about us." He looked at her accusingly.

She looked down and felt conflicted. She didn't want to hurt

Alex but no matter what she knew she didn't want to partner with him. Not after how he had been since the Draw. Not since she learned that her voice mattered too. They had started their fun alone in the safe house and others entered during. Tessa knew she wouldn't have wanted to stop.

Could she trust Anthony? She felt like she should.

"I want to trust you."

"Don't," he demanded. "My first priority will always be the cause, no matter what or how good you look without clothing on."

She looked down on herself, suddenly realising that they were both still naked.

"You want to be my partner, but—"

He put her hand up and interrupted her. "No, I want to have sex with you and work with you as a rebel and see where that goes. There's a difference."

She nodded. This was the set-up she wanted to have before. With Anthony, Tessa could have fun without commitment and make the Region a better place. What could be so wrong about that?

"Now let's get dressed and handle... that." He gestured to the screen, now filled with people.

She looked at the screen again, finding Alex and her brother still in the domed meeting space.

Tessa took a deep breath and started dressing.

CHAPTER 45

Alex

They sat out in the gathered hall for a while. The sounds of Tessa tested the acoustics of the domed room annoyingly well. The repetition of a name that wasn't Alex's made him tense.

"Maybe I should get some air," Alex said, standing up.

Dante caught him on the shoulder. "As much as I also don't want to listen to this, it isn't safe up there. They caught and killed one of us already today."

"I'm an Avarice," Alex countered.

"And Prudence was a Dealer," the girl with the piercings said. He had got her name before at the Draw, but needed reminding again. Her name was Veronica. "Sit down, Loverboy."

"Please don't call me that." He hadn't minded the nickname when he had heard it at first, but after hearing Tessa being with someone else, he felt like the title was no longer his. "Has anyone tried knocking?" he asked nobody in particular, pacing like a caged animal. He was growing fed up with the grunting and groaning.

"Avarice, just wait it out. Unless he is some sort of Fate, it can't last for much longer," Veronica said, but the last thing

Alex wanted to do was imagine Anthony being like a Fate for Tessa.

The screams were sharp and spaced apart now. He hated that he could picture exactly what was happening in there. He couldn't take it anymore when Alex heard her say she wanted Anthony to come inside her. It just solidified what he feared; that they were actually having sex. He was inside her. She had done more with someone she had just met, than him.

Alex did his best to breathe and calm down. He reminded himself that she didn't owe him anything. He was the one that messed everything up. He was the one who turned her down after she repeatedly attempted to salvage what they were trying to build.

He had given her a taste of this and then he abandoned her. Of course, she went elsewhere for release.

"I say when they come out here, we give them a standing ovation," Veronica suggested in a laugh.

Dante glared at her but the others in the room laughed and agreed.

"Thank the Fates they're done," Alex said when finally, the noises stopped. He sat down beside Dante.

"Unless they go for round two, or even three. Who knows how long they've been in there." Veronica was testing him and he knew it. Alex clenched his fists on his lap. "Hey, I don't blame him. I would if I could."

"That's plenty, Nico," Dante said to her in frustration.

Alex wondered if he had a nickname for everybody.

The door opened and as agreed, the rebels took a standing ovation.

Anthony revelled in it, taking a dramatic bow, but Alex stared past him to Tessa who locked their gaze.

Alex's shoulders drooped when he saw there was no regret in those eyes.

CHAPTER 46

Tessa

Anthony opened the door to The Circle and Tessa felt mortified when everyone got up and started clapping. Everyone, that is, but her brother and Alex, of course. Though she decided to own it. She was a woman, and Alex had made it clear a few times that he didn't want her now that she outranked him. She wanted to be with a man unthreatened by her potential.

She made sure to lock her eyes with Alex, allowing her confidence to radiate through her.

Tessa could have smacked Anthony for the bow but the rebels seemed to enjoy him playing along with their teasing.

"Why are you all here?" Anthony asked the group.

Everyone looked at one another as if they were unsure who should speak up for the rest of them.

"Okay, better question: what is *he* doing here?" Anthony asked, pointing at Alex.

Tessa saw the hesitation so she spoke up. "He's my personal assistant."

Anthony turned to look at her and his eyes turned dark and broody.

"Fucking Elites. Can't do a damned thing for yourselves." Veronica rolled her eyes.

"That's enough," Anthony said in a stern voice that made Tessa want to get excited again. "Tessa Gamble is now a senior member of the rebellion."

She watched Alex's reaction to that. Clearly there was going to be a bigger conversation later. However, she reminded herself that she didn't need to explain herself to anyone.

"Why didn't you tell us we could fuck our way to the top?" Veronica asked, picking at her nails.

Tessa reddened. That wasn't the intention of the arrangement but she could definitely understand how it could be seen that way.

Anthony walked over to Veronica and towered over her. "You have a safe space here. It would be a shame if you were no longer welcome." Tessa saw her gulp beneath his gaze and nod.

For the Low-Borns and Working-Class to have this sense of purpose, a place to go, Tessa could see that as being invaluable. There was strength and power in numbers. They looked out for one another as a community. She wondered if a Low-Born or Working-Class being removed from the rebellion was on par to an Elite not Drawing well.

Anthony raised his voice and it echoed off the domed ceiling. "As I was saying, Tessa Gamble is to be respected and welcomed here. Regardless of rank, we have always shown respect and dignity to one another." He went and stood beside her. She was amazed at him standing up for her. Taking control.

She wanted more.

"She Drew well. An ace is rare and provides opportunities not only for her but also for our cause as she answers to nobody. Our relationship is separate and is, frankly, none of your fucking business."

Tessa felt her chest constrict. She didn't trust him, but would he make such a public spectacle of someone he didn't care for?

"Where was you today?" a boy she recognised from the bushes piped up. Low-Born Tessa thought, based on the way he spoke.

"I was working."

There was a clip to the voice that suggested he was annoyed at being questioned.

"So yous call a meeting, right? Then you don't show. We couldn't get inside. The Dealer got caught, so she did!" the boy continued.

"Better her than the likes of us," a girl at his table said in response.

"She's dead," Dante snapped at her.

Tessa's mouth dropped and when she looked over at Anthony saw that, even though he schooled his face, he was surprised too.

"Still better her than any of us," the girl defended herself.

"The Elite are not all the enemy." Dante was clearly not in the mood.

"Sure, yous can say that."

"That's enough," Anthony barked. "Dealer Prudence was an asset and a kind person. She may not have done as much as we believe she could have but she fell to the Fates. This attack was a direct result of the oppression she orchestrated."

Tessa stared at him in shock. She had no idea where he was planning on taking his train of thought.

"For the system to change, we need to force their hand." Mumbles of agreement filled the room. He continued, "If Dealer Prudence couldn't make it out alive, what chance do the rest of us have?"

"You don't seem to be very upset that one of your own was caught and has fallen." Alex cut through the murmurs of the crowd. "Don't try and distract this group from your guilt. You called a meeting and weren't present. As a direct result of *your* actions, one of your own was eliminated from the Game."

Tessa saw Anthony's jaw tighten. "We all know the risks of going against your father, Avarice. You of all people should know this."

They stared at one another and she couldn't help but think that their glares weren't entirely about the current situation.

Tessa decided to speak up. "They found her as they could have found any of us. Why weren't you here?" She continued in a lower tone, "It could have been me, Tony."

Alex clearly heard her. "He meant for it to be you, Tess."

Tessa caught Alex's eyes and they were filled with fire. Alex had never lied to her before, and even though she knew Alex had heard her and Anthony, he wouldn't have started then. When Anthony didn't immediately respond she took a step closer to him and attempted to catch his gaze. He refused to let her.

"What you are suggesting, Avarice, is exactly why you shouldn't be here. You're just jealous that she was begging for *me*."

Tessa blanched and looked across at Alex who slowly shook his head. He may have angered her earlier and she always treaded lightly with him, but she trusted him. Alex was her greatest friend.

"Thought you said it was none of their business, Anthony?" Tessa challenged.

"You don't seriously believe him, do you?" Anthony turned and demanded.

She searched his eyes for a moment and they were filled with anger, but devoid of hurt. "You told me not to trust you, remember?"

He stared at her coldly.

"Enough of this pissing contest." Veronica stepped forward for the first time since getting scolded by Anthony. "Why is there a witch-hunt for us suddenly?"

Anthony turned to face Veronica. "Perhaps it was our show of force."

Tessa had heard enough. "It wasn't a show of force though, was it? Who knew a faulty boiler could be a show of force, Anthony?"

The room went silent as everyone waited for Anthony's response. Tessa could see he was agitated. His little games were falling apart around him.

"You don't believe the Elite scum, do you?" Anthony cried out.

"Didn't you just say I was an asset?" Tessa asked, hurt. She didn't expect him to lash out at her this way.

"That was when I thought your loyalties were with us! The people who cultivate, who build, who make your coffee in the morning and mow your grass." He was making the speech like he was going into battle, and the rebels were eating it up.

"We are the people who rent your houses at impossible rates, the people who are the pillars on which you Elite have built your empire. We carry all the weight, cracking and breaking under the pressures while you lot dare to question why we tire."

Tessa felt the shift in the room. He had warned her that they didn't do well with being cornered and she, with Alex's help, had done so in his own safe house.

Anthony was an Elite now, but he owned this rebellion. He was raised in this, spoke their language, lived their pain and realised the dream the Elite created for them. Anthony was the hope and he was using that as a weapon.

"We can help," Dante yelled over the mumbles of the crowd. "We can become the leadership, we can be the change."

"I'm hearing a lot of words there, Gamble," Anthony challenged with a smile. "This is bigger than some balls and nets. Our people are losing jobs, wages are being cut, all in the name of putting more money in your pockets."

"Yeah!" cheered the crowd.

"Violence is not the answer," Dante pleaded with them.

"Then what is? We try and join together and we cannot protest, we cannot unionise, we are unable to get a foothold to stay stable, let alone get out on top."

More cheers from the crowd. Tessa could tell Alex and Dante were both in a very poor position in the middle of this angering mob.

"Tony," she said in a loud whisper, only meant for him.

He turned with the ferocity she craved, but right now it made her terrified.

Anthony gave her a wicked grin. His eyes flicked between her eyes and her mouth. "You'll have to choose a side, sooner or later. You think you can be the hero of both, but you're only making yourself an enemy of either. Neutrality doesn't suit you."

"And what does?" she challenged.

He got closer to her, sharing the same air. "You're always welcome on my poker table, Miss Gamble." The smug grin she lusted for reappeared on his face. "You and I, we can *be* power, with you being an ace and my connections; we can right all of the wrongs."

"We can't do that with violence," she pleaded.

Anthony leaned even closer and she felt his breath on her lips. She could still smell herself on him and she hated thinking that she could probably still taste herself on him as well.

"Well, peace isn't working for us, Miss Gamble. It only works for the likes of you. This status quo doesn't benefit the likes of us. It is time for a change." He stared at her mouth. "You're either with me or against me."

He waited there and she was sure he wanted her to kiss him. To melt into him and follow his every word.

But she was her own person and she could, and would, make change without him.

Tessa pulled back and watched anger flash in his eyes.

"You and your kind better get out of here, then," he warned.

"Are you coming then, jack?" she questioned.

Anthony scoffed. "Rank means nothing to me. You could have been a Low-Born but if you think like an Elite, you are one. Come play poker anytime, Miss Gamble."

She stood toe to toe with him for a moment. She refused to let him dismiss her, though she knew they had to go before things turned violent.

Tessa turned away, releasing his gaze but she felt his burn on the back of her head as she wove through the rebels to get to her brother and Alex.

"We should be leaving," Tessa stated to her brother who then nodded to Alex. She allowed Dante to lead the way to the climb.

CHAPTER 47

Tessa

Tessa felt conflicted. She knew she had to do something but the Elite wouldn't like change and wouldn't let it come easily. There was no pleasing everyone, but she knew the elimination of one side from the Game wasn't sustainable even if it was possible.

Life couldn't keep being taken from either side. She was also foolish to think that turning a blind eye to any death caused by the system was okay. Like somehow there was a form of 'acceptable death'. Was execution really any different than dying of exposure or dying from not receiving necessary care? The Elite killed intentionally and ignorantly; both were murder.

The Elite, Working-Class, and Low-Borns were all people. Death was equal across all ranks. It could have been the one thing they had in common.

The climb was silent, as was the walk to the car. Luckily, no unexpected surprises were waiting to greet them outside.

Tessa opened the door and climbed into the middle seat of the bench of three in Dante's truck. She felt awkward sitting so close to Alex as he got beside her in the passenger seat.

When Dante turned the key and ignited the engine, it gave Tessa the courage to talk. She didn't want to be the one to break the silence so luckily the truck did it for her.

"Is Dealer Prudence actually…"

"Dead?" Dante replied softly. "We think so. On the broadcast—"

"They killed her on the broadcast?" she gasped in disbelief.

Dante just nodded grimly with his knuckles white as he gripped the steering wheel.

Tessa partially turned her body towards Alex but didn't want to look up at him, not this closely, anyways. And not with all of the unresolved conflict between them.

"Why do you think it was meant to be me?"

She felt his gaze on her and he waited until she finally looked up. He didn't look mad at her. There was something akin to an apology in his eyes.

"Your brother and I think that it is a bit coincidental for Largesse to have given you that talisman the day before a meeting that he called, where he neglected to show up, and where Dealer Prudence was caught and found guilty for having the same thing he gave you."

"I think you were right in thinking that he planted it on you, but I don't think we were right about why. I know I questioned it last night, Squirt, but I do agree with him. Also after that display in the safe house? He didn't deny it to you, did he?" Dante glanced over at her.

"No," she said quietly. She was embarrassed to have allowed herself to be ensnared by him in such a personal way. For some reason, though, she didn't regret it.

"Tess, I know this doesn't look good. But I also don't think my father would have allowed it to be stolen."

Her face snapped up. "You think your father is in on this too? That makes no sense. That would make him part of the rebellion."

It barely made any sense to her as to why Dealer Prudence was involved. At least she had motive.

"I have no idea. He must be against it, but he doesn't exactly lose out by being the only Dealer in the Region." He softened his face and gave her a soft grin. "We won't let anything bad happen to you, Tess."

She was confused. "You aren't mad?" Not that he had a right to be, but she was still surprised. Avarices didn't lose.

He gave a light chuckle and grabbed her hand. "I have been an idiot, Tess. I know that. Did I want to... hear how much of an idiot I was? No. I really, *really* didn't. I want you to know that I do care for you and we don't owe anything to one another right now. You asked me before if it would be all or nothing, and I thought that was how I wanted things. But I am just happy if I can get you any way that I can. I can be your assistant, we can hang out, we can have sex, whatever I can get, whatever I earn back, I want."

Dante cleared his throat loudly and Tessa figured that maybe this wasn't the best place to have this conversation.

"Though I know you aren't angry, I still want to apologise. I never meant to... I mean I just needed..."

Dante cleared his throat comically louder that time.

Alex smiled at her. "I know, Tess. Let's save your brother from choking to death, though."

She loved his big toothy grin. It was comforting and friendly. It was familiar. Tessa didn't think she would ever commit to Alex. He would make some other person happy forever and play well with them, but that wasn't going to be her. She did mean it when she said she wanted her freedom years before making any decisions. Once this whole mess was behind them, maybe she could finally live her life.

"What's the plan now, Squirt?" Dante broke the awkwardness of the truck and made Tessa think. The people of Cassino were unhappy and the rebels would thrive on that.

"We still play. Tony really showed his hand with that outburst."

Dante raised his eyebrow, entertained. "Tony, eh?"

She seemed to have said it so many times that it stuck. She turned red.

"Casual first name basis and fucking the leader of the rebellion, very nice." Everyone jumped and turned to the back. Veronica popped up and leaned her head on the back of the seat between Alex and Tessa.

"What the hell, Nico?" Dante said in frustration.

"We're on the same basis, your brother and I." She looked to Tessa and whispered loudly, "Right where you're sitting."

Tessa spun quickly towards her brother who was shaking his head while he rubbed the back of his neck.

"Didn't you say earlier you would sleep with Tessa?" Alex laughed.

She shrugged. "I would. The Gamble siblings are hot." Veronica said it so casually that it made Tessa laugh.

Alex laughed harder with Tessa. "Dante and Nico sitting in a tree…"

"You can't sing that when you've slept with my sister, Avarice."

"Well, technically, we didn't—"

Tessa wanted this leg of the conversation to end immediately so she interrupted. "Okay! Enough of that. I think we should ask Veronica why she's a stowaway."

"If you must know, I want nothing to do with your precious Tony anymore. After hearing about your assassination attempt, I take it you don't either?"

Tessa mused, "It does put a bit of a dampener on our relationship."

Veronica continued, "I also think that people can change. I've seen Dante do the small stuff but you can be Dealers, both of you. I thought turning the group against you when you could be the answer was dumb."

Tessa looked to Dante. "Dealer Avarice did tell me that you were scouted for leadership."

"Other than Dealer Prudence, who was already too far into the Game by the time we got to her, we've not had anyone important listen," Veronica nearly whispered.

"You are important, Nico," Dante said to her looking into his mirror. Tessa wondered how long he had been seeing this Working-Class girl. For all she knew, Veronica was the reason he volunteered at the Complex.

"Shut up, Dante, you know what I mean. Look, I joined the rebellion and it's been all talk and now, we are getting killed publicly. Retaliation will follow which will just go back and forward like that. Then where will we be? You said there was a better way? Well, I'm behind that."

Tessa grinned at her. "What happened to you wanting to watch the Elite struggle?" Recalling their first encounter at the Draw.

Veronica shrugged. "Do I want a bunch of snooty people who have no idea what real work and struggle is to learn a thing or two? Sure. There is a difference between ignorance and apathy. I know that now. Me hoping others suffer isn't going to help anyone. Knowledge might. If the three of you born and bred Elites can hear us out, why can't others follow you?"

Tessa had a lot of guilt regarding her ignorance. Empathy and sympathy could only be present if you were aware a problem existed. She wanted to learn, wanted to grow and wanted to be better. People at all levels just wanted to be able to live. That's all Tessa had ever wanted, anyway.

"Hey, Veronica?" Tessa mumbled.

"Hmm?"

"How much is it for a loaf of bread?"

Veronica laughed sharply in surprise. "I thought you'd never ask."

CHAPTER 48

Tessa

They arrived at the Gamble residence and entered the front door.

Veronica let out a long, low whistle. "Fucking hell, Gambles. We should have been having our meetings here." She plopped herself down on the couch in the lounge, easily making herself at home.

Tessa heard a large bang from the other room and looked at Dante.

He breathed, "The broadcast. It isn't pretty, Squirt."

"It repeats for you Elite lot too? I thought the torture was just for the low-lifes. One time our pad was broken and it took three days for the maintenance crew to come around and shut the damned thing up!"

Tessa had never even considered their broadcaster malfunctioning. Yet another thing she took for granted. She sighed loudly.

Alex took her hand. "I'll be there with you, okay?"

She wondered where this Alex had come from.

"Come on, Squirt. Mum?" Dante called out.

Their mum appeared and walked slowly down the stairs. Tessa thought she looked a bit out of sorts.

"I couldn't watch it or listen to it anymore..."

Tessa felt like she was about to understand why.

"Who is this?" their mum asked, gesturing to Veronica.

"I'm Veronica, Mrs Gamble." She stood from the couch during her introduction.

"Are you friends with Tessa?" her mum asked.

Dante cleared his throat to get her attention. "Actually, Mum, she's—"

"I know him from the Complex!" Veronica yelled excitedly in interruption.

Their mum smirked and looked between them, slowly nodding. Tessa knew her mother had instantly figured out just what Veronica was, but she wasn't going to drag it out of them.

"How was your meeting with the rebellion leader, Tessa?"

Veronica grinned widely and winked at Tessa. "She caused quite the raucous."

"Oh dear! Was everything alright?"

"Sounded like it to me," Veronica mumbled suggestively.

Tessa decided to jump in and take it from there. "We think it may not be best to fall in line with the rebels, anymore. It is a bit of a longer story so let's get the broadcast over with." Tessa had heard the bang again so she knew it wouldn't be long before it repeated.

Dante led, followed by their mum. Alex placed a hand on her back, gently leading her forward. It was both comforting and confusing. She hoped he understood that she was still angry and hurt, and that suddenly being affectionate wasn't going to make up for everything.

When the broadcast ended Tessa felt the world tilt. She felt hot and dizzy. She gripped the handrail behind the pad for support.

"Tessa?" Alex knelt in front of her. "Are you okay?" His voice was full of concern.

She felt the tears grow behind her eyes. "It's my fault." She tried catching her breath as it caught into a sob. She fell to her knees in front of Alex who took her into his chest and wrapped his arms around her.

"It isn't, Tess, it isn't." He was rubbing circles into her back and it reminded her of the circles Anthony rubbed on her hand earlier.

She pushed him away, suddenly filled with anger towards herself. "It is! That..." she pointed to the screen, "... was supposed to be me. If I hadn't made a fuss at the Draw, if I had just taken my card..."

"Then you would be in a worse position than Dealer Prudence, Squirt." Dante knelt next to his sister. "If it wasn't you making a fuss, it would have been something else. People took notice of your actions because of who you are and where you come from, which is exactly what we want. We want to make change."

"Not like this!" Tessa yelled, launching to her feet. "Nobody deserves this."

"Tessa Gamble, shut the fuck up." Everyone turned to see Veronica in the middle of the room. "You want the truth? Truth is, Dealer Prudence indirectly killed far more than one person. By playing their fucking Game, you supported those deaths and the squashing of everyone else that doesn't live on this side of those gates."

"Nico..." Dante started.

"No, Dante. She needs to fucking hear this. You all do." She was spitting mad. "People die. People make their choices, and they die. That is life. She played both sides and was found out. *She* took those risks. Even if it was meant to be you, the witch-hunt would continue. You know why? Because we aren't meant to win. We never have been. If *they* don't want us to, we won't. You were born a winner, Gamble. You were dealt a winning hand before the Draw even fucking happened. His daddy," she pointed at Alex, "didn't want you to win. Not with his precious baby boy anyways. So, he set you up to lose like the rest of us.

"Dealer Prudence gave every single person in that room the chance we were all promised from infancy. We actually had hope and due to the dangers of the hope that *she* provided, the fuse was lit. You dared to fan the flame, Tessa. You started a movement and the ball is rolling far too fast for anyone to catch it. If you lie low enough, the ball will eventually stop and people will forget. The Elite will no longer be as threatened and they can go back and bathe in champagne or whatever it is you fuckers do with your stupid amounts of money."

She paused for a moment, looking at Tessa who was too stunned to continue to cry or fight back.

"You can also use that ball and make sure she didn't die for nothing. Make those fuckers pay. For trying to kill you, for killing a lot of us, and for making the Game one that only they can win. My advice? Buck the fuck up and play to win. The Fate of Spades blessed you with ambition and pride so *use* it."

Tessa blinked at Veronica. There was so much truth and harshness to what she said. Now she also knew what her suit meant. She was proud and she was ambitious and those were not bad things, even if the other ranks thought so.

"With your ace, with us behind you, and the fire in your belly that we all saw at the Draw, the Fates can get you places. If they kill you? At least you're fighting and playing the Game for something bigger than yourself."

Tessa felt the last of some warm tears escape her eyes when she wiped them clean. Veronica was right, she couldn't wallow and weep. She was better than that. She was stronger than that.

Tessa had to play with the cards she was dealt.

She faced the room. "Mum, where's my talisman?" Tessa hadn't noticed how pale her mother had got and her hand was on her throat.

"Mum? What's wrong?" Dante crossed the room to her.

"Why are you all talking about Tessa nearly dying?" she gasped out. "And so casually."

They all looked at one another but Tessa spoke first. "If I tell you, will you stop me from seeing Dealer Avarice?"

"Why the hell are you going to see him?" barked Alex, still kneeling on the floor. "Isn't the point *not* to get caught?"

"Where's the fun in that?" Veronica asked, clearly enjoying the spark she had ignited in Tessa.

"Mum, it's all speculation that Tessa was meant to live the fate of the Dealer. We don't know anything." Dante rubbed his mother's hands in his own for comfort.

"I can't let you become your father." Her mum shook her head.

"Mum, for my plan to work I need Dad's talisman. You're going to have to trust me." Tessa couldn't have known what her mum went through when they lost their dad. All Tessa really remembered was her mum always being there, strong and resolute.

"I need you to promise me that you'll be careful. I can't lose you. Either of you." She looked down at Dante's hands around her own.

"Mum, I'll be as careful as I can. Though I do need to get to Dealer Avarice before Anthony does." Tessa pleaded with her eyes and her mother relented with a sigh and left the room.

"What are you planning?" Alex whispered and placed a hand on Tessa's back. There was a certain level of comfort by his presence and support, but she felt it had some sort of condition. She stepped away.

"Your father told me I wasn't his enemy, or that I didn't have to be one, anyway. I am going to call him on it."

"By handing yourself over to him?" he said in what sounded like a whole octave over his normal range.

"If what you're saying is true, Alex, your father already knows. I just have to play the card before he can."

"At least let me go with you," Alex said as a non-negotiable.

"No," Tessa said sternly. She was done allowing others to make her choices for her. "This whole mess started with him not wanting us together. I am going to run on the assumption that his opinion on that subject still stands. By now your sister has likely told him of your employment to me, so let's not push it."

Her mum entered the room holding the talisman and turning it over in her hands. "Funny how a little token can cause such trouble."

"That's the weird thing about taking something as a representation." Veronica found her voice again from across the room. "A coin is a coin, a bit of metal. We are the ones who give it any value. Just like the cards we are dealt in our Draw. They are all identical bits of paper with a different picture on them, and somehow that is the difference between owning a mansion and barely affording shoes. That token in your hand represents control, power, unity and freedom. All those things are far more dangerous than a couple of dollars."

Everyone stared at Veronica for a beat too long.

"Oh what, like I can't be smart and philosophical because I'm broke?" she challenged defensively.

Dante strolled over with a goofy grin that Tessa hadn't seen before and he put his arm around her waist. "No, Nico. You can be and you are. The problem is we haven't given you enough opportunity for us to see it."

She smiled at him like he was the only one in the room and everyone else in the room allowed them to have that moment.

Tessa walked up to her mum. "Dad fought for what he believed in and you both instilled in us the importance of trying, of giving chance, of finding friendship. You gave us a future, one that we didn't have to work for. But I want a future I *can* work for. I want a future everyone can live to see. That may well start with me, but I'm not alone." She clutched the locket her mum had given her. "I have you and I have Dad, and Dante, and

Alex, and everyone else who wants to root for the little people who never had a chance. This Game has taken so many people; it took Dad. If you give me that talisman, I can finish what he started. I can make sure he didn't die for nothing. I can make the man who created his ultimate loss, fucking pay."

Her mother's eyes watered and she smiled, handing over the talisman. "Language, young lady."

Tessa took the talisman and cried with her mum. She was going to change everything, or she was going to die trying.

***

"You know, I'm not a big fan of this," Dante said, pulling up to the Dealer Compound.

"You don't have to like it. As a matter of fact, I wager a lot of people aren't going to like what comes of this." Veronica had gone for the car ride. She took the seat between Tessa and her brother. Alex was relegated to the back.

"Your father told me that he isn't an ally but that he also isn't an enemy. Any clue on how I should play this?" Tessa asked Alex, turning around to face him.

"Very carefully." His smile wavered which gave away his nerves.

"I can't believe he was wasted on Elite education," Veronica grumbled.

Alex glared at her and Dante raised his eyebrow at Alex. That, Tessa decided, was a good time to leave.

When she grabbed the door to open it, she paused before sliding out of the truck. She turned back, looking at her little group of companions.

A movement didn't need to have masses or an army. It didn't require thousands of people. But the people it did have needed to be committed.

She needed to be committed.

Tessa looked at Alex. He was an Elite who fell in rank. She and her brother were both Elites that stayed in their place, one by the grace of the Fates and one by the system. Then this Working-Class girl who just wanted a chance.

Luck had its place in the world, but change wasn't bolstered by luck. It was forged through determination and risk.

Though she was lucky to get the card provided to her by the Fates, her action was her sacrifice. To everyone like Veronica, like her dad, and to her future children who didn't deserve labels and boxes, the limitations and caps that came from this broken system.

The Elites were playing baseball but giving the other ranks no bat. Every once in a while, one of them would step in front of the ball, sacrificing themselves and their safety to make it a little further, but that only worked on the hope to succeed off the chance of those that followed them.

How could you possibly keep score like this? You couldn't. That's what Tessa resolved. She didn't know what game she was walking into, but she would play like lives depended on it.

Because they did. On both sides.

CHAPTER 49

Tessa

Tessa was shown to Dealer Avarice's office. She didn't have to wait for an audience. As an ace, she could demand one. She hated the power that she had, but she needed to use it; it was the only way her plan was going to work.

"*But they, in their depravity, design greater grief than the griefs that fate assigns.*" Dealer Avarice snapped the book shut and placed it back on the shelf he stood in front of.

"Homer?" Tessa questioned in interest upon entering.

"I see you are well read, Miss Gamble."

"I would wager you knew of my interest in *The Odyssey*, Dealer Avarice."

He smirked. "Maybe I had heard such things. Dangerous to teach at such formative stages."

"Wouldn't you say there are more dangerous things being taught much more subtly?"

He grinned at that and nodded, gesturing to the seat in front of his desk. They both lowered into their chairs at the same time. "How can I help you today, Miss Gamble?"

She pulled out the talisman and played with it in her hands.

She twirled it between her fingers. She learned to spin poker chips in her hand as a child. Gambling on the education grounds was encouraged among the Elite. It taught risk, reward and the art of deception.

She saw his jaw twitch and his eyes widen slightly before quickly returning to their neutral place.

"You know, Dealer Avarice, if you wanted me, you could have just asked for me." He didn't reply so she got up and walked around the room feigning indifference. Her confidence was high again. She threw the talisman on the desk. Her voice was steady and strong. "You didn't have to fetch your assistant after me."

He was staring at the talisman on the desk. His hands were still folded in front of him. She continued, "You don't think I'm so foolish, do you?" She was playing every card she had. Tessa needed to keep showing face; she needed him eating out of her hands.

"To what are you referring, Miss Gamble? This talisman went missing from my personal effects. A relic from the rebels you once told me that you weren't a part of."

She tasted his fear, the concern of an Avarice losing. "Now how did you know it was called a talisman, Dealer?"

Without missing a beat, he replied, "Your father told me."

She didn't allow him to say anything more. She was unwilling for him to use her emotions against her. "Oh yes, I am sure my father told you a great many things before you Voided him. Just as I am sure you made every cent possible off his downfall?" Tessa knew she had no foundation for that claim, but wondered if he would admit anything. Refusing information often led to gaining other.

"And what do you know about his downfall?" A question she wasn't expecting, but luckily her back was turned to him while she skimmed the spines of the encyclopaedias on his shelf.

"More than you would like, Dealer. Hmm… *Dealer*. That's a fitting title, isn't it?" She was going to spell it out for him. She needed to know if her instincts were leading her in the right direction when it came to her father.

"Pharmaceuticals are honourable investments."

She flinched at the admittance and hoped he didn't notice. She brushed an invisible fluff off her arm just in case. She steadied her voice. "Yes, it is when they help people. When research and development can be done."

"Your father took them voluntarily. They helped him… settle… while he was incarcerated."

She had no idea that he started using when he was still in prison. Tessa wanted more information but felt that she was getting further from where she needed the conversation to go. There was also a fear of how she would do when faced with the wrong information.

"Anyways, I am here to take you up on your deal."

"Deal, Miss Gamble?"

"Oh, last time I was here you said you weren't my enemy."

He corrected her, "I said you didn't have to be my enemy."

She waved her hand. "Yes, yes. But you planting that bit of rock on me and then sending guards is pretty enemy-like behaviour, wouldn't you say?"

Tessa got him again, the set jaw, jutting his chin slightly to the left. She wondered quickly what her tell was. She sat back down and she gestured, telling him he had the floor to speak.

He wasn't taking his eyes off her. He was trying to dissect her intentions.

"I will answer all of your questions, Dealer. I am not mad. I'm merely disappointed. I thought we could have a good thing going, you and me. But then you tried having me killed…"

"I did no such thing. The officer acted on his own accord and has been dealt with."

"I watched the broadcast the same as everyone else. She was

to be eliminated from the Game. It just so happened to be a very public execution."

He looked down at his hands. "I never would have killed her."

"But you would have had to. You found a leader of the rebellion who admitted her guilt publicly. You know as much as I do what that means."

He took a deep breath. "I knew where her loyalties were, Miss Gamble, unlike some."

Tessa was greatly surprised to hear this. "You know I have no loyalties to anyone."

He pointed at her with his clasped hands. "That neutrality is just as dangerous as playing for both sides. We all saw how Dealer Prudence found that."

Tessa pressed her fingers together and observed the Dealer.

He knew, which likely meant she was a mole for him. Though Dealer Prudence still went against the Draw…

"So why hunt for me, then?"

He smiled and stood up, circling his chair. "'*All I have in mind and devise for you are the very plans I'd fashion for myself if I were in your straits.*'" Another Homer quote. "I may have provided the means of the capture but the facilitation was not mine."

"I believe we have already addressed that I know of your cooperation with the rebel leader." His spin to face her made her smile slowly. "Unless you didn't know he was the leader?" When he didn't respond she continued, "Well, he played the doting assistant well, then. Where, really, he is running the whole show." She knew pulling his pride was going to give her the most reaction, and therefore the most information.

"Every report you handled, every piece of intelligence, every task, was him all along. Did you believe that you were baiting the leader when you came for me?" He remained silent but his jaw was tightening. "The obvious choice for a bluff, don't you think? A daughter of the old rebellion leader. Brother and sister both act up against the process… no wonder you didn't want me for your son."

She paused, allowing him to speak if he wanted. When he didn't, she decided to quote *The Odyssey* as well. "*Few sons are the equal of their fathers; most fall short, all too few surpass them.*' See? I can quote things too. You destroyed your son's future over a girl who, in reality, had nothing to do with any of this. All I did was dare to take a warning seriously and play by the rules. He could have been great, your son. He and I could have even been a successful couple. Maybe had a successful family."

He pulled open the top drawer of his desk and threw another talisman on the desk. Tessa assumed it was the late Dealer's.

"She wouldn't tell me the true leader. It was too obvious of a give-away. I had no information that told me that she was leadership there." He sounded sad, almost hurt. Tessa was surprised that he could be so human.

"He used me as a pawn. He distracted you to make you see only me coming forward to attack. When I didn't fall, he gave you another. He was always shielding himself. If you had got me as you wanted, he would have been able to keep going. You found an ant in a colony, Dealer."

"Give me names," he stated.

"Well, you already know one. I won't give you any more… yet."

A small grin threatened the corner of his lips as he continued the quoting game. "*Her gifts were mixed with good and evil both.*'"

She smiled in return and replied with another quote from Homer. She could and would speak in this little code as well. "*I won't set foot on a raft until you show good faith, until you consent to swear a binding oath you'll never plot a new intrigue to harm me.*'"

He observed her further and she saw his mind working.

"We have a mutual target, Dealer Avarice. Though I cannot do much without power."

His eyebrow raised. "And which power could I give you that your rank doesn't already provide?"

"Dealerdom," she replied simply.

"Now, why would I want that, Miss Gamble, when it just so happens that I have all of the control to myself? The people must be so grieved over the loss of the late Dealer Prudence. I couldn't imagine restoring anyone to her position so quickly."

Tessa rose from her seat and wordlessly went towards the door. Her audience was the best card that she had always had. She had just shown him how harmless she was to him and highlighted how little he knew. The Dealer needed her, she knew that.

He let her get out of sight with the door closing behind her when he called her back in. She grinned before re-entering.

"Why wouldn't I just catch my assistant and handle him myself?"

"I'm sure that won't look suspicious at all: your assistant was found to be the leader and the late Dealer was a senior member? You're already skirting being guilty by association. Also, if I'm being honest, not too many people like you, Dealer. It wouldn't take much to push them against you. He is in the safe house just now if you want to get him. Not that you know where that is or you would have seized it already." She was testing him and she knew it.

"What is stopping me from seizing you right now?" Dealer Avarice asked in a way that was non-threatening, simply curious.

She wouldn't give him the reaction he was looking for.

"You can. It is your decision, Dealer."

His eyebrows shot up at her confidence and she was internally proud of herself for maintaining her resolve.

"Well, Miss Gamble. You and I are both aware that you have done more to uncover the rebellion that has plagued me in a matter of days than any others I have hired to do so over the course of your lifetime." He paused and gestured for her to sit again. She obliged. "What are your terms then, Miss Gamble? I assume you aren't simply interested in the title."

"Your son will be my assistant."

He laughed. "He isn't even of rank to enter the building, Miss Gamble."

"That changes as well, along with other limitations," she said so solidly that he was taken aback.

"You want to get rid of our whole way of life," he resolved for himself. "Why would I give you that? Why would I give you the key to everything?"

"I don't want to start over. I wish to make meaningful changes. Small steps at a time, starting with the citizens' inability to visit a building they, themselves, pay for. Also, they should be able to visit their leader; they do pay your salary, after all." She took a breath before continuing, "More opportunity for every rank, regardless of background, and—"

He interrupted. "And! Miss Gamble, you can't possi—"

She spoke over him. "*And* the Draw will be genuinely randomised and up to the Fates. Nobody will be able to buy a better place."

"That last condition will be the end of the township. There is a reason for this balance, Miss Gamble. Human nature will always create a discord of haves and have-nots. There will always be winners and losers."

"Is it really a game if it is rigged and fixed, Dealer Avarice? Those born in the Elite are very likely to stay in the Elite. That fact isn't lost on anyone. With what I hope, we can have mixed neighbourhoods and mixed schools. If people work hard, they can win. In the Elite's case, should they work hard, they won't lose out on anything."

He looked frustrated. "You expect me to make you a Dealer, anger the most powerful people in the Region, and ruin my own family?"

"You did that yourself when you fed your son a nine and allowed his sisters to make a profit off him," she spat back. That was personal. It was the first time that she allowed herself to show real emotion in the meeting but it seemed to hit home with the Dealer.

"Give me Mr Largesse and you have a deal."

She was surprised. That was easy. Too easy. "What?"

"You heard me. Give me the rebellion leader and you have a deal."

She paused a moment. There had to be more to this; there had to be something bigger going on. "And my suggested changes?"

He nodded. "Though it cannot all happen overnight, Miss Gamble. We would have more than one rebellion on our hands if we angered too many groups at once."

"Put it in writing and I will agree," Tessa said, raising her chin a little higher.

He smirked, clearly impressed by her commitment. He pulled out a sheet of paper and scribbled down on it.

"I want a witness," she then stated. He may as well scribble on a napkin if nobody was there to see it.

He looked up at her. "I cannot."

"Then how will I hold you to this?"

"You can't. You don't know if this is honest or true. This is, in itself, a gamble, Miss Gamble. Give me Mr Largesse and you have my word that there will be a Dealer Gamble."

Her mind swam. She was out of cards and knew that was the best deal she was going to get. She took the document he had just sketched and stood.

"I'll need those officers. Tonight."

Dealer Avarice simply nodded and Tessa left without another word.

***

"You *what!*" Dante, Veronica and Alex screeched in unison when she explained what had transpired.

"I'm sorry. You want to go back to the safe house? Tonight? Did you not notice the mob that was forming? I literally snuck out." Veronica was not in support of Tessa's plan.

"Tessa, you know I'm with you but this might be actual suicide." Alex offered his opinion.

She looked to Dante who gave her a face that told her nobody in the car liked her plan.

"You all know Anthony isn't an idiot and neither is the Dealer. I have to play them both to see any end to this."

They were waiting in the truck for the officers but Tessa couldn't sit still any longer so she opened the door.

"Where do you think you're going?" Alex questioned as if he were in charge of her. She hated that.

"Tell the officers to go straight there when you see them. I need to walk these nerves off and come up with something," Tessa said, hopping out of the truck.

"We can help, Squirt!"

"You are helping by doing what I ask. Please, Dante."

Veronica looked at Dante and turned to Tessa. "Take Avarice at least. I don't trust his daddy as far as I can throw him… and that man is a beefy son of a bitch."

Alex side-eyed Veronica and his gaze softened when they landed on Tessa. His eyes were pleading for permission.

She sighed loudly. "Fine. Come on, Alex."

Alex couldn't get out of the truck fast enough as he launched himself out of the back.

"We'll meet you at the house?" Dante asked.

Tessa nodded and waved over her shoulder as she and Alex walked down the path away from the truck.

"What is the real plan, Tess?" Alex asked once they were out of sight of the others.

She smiled. Even if he was an ass, at least he paid attention. "Where is your bike?"

"In front of the gates… why?"

"We're going to the safe house."

CHAPTER 50

Tessa

"I didn't bring my second helmet…" Alex admitted when they approached the bike. Tessa just stared at him.

That was not in her plan.

She looked between Alex and the bike. That was the fastest way to get there at that moment, helmet or not.

"Drive safely, okay?" She lowered her voice. It was a long ride from the Elite village to the safe house.

"Tessa…" He reached out to touch her face but she walked towards the bike instead.

"I just need to get there and I know Dante would force himself to come with me to get Anthony out."

"You don't think I would do that for you?" Alex asked, hurt.

"Alex, no. I want some backup just in case. Dante would just be… Dante." Tessa didn't know herself what she meant by that but Alex seemed to take that as an answer.

It made her think of how freely she could speak with Anthony. He was confident and sure of himself. Too bad he tried to have her killed.

"Why don't we go to my apartment first? It isn't very far and I can get the second helmet."

She nodded, still nervous about the ride. At least this one would be much shorter.

He got on the bike and put his helmet on. She climbed on the back, tucked her chin into her chest, and pinned herself tightly to his back. Before he kick-started the bike, she felt him rub her arm.

She felt comfortable with him, but no longer felt a want for him. There was a guilt she felt with the lack of electricity. Tessa decided to bury those thoughts for another day. She had no intention of doing anything further with him and she needed to keep her focus on the plan if it was going to work.

They really weren't on the road for very long when he pulled up on a stout red-brick building.

"Did you want to come in?" Alex asked, removing his helmet and running his hand through his hair.

"I think we should just get going if that's alright." She saw the look of disappointment grow on his face and refused to allow herself to feel any remorse. Tessa decided he was an adult and fully able to handle himself without her comforting him.

"I know I said it didn't bother me…"

"Alex," she groaned, not wanting to have the conversation in the middle of her plan to change everything. She couldn't understand how he couldn't see past himself. This was bigger than just the two of them, he had to understand that. There was no time for his desperation.

"It did though, Tess. I always thought I would be your first and I was going to be—"

She interrupted him. "I wasn't *your* first, Alex. I won't make you feel bad about that." Tessa was stern and to the point.

He played with his hair and put his helmet down. "I know but I wanted it to be you. Every time I wanted for it to have been you."

"I want to be clear, Alex. I don't want you to apologise for sleeping with anyone. I am also not going to apologise for sleeping with Anthony."

Alex winced at the mention of Anthony's name.

She continued, "You've had fun and I've had fun. Separately and together if you recall."

His eyes went wide. "What are you saying, like we are even now? Is that it?"

"No, Alex. I am saying we are both adults who have had sex. End of. I never owed you my first time, and if I am being honest, it is disgusting for you to have ever believed that. We have been friends our entire lives. Did I want to spend my freedom years with you? Yes. But our lives changed so quickly, Alex."

"Is it because he's an Elite now?" he spat at her and she was taken aback.

"When are you going to get it through your head that rank has nothing to do with this?" Did he not see that she was trying to change everything? Fight for opportunities for everyone, including him?

"Rank is *everything*, Tessa, don't you understand that? The only reason my father offered you anything is because you're an ace. The future we had, the future you want? Rank. Wealth. Power. You may not be as outwardly hungry for it as my father but at least he is honest with his intentions."

The words hit her like a slap. Alex was so hot and cold with her and she never knew where she actually stood. Tessa didn't want to regret their night in the tent, but she also felt like it made everything more complicated. She had to remember that his thoughts and actions weren't on her. This possessiveness was his own doing. She didn't have to engage.

Tessa remembered how it felt to be without clothing. She remembered what it felt like to don the dress for the Draw. It was the same feeling. It was her confidence, her control. Her fate was *hers* and hers alone.

She stood taller. "What do you want, Alex? Do you want to take me up to that apartment and fuck me? Have me beg for your name like I did his? Would that make you feel better? Would that pick your pitiful self off the floor?

"I am an ace and you are a nine. Those are the cards we were dealt. The discrepancy in our ranks bothers only one of us. So, you tell me, Alex. You tell me a solution that works for you and your fragile ego because clearly the person with the problem here is *you*."

His lips went taught and he stared down at her face.

"I owe you nothing, Alex. Too long have I let you take the lead and make me feel insecure. I won't be watching what I say anymore. I won't guard my actions or censor myself in front of you. I never should have." She felt the courage and confidence surge through her. "I owe myself my strength. I owe myself control. I owe *myself* pleasure in whatever way I see fit with whoever I see fit. I am done being small. I am done feeling lost. I am done with the guilt you attempt to lord over me."

She paused to take in the weight and the relief of her words. Today she stood up for those who had systemically been wronged. Though she never struggled inside the gates she realised she, too, needed standing up for. She needed help too and she had allowed others to feed off her lack of self-worth.

Tessa Gamble decided that she would live up to the ace that the Fates provided with the pride and the ambition that her spade blessed her with.

She grabbed his helmet, smacked it on her head and kick-started the bike.

***

She was filled with immediate regret as she went a singular speed the entire way since she didn't know how to change gears.

She didn't dare look behind her to see Alex, more out of embarrassment than anything else. Tessa had made this elaborate speech and then left on what may as well have been an electric scooter.

However, she surprised herself by enjoying the feeling of driving it. It stayed balanced on its own and luckily nobody was out this late for her to worry about colliding with.

She ran every single red light as she didn't know if she would start again if she stopped.

Tessa knew Alex would likely go back to the house and tell Dante what had happened. In fact, her new plan hinged on that possibility. She smirked when she thought of how proud Veronica would be of her.

Tessa barely recognised this version of herself. She had only felt so self-assured less than a handful of times. Tessa believed that her vulnerability released her from her cage. When she thought for herself and behaved freely it felt whole and complete. It felt right. It felt like her.

Who Tessa was expected to be was so restrictive, and yet she was born with endless options. She was raised with potential and educated to fulfil any capabilities. However, the most dangerous parts of her were squashed. Her care for others, her sense of justice, her empathy.

Those things had no place in the wider Game, not for the Elite. You couldn't ride on the backs of others while concerning yourself with their conditions beneath you.

She suppressed it. Turned a blind eye every time they drove to the lake. Of course, she saw it when they left the limits of the Region. The cracked walls, repeatedly painted bricks, and over-filled rubbish bins. She didn't care. She didn't want to properly *see* it. Why would she? It was never a part of her world.

But it was. All of this was her world.

And she was determined to change it.

CHAPTER 51

Alex

Alex watched her drive off on his bike with a mixture of awe and anger. Truth be told, he was embarrassed at how he had acted. He had lost everything and he really wasn't a good loser.

"Girlfriend finally break up with you?" he heard a familiar voice call from above. He stepped back from the building and looked up to find his sister on the balcony. "Before you ask, I heard all of it. Louise said she's buying this place for you. Never saw you as the gold-digging type, little brother."

He sighed. "What do you want, Laura?" Alex was in no mood for unexpected company. He just wanted to go and be of some use for Tessa and her plan, even if he did mess up... again.

"Come up, let's have a chat."

He groaned but relented. Where else was he going to go? Tessa had stolen his bike and though he was sure Dante would want to hear of his sister's whereabouts, he had no interest in admitting how much he must have hurt her.

Alex decided to take the stairs up to the apartment. The more he could delay this conversation, the better. As he approached the door, he heard multiple voices and tried to figure out who they all were before entering. Some were painfully familiar, but others completely new. Was this an ambush?

Laura must have got impatient because she swung open the door in front of him and gestured, welcoming him to his own apartment.

"Time to pick a side, Alexander." His father stood up from the chair directly across from the door.

Alex's entire family was here, along with a few rebels that he recognised from the gathering earlier.

His sister must have seen his confusion.

"I told you I have a lot of pieces in the Game. Several games really…" Laura said, sitting down.

That didn't answer anything Alex was wondering so he ignored her and just stared at his father.

"Didn't I warn you, boy, that you would sink with her? You have yet to heed my warning." Everyone was silent as the Dealer spoke and Alex was frozen in place.

"She didn't sink. Her rank is higher than yours," Alex defended.

His father grinned and looked at Laura as if his speaking to Alex was a waste of his time.

"She took the bait. Didn't I say?" Laura mused.

He wasn't a fan of his family speaking in riddles around him. His mind was trying to make sense of everything but couldn't. "Could we just stop with these games and tell me what's going on?"

"Oh, Alexander. Games are what we do." Laura grinned wickedly. "And Avarices always win."

He felt stupid. His family was speaking to him as if they were spoon-feeding him obvious information. However, none of it made any sense.

"You're going to get Anthony like you want…" Alex wanted to lead with any thought in hopes anyone would volunteer any more information.

"Is that what I want, my boy?" his father asked coyly, gesturing up at the hallways leading to the bedroom.

Alex's mouth fell open when he followed where his father pointed.

"I don't understand," he managed to choke out.

"You have proven yourself trustworthy so far, Alexander. Though you have remained by Miss Gamble's side, you have yet to work against the interests of this family," his father said, but Alex paid no attention.

His gaze was still fixed at the end of the hallway.

At Dealer Prudence.

Alive, looking well, and as if what he saw had never happened.

"Did you tell me the truth when you said you planted the nine?" he demanded of his father, still attempting to put all the pieces together.

"I have yet to lie to you, Alexander. I still expect great things from you, of course. You are an Avarice and always will be."

Alex turned his attention to the very alive Dealer Prudence. "Were you ever really part of the rebellion?"

Dealer Prudence smiled lightly. "Alexander, we are the rebellion."

CHAPTER 52

Alex

Alex did his best to control his reaction but when he looked at his father, the questions and hurt were clearly written on his face.

"We heard of Miss Gamble's disloyalty to you." He gestured to the rebels Alex had recognised from the safe house. "I would have liked to share in your surprise, however, I know all too well how the Gamble family can be."

"I have been a part of that family more than I have this one. They welcomed me when you turned me away for being a nine, something *you* made happen!" Alex raised his voice in defence. He may have been an Avarice in name, but he felt like a Gamble.

"Unfortunately, your sisters were too old to have luck with the eldest Gamble sibling. It is hard for separate years to mingle before adulthood... Luckily you and their youngest hit it off overly well."

"You used me to get to Tessa?" Alex did nothing to disguise his hurt. Not only did his father make him a nine for strategy, but his love was coordinated for it as well.

"Oh, my son." His mother found her voice. "We all use one another. We are all pieces of the greater Game."

"And what game is that, Mother?" Alex figured this was more than just getting rich quickly, it had to be.

She grinned. "The game for power."

His father got up from his seat and paced the room. "Alexander, you got uncomfortably close with Miss Gamble. I did not recognise that until it was far too late. I expected some form of intimacy, yes, but when there was talk of partnership?" He shook his head. "That was never part of the plan."

"And what was that plan?" Alex demanded. "To use me to get to them?"

"Precisely," his father said with absolute authority. "You were our long game, Alexander. You couldn't have possibly thought I ever approved of a genuine friendship between you and the daughter of a rebel leader?"

He hated the thought of that. He knew there was no real love in his family the way the Gamble family had. Alex loved the Gambles. He was one of them. Even all of the times he had messed up, Tessa forgave him and let him in. It was his own selfishness that got in the way. Her father and who he was never mattered to him because the Gambles were always kind and welcoming.

He turned to his sister. "How do you fit into all of this, then?"

Laura smiled. "You can call me the driver. All pieces continue to move because I will them to. We gave each of you a chance to prove your loyalty to the Dealers and the Region. Miss Gamble failed spectacularly. We continued to test you and you have yet to fail."

"You're not working *with* Largesse…"

"He's working for us," his sister completed.

"Why? Why fake all of this?" The rebellion. Love towards him. An orchestrated relationship. The luck of the Draw. It was all a lie.

"Hope, Alexander. It is an incredible motivator. When the older rebellion, led by Miss Gamble's late father, fell, we knew we needed to control it. Not eliminate it." His father picked up a baseball Alex had brought from the house. "Dealer Prudence became leadership for a while, rebuilding the rebellion in a manageable way. We continued to hire a cycle of Low-Born and Working-Class individuals who we could control who were compensated heavily for their contributions.

"Anthony was the most recent and current hire; however, he has always concerned me. His thoughts and actions are far too independent. I hired him as my assistant and decided I would keep him close... I also gave him the opportunity to pay off his debts, which he has done."

"What happened to the other leaders?" Alex asked, afraid he already knew the answer.

"Well, their families were also compensated for their loss. Though one less mouth to feed is sometimes a saving grace to these families. We also usually rewarded more than the person would contribute to their household, anyhow."

He threw the baseball at Alex, which he caught.

"Throw the ball into the air, boy," his father ordered and he did, catching it on its descent with ease.

"See how much easier it is to catch when you throw it for yourself? You know how hard, how high, how fast, and you threw it in a way you knew you would be able to control."

"Do all of the rebels work for you?" Alex didn't want analogies. He wanted facts.

His father laughed a single scoff and then coughed, as if his body was unfamiliar with humour. "Oh no, but we know who they all are thanks to our loyal employees." He gestured at the room around him.

"You see, my boy, people like instruction. They thrive on direction and fall in line accordingly. Though they do need prompting. They need a cause. Your Tessa gave not only the *true* rebels such a cause, but also those in the general public. She showed the Elite a new set of ideas. That unknown makes her a far greater risk than we can afford to have around."

"You told her you didn't have to be her enemy! She's trying to work *with* you." Alex had never been so torn, so hurt, so confused.

"She didn't have to be my enemy," he said calmly, despite Alex's anger. "Tessa Gamble chose this path. Every single step of the way she was defying what it means to be an Elite in Cassino. I know Dante Gamble is a rebel, but he did small things like buy nets for basketball hoops. I can allow that to slide; if anything it does me a favour. Miss Gamble, however, is a symbol. She is a voice. She is a danger to our way of life."

"She just wants to change what is wrong, Father. She wants to help people long term," Alex argued.

"At what cost?" Louise was finally done hearing others speak. "More opportunities for them mean fewer for us!"

"No, Louise, they don't. How could you be so selfish?"

Louise scoffed. "You just said to your little girlfriend that she was power hungry."

He paused and lowered his tone, full of regret. "I was angry."

"Good." His father walked over to him and squeezed his shoulder. Alex used to feel so deprived of his father's touch, that he hated how good it felt to get some.

"Let that anger fuel you. You, without knowing it, have been playing loyally for your family up until now. Play with us. We are the winning side, Alexander. Our family has a monopoly on this entire Region. We are on both sides for change and against change. Nothing can stop us."

Alex mulled this over. He had failed multiple times to repair the damages done to his friendship with Tessa. He loved her. Now, his family wanted him and needed him. Something he had always wanted. Could he turn his back on his own name? Could he turn his back on her?

"Tell me your plan," Alex nodded and his father squeezed his shoulder again.

"That's my boy."

CHAPTER 53

Tessa

Tessa arrived at the clearing and was very impressed with herself for not dying. The first step, getting there, was more difficult than she anticipated.

She stepped into the clearing after taking her helmet off. It was dark and she felt foolish for not taking a flashlight with her. Once the lights of the bike went off, she was left in complete darkness.

Luckily, she didn't have to wait long for the scouts to notice her.

"Thought we'd chased yous outta here." A boy she didn't recognise spoke.

"I was invited back anytime for a game of poker." She hoped they didn't know what was meant by that.

The two looked to one another and the one who didn't speak went off in the direction of the pit of death.

"Asking permission?" Tessa asked with a laugh.

"For the likes of yous? Yes." Clearly, this was a man of few words.

They weren't waiting long before the other scout returned

with a nod. She walked towards the pit of death and hoped her nickname wouldn't become accurate.

When the door was released, she fell onto the mat. She didn't land quite so clumsily this time, but still couldn't manage to stay on her feet.

"Back for more already? I must have played *really* well, then." She turned to see him wear the smug grin that she hated to love.

She didn't respond. He just walked in the direction of the office and she followed. The safe house was empty. Everyone must have gone home but Tessa wondered why he was still there.

He didn't even cross the threshold of the door before he took his shirt off.

She paused a moment as she felt the heat rush through her again. Tessa felt betrayed by her own body. He was the enemy. He wanted her killed. She couldn't understand why she still wanted to be on top of that table.

Then again, her tightening core said to her, why not take control? Make him trust her. Play his game in return and lure him to the officers who would be waiting outside.

"Are we in a rush?" she asked in a forced husky tone.

"Well, I haven't stopped thinking about you begging me for more." He went straight to the trunk this time and pulled out a condom. He was preparing and not questioning for a moment why she would come back other than to take part in sex again. Men really were stupid.

"Maybe I just came back for my dress..." she said, crossing the space between him and the table. She bent to look into the trunk and her dress was still there. When she stood up with it, she noticed his eyes were hungrily on her backside.

"Want me to put it on?" she asked with a smirk.

His eyes snapped up to meet hers. And then at her dress in her hands. He didn't have to know that the dress wasn't for him. It was for her.

She wore it as armour at the Draw and came out victorious. Tessa would do it again.

She turned her back to him, undressing as slowly as she could manage. She felt him watch her and she grinned. In one motion, she removed her trousers and her underwear. Glancing over her shoulder, she noticed the bulge fight against the fabric of his trousers.

"Do you really have to put anything back on?" he asked in a beg.

"No," she laughed, donning the dress. Her armour, clinging to her body, left little to the imagination anyway.

She walked past him and tilted her head up to his, sharing the same air, and barely skimmed her mouth on his before walking past him.

Tessa made sure to make eye contact before sitting at the table, surrounded by the chips still splayed on the floor from earlier.

"If you wanted to play strip poker, you probably should have left more clothes on," he grinned, walking towards her and tilting her chin up so their eyes met.

"Who says I want to play strip poker?"

She thought of Dante hopefully coming with backup once Alex got word to him.

"Oh?" He smiled playfully. "What are we playing for then?"

"I know, Tony," she said with a severity to her voice. Tessa locked her gaze to his.

His grin disappeared. "I was in the meeting when Avarice tried telling you." Anthony reached down to the floor and picked up a deck of cards, likely also lost in the frenzy of their earlier activities.

"So, you think after you try and kill me that I'd sleep with you?" she mused, plucking the cards from his hand and opening the box.

"You seemed to enjoy the fucking the first time. I don't remember hearing any complaints," he shrugged.

"Ah yes, but I didn't know then, did I?"

He watched her shuffle the deck. In addition to learning to spin chips in her fingers, she learned the art of show shuffling on the education grounds.

"See, Miss Gamble. Information and knowledge *are* valuable."

She tried to do her best not to stare at his bare chest. The Working-Class was evident in his body. He likely worked hard considering the muscles she could see flexing with each movement.

"What I can't understand, Tess, is if you aren't here for another ride on the table, and you think I tried killing you once, why come at all?"

"Why does anyone play poker? I came to make a deal."

His eyebrows shot up in keen interest. "You are not exactly in the position to make any sort of demand. Why would I give you anything?"

She shrugged. The shuffling continued and she was concentrating on her tricks. "Why would you fuck me?"

He laughed at that. "It's fun and you're attractive. That's all you need really."

"Well, I'm still attractive and this could be fun. What good is it to win without a proper game, Tony?"

She watched his mind turn. His face twisted in a strange way. He whispered, "You should have just joined the rebellion. I would have kept you safe."

"Safe?" She laughed lightly. "You tried having me killed."

They were both still speaking in low tones. Neither was willing to drop the sensual act. It was a play, it was for control.

"If you think I acted alone, you aren't as smart as I thought you were."

She collected the cards and packed them into a tight deck, placing them down on the table in front of her.

"So, you want me killed, and I want you gone. Is that it?" she offered.

His eyes lit up. There was something she hadn't caught yet. A move she couldn't see.

"A gamble, then, Miss Gamble. I win, you die. You win, you hand me over to Avarice like you want." He reached out his hand.

Her face dropped for a moment before she steadied herself. How did he know about the plan to hand him over? She had no time to figure it out. Those were the stakes inside and outside this poker game, anyway. He just knew more than she thought he did.

"Deal." She shook his hand and then distributed the cards.

Tessa would stall as long as she could, but she *really* hoped Dante would get there soon.

CHAPTER 54

Alex

Alex had taken his sisters' car to the clearing. The scouts didn't stop him or even greet him. They were expecting his arrival. Though he had been pricked, the door opened for him anyway. He didn't need Dante to come with him and for that he was thankful. Maybe this plan would work.

He landed on the mat and made his way into the domed gathering space.

"Sit down," he heard a stern voice say behind him. "I know who you are, Alexander Avarice."

They spent a moment searching the other's expressions. She started grinning and he returned it with a silent accord.

"Every coin has three sides…" she led.

"The heads, the tails, and the edge," Alex completed, smiling wickedly.

CHAPTER 55

Tessa

She was panicking on the inside but had nobody to blame but herself. Tessa was the one who decided to come here alone, to take the risk. She even dealt the damned cards.

They had both wagered and won then wagered and lost, as was the way with poker. But Tessa was done playing it safe. Although she knew she was fucked, she pushed all her chips in the middle and stared at Anthony.

There was already a substantial sum in the middle of the table, but given how things were going, she needed everything she could get. Her life was on the line.

Anthony looked at her. "I've always admired how bold you are. I think that is your sexiest quality."

"Not my ass then?" she joked casually, looking at her cards.

"You know I have you here," he said as he pushed all of his chips into the pot as well. "I'll let you in on something: this bet is not a life for a life."

She kept a neutral face, doing her best to suppress her fear. Tessa had to give him all of the pauses she could. She needed to delay; all of her hope was on Dante's arrival.

"It is just whether or not you live," he finished.

It suddenly hit her all at once. "Dealer Avarice," she whispered, finally realising.

"He played you like a fiddle. Every step of the way he was always several steps ahead of you. You fell right into his trap."

"I assume then that you aren't in any real danger if you do go to him?"

"Likely none, but it is never for certain. Dealers are fickle."

She tried to understand the implications of this. What it meant for the wider Game. They, themselves, made a deal. She could still create change, but she had to win. She had to stay alive.

"Who are you, really?"

"Oh! Tess, I am who I've said. Though I am not the *real* leader. That's Avarice. I'm just a token boy getting paid a fuck load of money to do the grunt work." He paused to play with his cards. "Now, where were we?"

CHAPTER 56

Tessa

Anthony looked up at her with the smug grin she came to hate. He had just put down his hand, and though it wasn't good, hers was still worse.

The only move she had left was to be confident. It had yet to fail her. Tessa clutched her locket. She had to bet on herself. Nobody else was going to do that for her.

She didn't let her defeat touch her eyes as she plastered on the widest grin she could muster and made a move to put her cards down. She took half of a small moment to rearrange her hand but that was the only hesitation she needed.

"Hang on there, Gamble." Anthony attempted to sound casual, but Tessa could hear the strain of panic in his heightened voice. She could tell he didn't want to be taken to the Dealer, potentially seen as a failure, or worse. She would use that to her advantage.

Tessa feigned shock. "You can't just back out of a game like that. We lay our hands down now, Anthony, a bet is a bet. A game is a game."

She made the move again and his hand went up to stop her.

"I told you to wait." He didn't want her alive. She was sure of that. Though she didn't understand where his hesitation truly came from.

"What could you possibly do with that hand, Tony?" She gestured to his upturned cards across the table. "You want another chance to pick up, what, another ten?" she scoffed. "Three of a kind won't help you now." As she made a third false attempt to drop her cards, he reached across the table to grab her wrist.

She glared up at him. "Let go."

His grip relaxed but he didn't release. She saw him twist slightly. Anthony was attempting to see her cards.

She closed the fan. The only card remaining visible was the highest in her hand: the ten of clubs.

"Not like you to cheat, Tony." She took her arm back and placed her cards face-down on the table. She was playing a dangerous game but little did he know; this game had suddenly turned into a game of wills.

"You must be really afraid of me falling uncontrollably in love with you. Commitment was never your strong point, was it?"

Anthony's cheeks flushed and she was proud at the sight. She had rattled him. This was clearly no longer about the game. This one, or the wider one.

"I didn't cheat." He played with his cards, lining them up and spacing them perfectly on the table before him. He had seen her card, she knew that. The odds of another ten being drawn were low.

She had him. While he was distracted, she glanced again at the door. *Where the fuck is he?* she thought to herself. Tessa wondered for too long. Clearly something changed in her face.

"Looking to leave so soon? The game isn't even over yet," he smirked.

"It would be if you stopped stalling." Tessa attempted to keep her careless demeanour as she rested her elbows on the table, evenly positioned on either side of her neatly stacked cards.

"Don't count your money, Tess. One last bet. Humour me."

More games. More bluffs. But Tessa had no choice, she needed backup and it had not yet arrived. "I am not agreeing to anything else. I've lived through this game, what makes you think I am willing to bet on it again?"

"I am no longer interested in betting on your life."

The door behind Anthony finally opened and Tessa's eyes widened in horror.

"I am more interested in betting on his."

She breathed hard. "Alex." Her mind spiralled. Him being there likely meant he had never gone to find Dante to tell him where she was. Dante wasn't coming, he couldn't be. Not if Alex was here.

His hands were bound behind his back and his legs were tied above the knees. He could do barely any movement other than a shuffle. Alex was covered in blood, a good amount of it too. Tessa hoped it wasn't all his, but she wasn't in the position to ask.

"You don't think I'm that stupid, do you, Tess? You insult me. As if you would come out here all on your own."

"Anthony, this has nothing to do with him."

"Nothing?" he barked back in a laugh. "He has everything to do with this. He convinced you to turn your back on us. On *me*." There was no hurt in his eyes, only anger. The girl who had brought Alex in the room didn't seem phased.

Anthony walked over to the girl and held out his hand, obtaining a pistol.

Tessa's stomach dropped and she felt the colour drain from her face. She knew her life was on the line, but it was all words up until that point. The physical element of death was now in the room and staring her in the face.

"Tony…" she pleaded.

"Don't you *dare* 'Tony' me. You had your chances. Now…" He swung the gun to Alex's temple. "One. More. Bet."

"What do you want?" Tessa was out of options. The game of confidence was lost before she even started playing. He had her and what mattered to her in his grip. She would have lost the poker game. She would have lost the mission to give Anthony to the Dealer. It was never about that stupid card game. He was stalling just as much as she was.

Anthony grabbed Alex by the shoulder and dragged him to the seat he had once occupied.

"Sit." He forced Alex down. "Good boy."

Tessa looked at Anthony in disgust. She knew only one of them was going to make it out of this alive. It didn't take a genius to figure out that the odds weren't great.

She looked over to Alex with a pleading look. "I am sor—"

Anthony backhanded her with the gun in his hand and a surprise squeak escaped her lips. She brought her hand up to hold her face. Her cheek ached and her lips tingled. She pressed her fingers lightly against her lower lip and they were covered in blood.

He grabbed her chin and jerked it up towards his face. "Don't you *fucking* talk to him. Can't you see, Tess? I always get what I want. One last bet; you should have taken it before he got here."

She didn't understand what he meant and she wasn't interested in any more of his games.

"What's the game?" Alex croaked out. Tessa's heart felt like crumbling. He sounded awful. Anthony must have agreed with her assessment because a wide grin crossed his face.

"What a great question, Alex. Good boy!" Anthony ruffled Alex's hair like he was a dog. It made Tessa want to scream but there was little she could do against someone with a gun.

"The game is simple." Anthony walked over to Tessa and spun her chair with ease. Once her back was to the table he knelt in front of her and his hands ended up on top of hers on either side of the seat where she hung on to. He grinned wickedly before standing up and gripping her by the chin. He brought his face lower to hers. "You aren't going to move. If you do, you both die, got it?"

She gave a slight nod in agreement, though it was hard against the grip he had on her chin. He released it by throwing her head to the side, almost knocking her off the chair.

Her mind was racing. There had to be a way out of this.

"Now, Alex. I know you aren't much of a gambler, but since you are an Avarice, I take it you know how to play poker. In front of you is my hand. As you can see, it is face up. Pair of tens. Across is Tessa's hand, obviously faced down. Pick the winning hand of the two, and you win. Though, do it quietly, of course. Wouldn't want to spoil the fun."

Tessa froze. The devil he knew or the devil he didn't. If Alex took the hand in front of him, she would die. If he chose her hand, he would die. The worst part of it all was that she didn't know which one it was going to be.

The silence in the room was as lethal as the bullet in the barrel of that gun. It was only interrupted by the sound of her cards flipping over behind her.

"Oh, *very* interesting." Anthony sounded amused. "What a fun game. It is a good thing I didn't play. I would have lost."

He whispered, breath tingling against her ear, "You played well, Miss Gamble."

Bang.